PRAISE F

...refreshing, funny, emotionally charged, and very entertaining to read.

— CAROL, TIL THE LAST PAGE

There is humor, there is heart and there is heat in this story! I absolutely loved it! . . . Mari and Liam delivered. Yowza, their chemistry was palpable.

— BIBLIOPHILE CHLOE

PETAL PLUCKER

Funny, charming, and utterly captivating! I devoured this sparkling read.

— ANNIKA MARTIN, NEW YORK TIMES BESTSELLING AUTHOR

Petal Plucker was funny, entertaining, fresh and fan-yourself-worthy . . . Their enemies-to-lovers romance is both charming, tender and steamy, and you'll love both of these characters (and their families!) and their sigh-worthy happily ever after.

— MARY DUBÉ, CONTEMPORARILY EVER AFTER

Morland has created a masterpiece of a romance . . . one of my favorite [books] of the year.

— CRISTIINA READS

Humorous, raunchy, and refreshing, Petal Plucker has rightfully earned its way, in my opinion, as one of the best romantic comedy [books] this year.

— CAROL, TIL THE LAST PAGE

My One and Only

This book was gripping, well written & the chemistry between the characters sizzled throughout this wonderful read.

— AMAZON REVIEW

All I Want Is You

Another heartfelt, steamy, terrific story. This is an author who really knows how to create a story that catches a reader's attention and characters that capture her heart.

— BOOKADDICT

TAKING A CHANCE ON LOVE

Thea and Anthony are in for a surprise when it comes to the language of the heart . . . I am in awe.

— HOPELESS ROMANTIC BLOG

THEN CAME YOU

This story really pulled all my heartstrings. This was truly a beautiful story and makes you believe there really is true love out there.

— MEME CHANELL BOOK CORNER

ALSO BY IRIS MORLAND

LOVE EVERLASTING

including

HAZEL ISLAND

One Perfect Summer

Forever Mine

THE YOUNGERS

Then Came You

Taking a Chance on Love

All I Want Is You

My One and Only

THE THORNTONS

The Nearness of You

The Very Thought of You

If I Can't Have You

Dream a Little Dream of Me

Someone to Watch Over Me

Till There Was You

I'll Be Home for Christmas

THE HEIR AFFAIR DUET

The Prince I Love to Hate

The Princess I Hate to Love

HERON'S LANDING

Say You're Mine

All I Ask of You

Make Me Yours

Hold Me Close

THE FLOWER SHOP SISTERS

War of the Roses

Petal Plucker

He Loves Me, He Loves Me Not

Oopsie Daisy

FOREVER MINE

HAZEL ISLAND

IRIS MORLAND

BLUE VIOLET PRESS LLC

To my nephews, who I hope don't read any of my books until they're at least fifty years old.

FOREVER MINE

CHAPTER ONE

Jack Benson considered his options: get up and leave without a word or suffer through the indignity currently being hoisted upon him.

"Come on, smile!" said Gigi, the woman he'd been seeing off and on for three months. "Why can't you ever smile for a picture, at least?"

Jack forced himself to smile. Apparently, that wasn't good enough for Gigi, because when she looked through the photos, she made annoyed noises at every single one.

Jack was a fisherman, for Christ's sake. He didn't give a shit about social media, and he sure as hell didn't give a shit about taking selfies, either.

Gigi, her mouth in a pretty pout, wrinkled her nose at him. "I can't post any of these. My friends don't believe that I even have a boyfriend."

Jack, lounging in his bed, sat up at that pronouncement. "Whoever said anything about 'boyfriend'?" he rumbled.

Gigi fluttered her eyelashes. "It's been four months."

As if time were the sole marker of a relationship. Jack

had to restrain a snort. Gigi wasn't a bad sort. She was the type of woman he'd always preferred: pretty but easily bored. Because once these women got bored, they left. And that was how Jack liked things.

Jack wished he had a bottle of whiskey on his bedside table. Instead, he went to his tiny kitchen, made them both two mugs of coffee, and handed one to Gigi.

"Look." He cleared his throat. "I'm not a boyfriend kind of guy."

Gigi laughed. "Every guy says that."

"I'm not every guy."

She pouted again, not even touching the coffee he'd given her. "Do you have nothing else to say?"

"What do you want me to say?" Now he was just confused.

Gigi quickly bounced from his bed and slipped on her clothes, shooting him daggers as she did so.

"You know what I think?" she said tightly.

He didn't think it wise to reply to that question, either.

"I think you don't know what you want. Any guy would love to be with me, so it's not me. It's you. You're just messed up." Gigi grabbed her purse and, after she checked her hair in her compact, gave him the finger before flouncing out to her car.

Jack winced when he heard her tires peeling out. He just hoped she hadn't run over his freshly planted sod.

Pulling out a bottle of whiskey he stashed under his mattress, he poured some into his coffee. Then he did the same thing with Gigi's leftover mug.

Jack had worked as a fisherman on Hazel Island, a small island in Puget Sound, for over a decade. On his boat, the *Perseverance*, he was at home. He didn't have to deal with people demanding things from him that he didn't have. It was just him, the sea, and the stink of freshly caught fish.

Not that fresh fish should literally stink. He'd learned that quickly when he'd started. He'd been amazed to find that fish straight from the water smelled and tasted of the ocean itself. He never sold fish that actually stunk—only a hack who didn't care about his catch or his customers would do that.

Jack pulled in a net filled with salmon, the fish wiggling and flopping about in one last attempt at freedom. But the net was lighter than usual, and when he looked it over, he realized he hadn't caught nearly as many as he'd expected.

And the salmon—they were strangely small, not at all like he'd been used to catching over the years.

Jack used to catch crabs primarily. Within the last year, though, he'd begun fishing for salmon as his main source of income. Crab fishing in particular had started to dry up due to overfishing.

Although the waters around Hazel Island were vast, they only had a few different species of fish available for commercial fishing. When Jack had moved to the island, he hadn't realized that there were better fishing grounds elsewhere in the Sound. At that point, though, he'd already felt at home on Hazel Island and hadn't wanted to leave.

Jack grunted. There were ups and downs with this business: bad weather, bad catches. Some years, he struggled to keep up with all the fish he'd catch. Other years, it was like the entire ocean was devoid of life. Feast or famine–that was the life of a fisherman.

But it was always temporary. This, however... Jack had a sinking feeling in his gut that this was a bad omen. He'd naively assumed the overfishing wouldn't be an issue like it had with crabbing.

Based on this catch, he had a feeling he wasn't going to be so lucky a second round.

By the time he returned to shore and began packing the salmon for sale with the help of a few guys he hired seasonally, he was in a dark mood. If the other guys noticed how pathetic this catch was, they didn't mention it.

Hazel Island was a sleepy town with no more than a thousand residents. The population swelled with tourists in the summer, but now that it was fall, the island activity had slowed down.

Jack made his usual stops at the various grocery stores and restaurants that bought salmon directly from him. His last stop was the Hazel Island bed and breakfast.

Gwen Parker, the owner, stepped outside the moment he turned off the engine of his truck. "Oh good, there you are! You're late," she teased.

Gwen had moved to Hazel Island five years ago to open her bed and breakfast. With her red hair, freckles, and wide smile, she'd quickly become a favorite in the community. She was always friendly, always willing to lend a hand or an ear. Her business had taken off and had yet to slow down. She'd somehow managed to draw in tourists for the rainy winter months when no one else on the island had done so.

Gwen Parker was a marvel that Jack did not understand one bit.

He looked at his watch. "I'm not late," he replied.

"You're usually here by eleven. It's eleven-thirty."

He looked around when he entered the kitchen of the bed and breakfast. Based on the quiet emanating from the dining room, they weren't busy.

"Sorry," he said gruffly. "I'll put these in the fridge."

He carried in Gwen's usual order, setting them in the same spot, something he'd done for five years.

When he returned outside, Gwen was standing by his truck, her head cocked to the side.

The sun had begun to shine through the clouds, and it made the strands of gold in Gwen's hair stand out. Jack had always wondered how many colors her hair held.

He'd wondered it, but he'd never, ever, attempted to see it for himself.

"You might be interested to hear Gigi came by this morning for some breakfast," said Gwen, her tone casual. "She seemed very put out. She asked for hash browns, which she never does."

Jack gritted his teeth. "So?"

"Aren't you two seeing each other?"

"No." He paused. "Not anymore."

"Ah. Well, she told Darla all about it, apparently. She was spitting mad. Said men were absolute beasts and she hoped a certain fisherman fell off his boat and drowned." Gwen's lips quirked. "I think you made her mad. I've never seen Gigi say anything mean about anyone. I think she's even nice to mosquitoes."

Jack let out a reluctant laugh. "I probably screwed that up," he admitted. He peered more closely at Gwen. "Since when do you care?"

Gwen seemed taken aback. "We're friends, aren't we? And I thought, you know, I could give you some advice—"

Jack groaned.

"From a fellow woman. That's all. I'm just saying, you might need to be more upfront with women in the future. If they think you want a relationship but you don't—"

He held up a hand. "Gigi knew the rules. She thought she could change them. Nothing more to it than that."

"Oh." Gwen looked embarrassed. "Sorry."

"Nothing to be sorry for. We had our fun, it's over." He jangled his keys, hoping Gwen would take the hint.

"Are you going to be single for the rest of your life? Sounds pretty lonely to me," said Gwen.

What had he done to deserve this? First, Gigi throwing a fit. Next, Gwen prying into his personal life. He and Gwen might be friends, but they weren't friends of that sort.

Jack Benson didn't have any friends he talked with about those things. That was what women did: talk, talk, talk. Talking about their feelings until you wanted to get on the nearest boat and sail until you hit the edge of the world.

"Are you offering to fix that problem?" he drawled. "Because it sounds to me like you're interested."

Gwen blushed. Being a redhead, she blushed easily and often. It was one of the things Jack found charming about her.

"I am not offering to fix anything. I'm just wondering." She spread her hands. "I just want people to be happy."

"Then how about you stick to making your customers happy. I'm doing just fine on my own."

"Sounds like someone doth protest too much."

Jack shot her an annoyed look before he took off.

THE DAY JACK had met Gwen Parker, she'd been covered in paint splatters, her hair a mess. She and her older brother, Elliot, had been working on the bed and breakfast all summer long. When Jack had heard that someone had bought the old, boarded-up house on Main Street, he'd assumed the new owner would simply bulldoze it.

Jack knew everyone on Hazel Island, even if he didn't make a point to be friends with them. When he stopped by the house-in-progress, he had to sidestep a hole in the porch. When the boards under his feet squeaked ominously, he prayed he didn't fall through to his doom.

Gwen had opened the door with a flourish. She'd smiled at him, and that smile had been like a punch to the gut. Jack was hardly a guy who used fancy words, but the word *radiant* had been the first thing that had popped into his head.

Gwen was radiant: from her bright hair, to her smile, to the way she moved, like some mystical spirit. She did everything with energy.

He introduced himself, and she shook his hand, her grip surprisingly strong despite her size.

"I'm in desperate need of fresh salmon. I've heard you're the guy for the job," she said brightly.

"Yeah, that's me."

"I honestly don't know anything about what makes any fish good or not. I've eaten my fair share of sushi, but if you handed me a tuna, I couldn't tell you if it was a good one or not."

Jack listened as this woman he'd never met chattered on.

She didn't come up for air. He wondered if there was something wrong with her.

Or maybe, just maybe, she just *liked to talk to people.* He shuddered internally at the thought.

"If you're worried that I'd screw you over," he said, "you don't have to be. Ask anyone on the island. They can vouch for me."

Her eyes widened. "Oh! Of course not. I didn't mean to imply that. I'm sure you're very honorable. The most honorable fisherman there is."

He eyed her. Was she messing with him? But based on her expression, she seemed entirely sincere.

He couldn't help but notice that she wasn't wearing a wedding ring. Her brother was helping her renovate the place, so she must not have a boyfriend or fiancé. That surprised him. Gwen didn't seem like the type of woman who would do well on her own. She needed to talk too much.

She'd hate how Jack lived: in a tiny house, isolated from humanity, no computer or internet. He had a radio and not much else for entertainment.

"Are you from Hazel Island? A lot of people seem to have been born and raised here. It's not like Seattle. Everybody is a transplant there, it seems like," said Gwen.

"I've been here for a while," was all Jack said in reply.

Gwen glanced at her phone. "Oh, crap, I need to meet my brother. I lost track of time. It was nice to meet you. If you're ever free, please stop by when we're open for a bite to eat."

Jack just nodded. He had no intention of coming to this little hole in the wall that would probably go bankrupt within a year. Not that Gwen Parker seemed out of her depth. It was just the nature of this island that small businesses either sank or swim given the fluctuation of the local economy. If you didn't know how to save during the months of good business, you wouldn't have enough to sustain you through the leaner months.

Gwen's phone rang right before Jack left. He watched as her face turned pale. The phone kept ringing, Gwen staring at the screen, like she couldn't decide if she wanted to answer it.

That was his cue to leave. But the sudden vulnerability of her expression compared to how she'd been just minutes earlier pierced something inside him.

Finally, her phone stopped ringing. When she looked up, she started, as if she'd forgotten about Jack's presence.

"Spam call," she said, clearly lying, considering she wouldn't meet his eyes. "They're the worst, right?"

"I wouldn't know. I don't have a cell phone."

Gwen gaped at him. "Seriously? How do you call people?"

"I have a landline."

"Well, you're maybe the last person on earth that does. Even my dad has a cell phone, and he barely knows how to print something."

Gwen's phone started ringing again. This time, she turned it off and shoved it into her pocket.

"Somebody bothering you?" said Jack. *Why do you care?* he asked himself.

"Oh, just my husband." She grimaced. "I mean, my ex-husband. We're separated."

Ex-husband. So she'd been married—was still married,

technically. Jack didn't know why that angered him. Was it because she was still legally bound to another man?

Or because she was free to date other people?

"He keeps wanting to talk. I don't know what there is to talk about. I already served him the papers. Now suddenly he's got cold feet." Gwen made a face. "I'm sorry. TMI. You don't care, I'm sure."

Jack saw the way her shoulders hunched. He noticed the circles under her eyes, and how she kept touching her back pocket where she'd put her phone, like a weird talisman. He had the sudden urge to keep her safe.

"Don't apologize." His voice was gruff. "You don't have anything to be sorry about."

She looked a little stunned at that pronouncement.

As Jack drove to his next stop, he kept seeing her face in his mind's eye.

As the weeks, the months, the years passed, he and Gwen fell into a routine: he'd come by every Tuesday and Thursday with a fresh catch. He never told her that he under-charged her, especially when she first opened the bed and breakfast.

She'd make sure to have a fresh cup of coffee–sugar, no cream–ready to hand to him. Sometimes she'd ply him with a donut or pastry, although she soon discovered he preferred savory things. So she started making him breakfast burritos, telling him he was her guinea pig for new items on their menu.

Jack heard through the grapevine about Gwen's divorce being finalized. When he saw her the following morning, he could tell she'd been crying. He made sure to charge her less than half for her salmon without her knowing about it.

When he heard she was dating someone, he didn't accept the coffee or breakfast items, telling her he'd already eaten. It felt odd, accepting her gifts when she should be giving them to the man she was dating.

As the years passed, they formed a friendship, something Jack had never had with another woman. He watched as Gwen gained confidence in running her business. He watched as she dated one man, then another, the relationships never lasting long. He watched as she became a pillar of the community, even though Hazel Island was a difficult place to be accepted if you hadn't been born there.

He watched Gwen because if he could do nothing else, he'd look out for her as long as he was able.

CHAPTER TWO

G wen Parker knew the answer before the bank loan officer opened his mouth.

"Unfortunately, Mrs. Parker..."

"Ms.," she corrected automatically. "Parker is my maiden name."

The loan officer shuffled the papers in front of him. "Pardon me. Ms. Parker. Yes, unfortunately, we are not able to extend a loan to you at this time."

Gwen felt heat creep into her cheeks. "May I ask why?"

"Unfortunately," the loan officer said for a third time, making Gwen hate the word, "your credit is not adequate for the bank to feel confident that you will be able to repay a loan of that size. That being said, we may be able to extend an offer of credit to you. Let me see..."

He looked at his computer monitor. "At 17.9% APR."

Gwen had to stifle a laugh. The business loan she'd applied for? The interest was capped at less than half that rate. The last thing she needed was to get a credit card and make her credit worse.

She thanked the loan officer after he did his best to get her to sign up for some other product. As Gwen left the bank, she saw at least three people who looked like they wanted to stop to speak with her. But she ignored them, hoping they wouldn't be offended.

Living on a small island was both a blessing and a curse, Gwen found. Blessing, because it was like living in paradise. A curse, because everybody knew everybody and there were no secrets here. It was as if the gossip grapevine was baked into the very earth itself.

"Gwen! Is that you?"

Gwen looked up, and belatedly realized she'd made eye contact. Now she was well and truly caught. Normally, she didn't mind stopping to chat with people. She was the owner of the local bed and breakfast: it was her job to be personable.

She just wanted to go home and brood. Judy Turner, though, always wanted to talk and was the biggest gossip on Hazel Island. Since her husband had passed away two years ago, she'd had no one to tell her to leave off.

"So nice to see you!" Judy gushed. As she approached, Gwen could smell her perfume, a scent that was a combination of roses and cotton balls. It always made Gwen want to sneeze.

"Hi, Judy. How are you?"

"Oh, you know me. The arthritis in my knee just keeps getting worse every year. I tell my doctor that, but he keeps telling me, 'Judy, if you would go for walks, it would help.' But how am I supposed to walk with a bum knee? Makes no sense."

Judy also tended to complain about her every health

issue. Gwen had already heard accounts of pretty much every organ and limb in Judy's body: knees, hip, gallbladder, lungs, and then some.

Gwen realized too late that she was holding the loan documents in her hands, and Judy's eagle-eyed gaze zeroed in on them before she could stash them in her bag.

"Are you buying another building in town?" Judy tried to look more closely at the top piece of paper, but Gwen folded them in half to block her view. "You know, the Wrights are selling that old house down by Terrace Avenue, you know, the one where the kids all go to mess around?"

Gwen hadn't told anyone about her plans to expand the bed and breakfast. She wanted to open a restaurant right next door. After five years of business, Gwen had felt that it was time to push herself to expand the business.

But now that she hadn't gotten the loan, it seemed less likely that this restaurant dream of hers would come to fruition.

"I'm just talking to a few people," hedged Gwen. "Nothing has been decided yet."

Something in Gwen's tone must've had an edge because Judy seemed taken aback. "I didn't mean to pry, dear. You know me. I'm too curious for my own good. Not much else to do since Frank died, you know."

Gwen was about to apologize, but was stopped when a male voice said, "Afternoon, ladies."

"Oh, Jack, how wonderful to see you," said Judy. "How are the salmon? I've heard things have been terrible lately. Do you even catch any? I would imagine your nets are rather empty lately!"

Fortunately for both Gwen and Jack, Judy realized that the bank would close soon, and she hurried inside.

Jack towered over Gwen. When he folded his arms across his chest, she had to stop herself from gaping at the muscles in his tanned forearms.

"If we walk fast, she probably won't catch up to us," said Gwen.

Jack's lips quirked upward in a rare smile. "Are you trying to get away from the old lady?"

"If she asks me one more question, I might lose it entirely."

Jack, being Jack, didn't press Gwen for an explanation. That was something she'd always appreciated about the rugged fisherman. He didn't waste her time.

He was direct, and he didn't try to meddle in her life. They had a friendship based on business and mutual respect. And Gwen was fine with that.

And if she ogled him out of the corner of her eye, what of it? She was human. Nothing was going to happen between them. They'd known each other for five years, and Jack hadn't so much as said something flirtatious to her. Gwen knew she wasn't his type.

Jack seemed to like the girls who didn't live on the island full time. Any time Gwen had a group of attractive, single ladies at the bed and breakfast, she knew one of them would end up going home with Jack.

It didn't bother her. Jack could do what he wanted, even if Gwen didn't understand why he preferred women who didn't stick around.

Gwen sat down on a bench that overlooked the water. It was one of her favorite spots, especially at sunrise. She liked to come here and meditate before the bed and breakfast opened for the day.

Jack didn't say anything; he didn't even sit next to her. He stood and gazed out at the horizon. Gwen wondered if he'd forgotten she was even there.

"Why were you at the credit union?" Jack glanced at her.

"Is it so odd that I went to the bank?"

"No. But that isn't your bank."

Jack might not be particularly verbose, but he was observant. He'd probably noticed that she would walk to First National—the other bank on the island–every Friday to deposit any cash or checks.

"I'm trying to get a business loan," she replied.

Jack didn't say anything, which only made her want to explain herself more.

"I have an idea, but I need funding. Nothing more complicated than that." She shrugged, making certain that the paperwork from the bank was hidden from Jack's view.

"An idea for what?"

This was where Gwen hesitated. She didn't know why, but she was afraid that talking about her restaurant scheme would somehow jinx it. *Or you don't want people to tell you it's a terrible idea.*

She'd already gotten her fair share of judgment from her dad and other family and friends about her opening the bed and breakfast. She didn't need a repeat of it.

But Gwen knew that Jack wouldn't judge her. He never had, in all of the years she'd known him. Early on, she'd thought he wasn't even listening to her, he'd been that stoic. But as she'd gotten to know him, she realized that he listened. He just preferred to speak when he felt it was truly necessary.

"I want to open a restaurant next to the bed and breakfast. We've already seen a lot of success with expanding our breakfasts to those who aren't staying at the inn. I think there's a real need for a homey kind of place here. Especially since Sutter's closed down a year ago..."

Gwen sighed because she was getting excited. She knew it was probably foolish to get excited. "But I was denied for a loan. The credit union denied me, too. So I'll have to figure out another way to get funding."

She could ask her brother Elliot, but he and his wife Bekah had a young daughter to think of. Her dad didn't have much in the way of savings, either. And Gwen didn't have any wealthy friends she could go to for a loan.

Jack sat down next to her on the bench. He stretched out his legs and then his arms across the back of the bench, as if he needed to take up as much space as possible. With any other man, Gwen would find that annoying. In Jack, she found it rather endearing.

"Who else have you asked?" said Jack.

"No one. Besides the banks, you're the only other person I've told about this. So please don't tell anyone else."

Jack grunted.

"It's probably a crazy idea, anyway. I know restaurants are one of the hardest businesses to get off the ground. Most fail within five years. The margins are razor-thin. Even if I secured funding, I could just as easily screw this all up."

"You won't screw it up."

Gwen looked up, surprised at the serious note in Jack's

voice. He quickly looked away and added, "You haven't screwed up yet with your current business."

"That you know of." She chuckled. "I'm just good at making things look good."

Jack stayed silent, and Gwen wondered what was turning in that brain of his. Despite knowing him for five years, she always felt like she'd never really *known* him. He had hidden depths to him. Any time she'd tried to get him to talk about his history, he'd skirted the topic. She didn't even know when his birthday was.

"Have you thought about talking to Luke?" said Jack.

Luke was the eldest son of the Wright family, who'd lived on the island for three generations now. They owned multiple businesses in town and had the biggest house on the island. They were one of the few families that lived outside the main part of town, high up on a clifftop that overlooked the ocean.

Everyone knew the Wright family had money. But that didn't mean they were particularly interested in giving it away.

"I don't really know him. I think I've spoken to him five times? Maybe?" Gwen could see Luke's face in her mind, his easygoing smile, but he'd always seemed untouchable to her. The golden boy with privilege dripping from his very pores. He exuded money and class that Gwen couldn't relate to in the slightest.

"I know he wants to invest more in businesses on the island," said Jack.

"You're friends with him, right?"

Jack shrugged. "Of a sort. He likes to tell me things

because I don't give a shit about his money like most people."

"I think that might be one definition of friendship." Gwen smiled.

"I can talk to him for you. See if he'd be interested. Even if he isn't, he'd keep his mouth shut, if that's what worries you."

Gwen's heart squeezed. She'd been so certain that this idea of hers was doomed to fail, but Jack was giving her a potential lifeline. She suddenly felt like she couldn't possibly deserve it.

Then again, Luke Wright would be the one to make the decision. Not Jack.

"If Luke agrees to finance you," continued Jack, "I'll match that amount."

Gwen stared. "You have that kind of money?" was her first reaction. Then she blushed. "I'm sorry. That was rude. That's extremely generous of you—"

"I'm doing it for selfish reasons, too. Another restaurant means another customer for me. I'd want a stake in the business and a guarantee that you'd only buy fish from me." The corner of his mouth quirked up. "Assuming I can deliver, that is."

"It's still generous of you." She was looking at her hands. "I hope you don't think me telling you about this was me asking for money."

"Gwen, look at me."

She did, and his dark brown eyes were totally serious.

"If anyone deserves the money, it's you," he said.

CHAPTER THREE

E arly that morning, Gwen watched as the group of middle-aged women who'd booked almost all the inn's rooms got ready to go hiking. It was already raining, but that didn't stop the group that had dubbed themselves the Furies.

Apparently, they all loved Greek mythology and loved to imagine themselves as terrifying monsters. When in reality, they were mostly polite older ladies with a love for extra-hot coffee and gaudy scarves.

The leader of the Furies, Helen, was going around to each member to inspect their pack and footwear.

"Alice, you can't wear sandals. We're going *hiking*, not a jaunt to the beach," said Helen.

"These sandals are specifically for hiking! I got them online."

"That's not a thing. There are rocks, and it's raining. Go put on the right shoes. I'm not carrying you when your feet start to hurt."

Alice grumbled but did as she was told. Helen was a tall,

thin woman with a pointy chin, a pointy nose, and a decid-edly pointy personality.

When she'd first booked the rooms, she'd told Gwen that she didn't want "any of that extra crap that costs an arm and a leg." Gwen had assured Helen that there would be no "extra crap" on the bill.

Another member of the group had donned a hat with a mosquito net, even though there weren't mosquitoes on the island. Another woman was hurriedly putting on mascara before Helen returned. Helen didn't approve of makeup while hiking, either.

"Where are the lunches?" Helen appeared in front of Gwen like an apparition. "I don't see the lunches."

Gwen gave Helen her best the-customer-is-always-right smile. "They're being finished up right now. Jocelyn wanted to make sure everything was as fresh as possible."

Helen harrumphed. "You made sure my lunch was vegan? And no mushrooms, peppers, or olives?"

"Of course. I made a special note for yours."

Helen didn't look convinced. Gwen crossed her fingers that Jocelyn had paid attention to Gwen's note about Helen's lunch.

Alice had returned wearing boots that, based on how shiny they were, would be mud-splattered by the time the group returned. After Jocelyn and the staff gave everyone their bagged lunches, the group was off, Helen in the front issuing directions. It was rather like watching an army going into battle, if that army wore Lululemon sweats and over-sized rain hats.

"Did you make sure Helen's was vegan?" said Gwen to Jocelyn.

Jocelyn Gray, who was the older sister of one of Gwen's dearest friends, had studied at a culinary school in New York City and had even spent a summer in Paris. She'd only returned to the island to help care for her ailing father. Unlike Alex, Jocelyn's sister, Jocelyn was straightforward and rather mysterious to Gwen. Alex tended to overshare where her sister simply didn't share.

"I made her a mushroom wrap," replied Jocelyn.

Gwen's eyes widening. "No mushrooms! Please tell me you're joking."

Jocelyn's expression remained bland until she started laughing. "You look like you were about to shit a brick. I promise her wrap was without any animal products, mushrooms, peppers, *or* olives. So basically, it's made up of air and bitterness," added Jocelyn wryly.

"Geez, give me a heart attack, why don't you? I already had to listen to her complaining about the coffee being too strong."

"Didn't she just complain a few days ago that it was too weak?"

"Exactly."

Jocelyn chuckled. "I have to admit, I've been enjoying cooking for everyone. I thought this gig would just be reheating old bagels, but I can make my own dishes. I appreciate that."

"Reheat old bagels? Now you're insulting me," joked Gwen.

"Hey, I'm just going off every other hotel I've stayed at."

Gwen was shuffling papers from the front register, returning pens to their cups and wiping down the counter. The entrance to the bed and breakfast was an open room that served as a dining area. Behind that were Gwen's office and the kitchen. There were two large rooms on the first floor, along with five rooms upstairs.

The inn had once been a house that Gwen had converted.

She'd made certain to retain its early twentieth-century charm, including all the random nooks and crannies that were common for these types of houses in the era. Although at times she wished for new pipes and central air conditioning on the warmer days, she wouldn't change this place for the world.

Next door was a small plot of land with another old house on it that the Wright family had owned up until a few years ago. Due to its small size, it had never been turned into a business like a lot of places on Main Street. It was where Gwen wanted to open her restaurant—and ideally, with Jocelyn as its head chef.

Gwen gathered her nerve. "Do you know what you'll be doing in the next few months or years? Will you be staying on the island?"

"I don't know. Dad isn't getting better and can't take care of himself. And it's too much to put on Alex completely." Jocelyn shrugged. "More than likely I'm stuck here for a while."

"I haven't told anyone this—" *except Jack Benson, that is* —"but I want to open a restaurant next door. And I'd love for you to be the head chef." Gwen said the words in a rush.

"What kind of restaurant?"

"American, comfort food. Something that's both high-end but...not." Gwen laughed a little. "I should add that it might not happen. I'm still working on funding. I want to buy the house next door and convert it like I did this place. It might be a pipe dream, but you're so talented, you deserve a position as a chef. Not just as a maker of sack lunches."

Jocelyn was leaning against the counter, considering Gwen's words. Gwen couldn't tell by her face what she was thinking. Was she trying to figure out how to let Gwen down nicely?

Jocelyn was hardly a self-taught cook. She'd graduated from one of the best culinary schools in the country, for God's sake. Her food had already won awards. The fact that she'd had to give all of that up to move to Hazel Island was a tragedy.

"I get to create the menu, the dishes, and have complete control of the kitchen?" said Jocelyn.

"Absolutely. I only know how to reheat bagels, remember?"

"Then I accept." Jocelyn put out her hand. "For whatever that's worth. But if you want to make this happen, I'll help you however I can."

Gwen shook Jocelyn's hand, laughing incredulously. Butterflies filled her stomach. Jocelyn agreeing to this scheme, Jack helping her find funding–it made it all too real. Now she had to figure out how to do it.

"Although when you say complete control of the kitchen," said Gwen, "do you mean I have no oversight at all?"

"I mean, I don't want anyone who isn't a chef to come in and tell me how to do my job."

As the owner and manager of the inn, Gwen planned to have the same role in the restaurant. The thought of giving that control to another person made her queasy.

"I need to be able to oversee my own staff," said Gwen.

"Micro-managing doesn't help anyone."

Considering Jocelyn was helping on an as-needed basis at the moment and was being paid as an independent contractor, she had more leeway in speaking to Gwen than the other members of her staff. Jessie, one of the maids, walked past the two of them and raised an inquisitive eyebrow that Gwen ignored.

"Perhaps we should go to my office," said Gwen.

"There's no one here."

"You will be my employee and will report to me. Your cooks will report to you. I have no interest in interfering in your decisions as a chef, but the restaurant overall will be under my direction."

Gwen had learned over the past five years to stick to her guns. She liked to think she was a fair boss, but she didn't mess around, either. She expected good performances from all her employees, including herself.

Jocelyn just narrowed her eyes. "I don't like being told what to do," she finally said.

For whatever reason, that admittance made Gwen laugh. "Now I get why Alex says you're bossy."

At Gwen's remark, Jocelyn's expression turned a little cold. "Of course Alex says that about me to other people."

Gwen had a feeling she'd stepped in something, but she didn't know what it was. As Alex's friend, Gwen had only heard snippets about Jocelyn. Alex had always sounded like a younger sister ripping into her older sibling when she'd described Jocelyn. But now Gwen wondered.

"You know Alex," said Gwen, trying to lighten the mood. "She says a lot of things."

She continued, "We can discuss the details later, but I promise that I don't want to micro-manage you or anyone else. Just ask my staff. I think they'll tell you I prefer to trust them to do their jobs than be constantly standing over their shoulder."

Jocelyn said she'd think about it, and they both returned to work.

GWEN EVENTUALLY WENT to her office to be alone for a few moments. She'd naively expected Jocelyn to either say yes or no, not for her to negotiate. Of course she would negotiate, Gwen reasoned. Jocelyn was a talented chef, and she didn't want to waste her skills.

She took a deep breath, then another. She hated conflict. She hated when people were upset with her. Even though she knew that, logically, her discussion with Jocelyn had been just that–a discussion–she still felt that familiar anxiety surfacing.

Her ex-husband had loved conflict, or at least, that was what it had felt like to Gwen. Tim had liked to pick fights with not only her but anyone else close to him. At the beginning of their marriage, Gwen had tried her best to keep Tim happy and to avoid any possible conflict.

If it had meant that she'd had to load the dishwasher the way he liked it, or that she'd needed to wash his clothes in a particular brand of detergent, she'd done it. She hadn't minded. She'd wanted to make her husband happy.

Tim Harrington had been Gwen's high school sweetheart. He'd been a year older than her, and when he'd asked her out, she'd jumped at the chance. Who would've said no to the cute basketball player with dreamy blue eyes? He'd taken her for burgers and milkshakes, and it had been Gwen's dream come true.

They married when she had just turned twenty. Both of their families told them they were too young, but Gwen was in love. Tim was her soulmate. Why wait to marry when she already knew they would?

The first year of marriage was blissful. Gwen graduated from college while Tim worked at his dad's construction business. They bought a little townhouse in the suburbs of Seattle. They talked about having kids one day.

Gwen had nothing to complain about. If their sex life was lacking, what of it? No one's marriage was perfect, Gwen had reasoned. Besides, they had all the time in the world to learn. Gwen had been a virgin when she'd first started dated Tim, while Tim had only had sex a few times with his previous girlfriend.

Tim was attentive, at least at first. But as the months, and then years wore on, Gwen could tell he was frustrated that she needed too much foreplay. When he complained one evening that she took too long, Gwen did what she always did: she worked hard to make the other person happy.

The foreplay dried up. Soon, Gwen found sex a chore with her husband. He never hurt her; he just didn't seem to *see* her. The sex would last a few minutes and then Tim would fall asleep, snoring loudly as Gwen stayed awake, wondering why she couldn't just enjoy sex for once.

One night, four years into their marriage, Tim stopped in the middle of sex and rolled off her. He made a disgusted sound.

"Do you have to just lie there?" he snapped.

Gwen could feel herself freezing up. She wrapped her arms around her middle.

"It's like fucking a dead person. It's creepy." Tim sat up. "You're my wife, right? Because sometimes you act like you hate me."

"I don't hate you." And she didn't. She loved him, dearly.

Tim sighed. "I'm tired. Let's just go to sleep."

They didn't talk about that night again. They had sex a few more times, but eventually, the sex disappeared entirely.

Tim picked fights with her more often, mostly about stupid things. But one day, it came to a head, when he told her there was something wrong with her.

"You're–I don't know!" He gesticulated wildly. "I don't know what's wrong with you."

She vowed to do better. She tried to seduce her husband, but in the middle of sex, she froze up. It was like being trapped in some nightmare. She told him they had to stop, and although Tim said nothing, his frustrated sigh said everything.

Tim strayed. Gwen knew it, but she was too tired to be upset about it. When she came home to find him in their bed with his mistress, though, she decided she'd had enough. She filed for divorce and moved out. Then she'd moved to Hazel Island for a fresh start.

Gwen took a deep breath again. Jocelyn wasn't Tim.

Even though she had the urge to go back and say she'd do whatever Jocelyn wanted, she resisted.

And then, for some odd reason, she saw Jack's face: the lines of his jaw, the creases in the corners of his eyes. How he'd stepped up to help her. Why? They were friends, yes, but she didn't think they were that close.

Her heart fluttered. She could dream of Jack as much as she wanted. He wasn't interested in her romantically, and she knew she shouldn't date, anyway. Not with her issues. What guy would want to be with a woman who froze up during sex? Who was incapable of one of the most basic things on earth?

Gwen wiped away a few stray tears before returning to run her business. She might not have any romance in her life, but at least she had the inn to keep her occupied.

CHAPTER FOUR

J ack gazed up at the entrance to the Wrights' house and wondered what the hell he was doing.

House? No, it was a mansion. Maybe even an estate. Jack didn't know what the difference was, nor did he care. All he did know was that the house was designed to intimidate.

The drive to get to the place was down a private road that ended in a gate, where Jack had to state his name and purpose before being allowed to enter the grounds.

The house sat atop a cliff. It was two stories, the white stucco blinding in the sunshine. With multiple decks encircling the house, it was built to showcase the magnificent views. To the east were the blue waters of Puget Sound. On cloudless days, you could see the snow-capped peak of Mount Rainier. To the west were the tall evergreens that made up the middle of Hazel Island.

It was an oasis within an oasis. A place where Jack assumed nothing bad ever happened. Money had a way of making life so much easier.

"Jack, what are you doing out there?" called a voice.

Jack tilted his head back to see Luke Wright standing on the deck some thirty feet above where the front door was located.

"I'm here for you, obviously," rumbled Jack.

"You might ring the doorbell. It's a thing people do when they come to people's houses."

Jack ignored that. "Then how about you come down here and open the door already."

Within seconds, Jack was inside, and Luke was giving him one of his infamous bear hugs. Luke was one of the few people that Jack allowed to hug him. In all honesty, he couldn't think of another person who'd hugged him since he'd been a child.

Jack had been here on a few occasions, but every time he entered the place, he marveled at it. Luke, though, was used to it. He'd grown up here, after all.

"Let's go upstairs and talk," said Luke. "How are you, by the way? You've been impossible to pin down lately."

"I'm busy earning a living." He shot Luke a wry look.

Luke, good-natured as always, just laughed. "Who else would tell me to eat shit but you?"

They went up the carved, wooden staircase, Jack quickly getting lost as Luke took him to one of the many open-air decks.

"How many rooms do you have anyway?" said Jack.

Luke shrugged. "I can never remember. Ask my dad. He'll tell you about every single one."

Jack had met the patriarch of the Wright clan once. He'd seemed nice enough but distracted with business matters. Their mom apparently preferred to lounge all day with her cadre of tiny, yipping dogs.

"Are you living here now?" said Jack.

Luke had his own place in both Seattle and on Hazel Island. Jack had been surprised when Luke had asked him to come to his parents' place.

"We're dealing with some family stuff right now. I'm only here temporarily." Luke didn't explain further.

Gazing out onto the horizon, Jack suddenly wished he'd asked Luke to come to him. Luke had an advantage, being in this place that reminded Jack of how little he'd accomplished in his own life. He lived in a tiny house all by himself. He spent his days with fish. What did he have to show for himself? Certainly not a mansion like this.

Luke got them both drinks, Jack nursing his beer instead of getting to the point of this little meeting. He'd never asked his friend for money. It went against everything Jack stood for.

But for Gwen...he'd grit his teeth and do it.

"So, are you going to start the conversation, or am I?" Luke grinned. "You look like you're going to shit your pants, Benson."

"Don't make me throw you off this deck." Given that Jack was quite a bit larger than Luke, it wasn't out of the realm of possibility.

"Always so pleasant. You said there was a business venture you were interested in. I think that means you want my advice. Yes?"

Jack glowered and shot back, "I don't want your advice; I want your money."

Luke's eyes widened, then he started laughing. He kept laughing until Jack wondered if his friend had finally lost his mind. Wiping away tears, Luke said, "That's probably the worst request for money I've ever gotten. Zero subtlety whatsoever."

"Then if you're not interested—" Jack rose to go, but Luke put out a hand.

"Unruffle your feathers. I'm fucking with you. You're always so stoic and serious, sometimes you have to poke the bear."

"Bears can tear your head off," groused Jack.

"Not if they want some of that sweet, sweet money. Or honey. I think this metaphor might be getting away from me, in all honesty." Forcing himself to be serious, Luke added, "Start from the beginning. I promise I won't interrupt."

Jack was skeptical, but he gave Luke the speech he'd rehearsed in his mind as he'd been driving up to the Wright place.

Another restaurant will benefit not only my own business but the island's economy. This in turn would bring in more tourists. If you could match the loan I plan to give, the restaurant could get off the ground and hopefully make a profit much faster.

But Luke seemed like he was barely listening at this point. "I don't care about the economic prospects. I care about why you want to do this. As far as I know, you aren't the type to throw your money away on a small business. Especially not on restaurants, which are often doomed to fail."

"I already gave you my reasons."

Luke eyed him. "You said this would be next to the bed and breakfast. Will it be connected to it?"

Jack hadn't mentioned Gwen's name because it felt almost like bad luck to do so. *Or maybe you don't want Luke peering more closely into your reasons.*

"Aha, I love when I'm right." Luke set down his beer. "Now it all makes sense. You're doing this for Ms. Parker. The redhead."

"This has nothing to do with Gwen." Jack was clenching his jaw so hard he had to force the words out.

"She's very pretty. I don't blame you. She talks too much, though. The last time I spoke to her, I could barely get in a word edgewise, and God knows I never have that problem normally," said Luke.

"You don't know what you're talking about," said Jack in a harsh tone. Forcing himself to stay calm, he added, "This will help Gwen. But it'll help a lot of other people, too."

"Hmm."

Silence settled between them. Jack began tapping his fingers against his knee. Was he going to have to beg Luke? He wasn't that desperate. Besides, he had too much pride. He'd rather get the money from someone else.

Who else has that kind of money? That was the problem. Jack didn't know anyone else who did. He could go through a bank, but his credit history was negligible. It had seemed pointless, given his lifestyle, until this moment. Now Jack regretted how committed he'd been to living off the grid.

"I'm not going to tell you yes," said Luke finally. "I want Gwen to come to me herself. If she can put together a business plan and some financials, show me the ins and outs of this venture, I'll definitely consider it. She's already been successful with the bed and breakfast. Clearly she isn't an idiot with business."

Jack let out the breath he'd been holding. "I'll let her know," he said.

"You know, it's funny. I've known you since you moved here, and I do think of you as a friend. But I don't think I really know you. You've always been a mystery. You keep to yourself. You're still single at your age—"

"Get to the point, Wright."

"I'm just saying that it's *interesting* that you suddenly want to help a woman, and not only that, but you were willing to ask for money on her behalf. You've never, in all the years I've known you, asked me for money." Luke's eyes flashed. "And God knows I'm used to people asking me for money."

"You know I wouldn't ask if I didn't think it was worth doing."

"Of course not. I trust you way more than most people. You never bullshit me. That's invaluable, my friend."

ON HIS DRIVE HOME, Jack's mind wandered. Luke's answer hadn't been what he'd been hoping for, but at least there was still a chance of funding for Gwen. Would Gwen be pleased? Or would she find it too much of a pain to put all of that together without a guarantee of getting a loan?

Jack had always been more of a saver than a spender. He'd had to be, when he'd had to buy groceries and pay the bills as a kid. He and his younger brother Danny had had to shift for themselves. Their mom had been an addict who'd spend their last dime on drugs instead of on food. By the age of seven, Jack had known to hide any money or benefits from their mom so she wouldn't spend them first.

As soon as Jack had gotten away from their mom–leaving Danny behind, for which Jack still felt guilty–he'd begun scrimping and saving. He'd work any jobs he could, especially ones that paid under the table.

When he finally had enough to get out of Seattle, he'd moved to Hazel Island on a whim. He'd wanted to get as far away from the city as he could, and he only had enough money for the trip to the island.

Once he'd arrived, he'd looked for work, but despite getting a few odd jobs here and there, he struggled. It was only when a local fisherman hired him to help out during fishing season that Jack learned the trade. And when he'd saved enough, he'd bought his own boat and begun his life as a fisherman.

A few years after he'd started working as a fisherman, Jack had been able to buy the small plot of land where he'd built his tiny house. He managed the upkeep himself. He'd done such a great job of living independently that Jack had almost convinced himself he could be alone for the rest of his life and remain content.

He enjoyed women here and there, of course. When he had an itch, he'd get it scratched and then move on. No strings, no commitment. His life was just fine that way.

And now at age thirty-five, Jack had a nice-sized nest egg. He could spare a portion of it for Gwen. Besides, he would reap the rewards eventually. *I'm doing it for myself*, he kept telling himself. *This isn't for Gwen.*

He'd always shifted for himself. It was easier that way. He knew what happened when you had to depend on someone else: they let you down. Better to keep people at arm's length, he figured.

He kept telling himself that, even as he returned to a silent house and a cold bed.

CHAPTER FIVE

"You should come out with us," said Alexandra Gray, Jocelyn's younger sister. A curvy brunette with boundless energy, Alex was one of those people who could cajole anyone, man, beast, or plant. Gwen was pretty sure Alex had sweet-talked her latest plant that she'd added to her bookstore into growing three leaves in a week.

Gwen glanced up from the papers strewn about her desk. "I have to finish this up. I'm already way behind on this month's accounts."

Alex slipped into the ratty chair across from Gwen's desk and pouted. "You always have an excuse. I've been very understanding, you know, but the last time you went out was two months ago. I remember. You said yes and I nearly dropped a book on a customer's head when I was shelving."

Alex owned the little bookstore on Main Street, the only one on Hazel Island. Despite essentially having a monopoly on books, Gwen had heard through the grapevine that Alex's business wasn't doing well. But Alex, as sunny as ever, had never let on to Gwen.

"Have you ever dropped a book on a customer's head?" said Gwen, genuinely curious.

"Only on purpose." Alex grinned. "Come on, you need to have some fun. You've been working your ass off. But you can't go, go, go forever. A girl's gotta let loose, have some drinks. Maybe find a guy to nail."

Gwen shot her friend a dark look. "I'm not nailing anyone."

"When did you turn into such an old lady?"

Alex said the words lightly, but they still stung a bit. Gwen had turned into something of an old lady: going straight home after work and heating up some frozen meal and watching TV.

She often fell asleep on the couch and woke up to infomercials at three AM. Nothing like getting yelled at by a man obsessed with laundry detergent to make a girl rethink her life choices.

This work could wait. Gwen was just giving excuses, and she knew it. Closing her laptop, she said to Alex, "Okay, where are we going?"

Alex clapped her hands. "There you go! Come on, we can get changed at my apartment. If we can get Felicity to join us, it'll be an even greater miracle."

Felicity Linden was even more of an introvert than Gwen. She worked from home as a writer, although she refused to disclose what, exactly, she wrote about, despite Alex's best efforts otherwise. Shy and quiet, Felicity tended to fade into the background. Gwen often noticed that she let her hair hang in her face to cover up the large birthmark on her face.

But the stars must've been aligned because Felicity joined

Gwen and Alex at Deja Vu, the bar that functioned as a club on Friday and Saturday nights. Gwen had been surprised when it had opened: Hazel Island wasn't known for attracting a lot of young people. But to her surprise, the club was absolutely packed with people who couldn't be older than college-aged.

"Where did all of these youths come from?" joked Gwen to Alex.

"There might be a rumor that you can get in without showing ID. Apparently, the enforcement is rather loose," said Alex.

Felicity, wearing her usual black without an inch of skin showing, frowned. "There are underage people here drinking?"

"I know nothing, I see nothing. Besides, it's just a rumor. Maybe all these youths are thirty, flirty and thriving." Alex then handed Gwen and Felicity drinks. "Cheers to us! Old enough to drink but not old enough to give up on having fun."

Gwen could cheer to that. She found herself finishing one drink, then another in quick succession. The alcohol made her feel warm, and suddenly all the worries that had been pressing on her faded away.

Alex had been right: she'd needed to get out.

The club pulsed with music, so loud that Gwen knew she'd probably be half-deaf when they left. But that was the handy thing about booze: you suddenly didn't care about the details. She and Alex danced with a group of guys, Felicity even dancing a little.

As the night wore on, Gwen could feel her internal old lady coming out. She was sweaty and tired, and the alcohol buzz was wearing off. Suddenly, she felt claustrophobic. Heading to the restroom, she nearly collided with another woman, who shot her an annoyed look. "Watch where you're going," she said.

The single-stall restroom was blessedly dim. Gwen didn't want to know how dirty it actually was. Splashing cold water on her face, she took in one deep breath, then another.

"Why am I always like this?" she said to her reflection. "Why can't I just have fun for once?"

Her reflection didn't have an answer. Sighing, she wiped her hands off on her pants since the paper towel dispenser was empty. When she returned to the dance floor, she couldn't find Alex or Felicity.

One of the young men they'd been dancing with earlier sidled up to Gwen. Putting his hands on her hips, he said in her ear, "Does the carpet match the drapes?"

Gwen reared back. The man didn't let go of her hips. "I need to find my friends."

"I've never fucked a redhead. How about you pop my cherry?"

Gwen grimaced in distaste. "How about not." She pushed the man's hands away, but that only seemed to embolden him.

Pushing back panic, she struggled to free herself, but the crowd was so thick that she couldn't get away. The man started grinding on her as if her struggle meant that she'd consented.

Where were Alex and Felicity? They wouldn't have left without her, would they? But maybe they'd been so drunk that they hadn't realized Gwen had gone to the bathroom. And if they were looking for her now...

"Let go of me," said Gwen. When the man seemed not to hear her, she yelled, "Let go of me!"

He let go, but only because a figure came up behind him and grabbed him by his collar. Then the man was sprawled on the dance floor, swearing, as Gwen stared in confusion.

Then the figure said in Jack's voice, "Come on."

Within seconds, Jack led her out of the club. Gwen gulped in the cool air, wiping sweat from her forehead. Nausea made her stomach roil, and she had to take a few deep breaths before she felt like she wouldn't vomit on the sidewalk.

Then as she looked up at Jack's face, she almost felt like puking. He looked *pissed*. And at her.

"What the hell were you doing?" he said, his voice harsher than she'd ever heard it. "Are you fucking insane?"

Although her buzz had been waning, she wasn't entirely sober either, so it took a moment for her to understand his question. Then she bristled.

"Are you blaming *me* for a guy manhandling me? Seriously?"

"I'm blaming you for being alone in a club and getting drunk—"

"I'm not alone. My friends..." Gwen looked around, but there was no sign of Alex or Felicity. "I don't know where they went."

"Some great friends you have."

"Why are you being such a jerk? And another question—what are you even doing here?" Gwen looked Jack up and down: he wasn't exactly dressed to go to a club. He was still wearing his fishing boots and jacket. She could even smell a whiff of fish on him. If he'd wanted to find someone to take home tonight, he hadn't even tried.

That thought made her belly twist. *It's none of my business what Jack does with his nights,* she reminded herself.

"It's a small island," said Jack, his arms crossed.

"When is the last time you ever went to Deja Vu? Because I'm pretty sure you'd rather get eaten by a bunch of eels than go to a club like this."

His lips twitched. "Maybe I was trying something new."

Gwen felt heat move through her veins. Maybe it was the moonlight highlighting the angles of Jack's jaw, or the way his forearms bulged. Maybe it was the memory of the warmth of his hand in hers. But she felt the urge to snuggle into his embrace, run her fingers along his stubbled cheeks—

She forced herself to put her hands in her back pockets. "Well, thanks for helping me back there. That guy was getting way too handsy."

Jack's expression darkened. "Handsy? I watched as you tried to get away from him. You're lucky he didn't follow you to the bathroom and do something worse."

"He was just a drunk asshole." Gwen swallowed. "It happens."

"That doesn't mean you shouldn't be careful. If you'd gotten hurt..." Jack looked away. "Just promise me you'll be more careful in the future, okay?"

That dangerous warmth inside her body only increased. Jack had been worried about her. Scared for her, even. It melted any anger she felt at his words.

"I will be. I promise." She shrugged. "I don't usually get drunk and go to clubs, you know. Alex wanted me to get out."

"Alex needs to find better ways to have fun."

He sounded like a grumbling old man and Gwen had to restrain a laugh. Reaching out, she touched his forearm. His gaze shot straight to where her hand sat, and she felt the look like a brand.

"Thank you," said Gwen solemnly. "For always looking out for me. You've been a good friend."

Something crossed his face, something Gwen couldn't name. She hadn't yet removed her hand. Feeling awkward, she tried to move away, but he only caught her hand in his.

"Gwen," he rumbled. He cupped her cheek. "Gwen," he repeated on a sigh.

Then he was leaning forward, and Gwen's toes curled in her boots as she awaited his mouth pressing against hers. She felt the warmth of his breath on her cheek. Her heart fluttered with anticipation.

But then she felt a cold wash of anxiety. Something must've changed in her expression because Jack flinched.

"Gwen! Oh my God, there you are!" cried Alex.

Jack let go of her so quickly that Gwen nearly stumbled to the ground. Alex then was at her side, Felicity right beside her. Jack had already backed away from Gwen, like he'd discovered she had the plague.

"Are you okay? I'm so sorry we lost each other. We were still inside, waiting for you, but when you didn't come back from the bathroom we were worried—"

Gwen held up a hand. "I'm fine. I've just been outside

talking to Jack. I should've let you know first." She eyed him. "Isn't that right, Jack?"

"That's right," he replied. Then, as quickly as he'd appeared, he said goodbye to the trio and walked away into the night.

"What was he doing here?" Felicity frowned.

"Maybe he's gotten into clubbing," joked Alex.

Gwen was staring at his retreating back. He'd been about to kiss her–hadn't he? Or had she imagined the entire scenario?

But she could still feel his breath, the warmth of his hand. She could see his dark eyes on her face, drinking her in. Her brain struggled to understand, but her body knew exactly what had happened.

"Too bad he's such a grump because he's super hot," said Alex, breaking Gwen's reverie. "Although I'm not convinced he can actually have a conversation. I think he's only ever spoken five words to me, total."

"He only talks to people when he needs to." Gwen knew her tone was sharp, so she softened it as she added, "Unlike some people, who just chatter away."

"Me? Never. And anyway, pot, meet kettle. The only person here that can match Benson for silence is our dearest Felicity here," said Alex.

Felicity smiled a little. "Someone has to listen to the chatterboxes."

"See? It's a symbiotic relationship," replied Alex, laughing.

By the time Gwen returned home, it was so late that she knew she'd have to have her assistant manager fill in for her tomorrow. Or today, she realized, looking at her phone.

As she closed her eyes, though, she wasn't thinking about work. She was thinking only about Jack.

She flung a pillow over her face, groaning in despair. Why had she frozen like that? Did she subconsciously not want to kiss Jack Benson?

No, I do. I think I've wanted to kiss him for a long time, she admitted to herself. So why the nerves?

Gwen wanted to tear her own hair out in frustration. She just had to be her own worst enemy, and now, Jack would never initiate something with her again.

Despite her best efforts, tears sprang to her eyes. She heard Tim's voice in her head all over again: *what's wrong with you?* There must be something truly broken inside of her, she thought. Because what sane, heterosexual woman would reject a man like Jack?

Swiping away the tears, she eventually fell into a restless sleep.

CHAPTER SIX

G wen was avoiding him.

He knew when someone didn't want to talk to him. Although Gwen was her usual kind self, she had a reserve about her that made Jack seethe. When she handed him his morning coffee days after their aborted kiss, she looked like she wanted to bolt as fast as she could.

Jack didn't understand it. He might not be the greatest at understanding a woman's feelings, but he understood signals. Gwen had done everything he'd expect from a woman: she'd tilted her head back, her pupils had dilated, and she hadn't removed her hand from his arm. She hadn't pulled away at all–at first.

But then he'd felt her stiffen. When he saw fear in her eyes, he'd felt it like a slap to the face.

Tossing a net overboard, Jack said to himself, "What the fuck was that?" Of course, no one answered. No one else was around for miles. Only the sound of the waves lapping, along with the occasional gull crying out, punctured the silence around him.

Normally, he enjoyed the solitude. But his head was all messed up, and he could barely concentrate on fishing. It had been a week since that night he'd pulled Gwen out of Deja Vu. He'd seen her three times, and all three times, she said hello and goodbye as quickly as she could.

"Benson, what the fuck are you doing?" he said, shaking his head. He was being an idiot. If a woman didn't want him, well, that was that. No reason to have a breakdown over it. He could find another woman to warm his bed easily enough.

He didn't just want a warm body, though. And the mere thought that Gwen had reacted in fear to his touch made him feel like his insides were all tangled up. He hated it. He never wanted her to be afraid of him.

As he turned the boat to return to shore, he felt doubt creeping in. He must've misread her signals. He'd been too pushy. She wasn't like the women he usually pursued. She was sweet, innocent. If she hadn't been married previously, he'd almost think she was a virgin.

A dark cloud hovered over Jack when he returned to shore, matching the gray clouds amassing in the sky. A rainstorm was coming, and the second he closed his truck door, the rain started falling.

He didn't need to go into town this morning. But he found himself driving there anyway. He had to see Gwen. He had to—he didn't know, exactly.

Why does it matter? She's not your girlfriend. She's just a friend.

And that must be it, Jack realized. She saw him as a friend and nothing else. He'd misinterpreted her friendliness for flirtation.

God, he was a fucking idiot. How could he be so blind?

When he parked his truck behind the bed and breakfast, Jack didn't think about what he was doing. He simply went into the kitchen like he did when he dropped off a fresh catch.

"Are you looking for Gwen?" Darla, one of the maids, asked him near one of the walk-in freezers. "She had to run an errand, but she'll be back in an hour or so."

"Can you tell her I was here? I need to talk to her."

Darla gazed at him speculatively. "Of course," she said finally.

Jack hated the way she was looking at him, like she could see right through him. He returned to his truck, only for him to pause when Gwen's red sedan pulled up next to him.

It was raining harder now, but Jack didn't make a move to get into the dry warmth of his truck. Instead, he went to the driver's side of Gwen's car and knocked on the window.

"Jack!" cried Gwen. She unrolled the window. "What in the world—?"

"You've been avoiding me," he shouted against the noise of the rain and wind. "Why?"

She stared at him. "Jack, it's raining—"

"And I'm a fisherman. I won't fucking melt."

Sighing, she turned off the ignition to her car and then gestured for him to get into the passenger side. Jack barely fit, even with the seat pushed all the way back.

"Is this a car made for ants?" he groused. He grunted when he bumped his head against the ceiling.

"Don't criticize Lola. She's a good car." Gwen patted the steering wheel.

Neither said anything for a painfully long moment.

"Why are you avoiding me?" he said, finally. He hated how he sounded like he was pleading with her.

"I'm not avoiding you. I let you get into my car. I've spoken to you multiple times this week."

"You know what I mean."

Gwen glanced over at him. She was gripping the steering wheel, white-knuckled. Jack could feel the tension vibrating between them.

"What happened Friday night..." She swallowed. "I'm sorry if I gave you the wrong impression."

Well, that was as clear as mud. Gritting his teeth, Jack replied, "Explain."

"What's there to explain? I screwed up, and I got you caught up in it." Her voice lowered to a whisper. "I'll always be a disappointment. It's better this way."

Jack felt like she was speaking a foreign language. "So you're saying you don't want me," he said flatly.

"I don't know what I want." Her expression was sincere, at least. "Which means it's better if we act like it never happened."

Jack didn't need an interpreter to understand that. He'd been right: Gwen saw him only as a friend. Even as his pride smarted and the caveman part of his brain wanted to prove her wrong, he'd respect her decision.

But what the hell did she mean that she'd always be a disappointment? He'd been the one forcing something that would never happen.

"I get it. You don't have to keep explaining," he said.

"I really am sorry." Her voice trembled a little.

"Nothing to be sorry for."

GWEN SPENT the next few days wallowing. She saw the look on Jack's face when she'd rejected him, and her heart felt bruised all over again.

It's better this way, she told herself. *I can't give him what he deserves.*

She told herself that, but it didn't make her feel better. It made her feel even more broken. She wished she was brave like Alex, who'd gone swimming with sharks and climbed to the base of Mount Everest. But instead, Gwen was practically scared of her own shadow. She hated herself for being so weak.

She'd never told Alex or Felicity about why, exactly, her marriage to Tim had failed. For all they knew, they'd simply grown apart, a narrative that Gwen had done nothing to contradict.

Alex probably wouldn't understand, Gwen had always figured. It wasn't that she wouldn't be empathetic, but her advice generally tended to boil down to "cheer up and move on."

"You look like someone just died," said Helen, startling Gwen out of her thoughts. "Did someone die?"

Gwen let out a laugh. "Not that I'm aware of."

"Then you should smile because you're alive and so is everyone else you know. Nobody wants an innkeeper who looks so glum."

"You're not smiling." Blushing, Gwen added, "Sorry, that was rude."

Helen only laughed, a laugh that sounded like a crow

cawing. It was slightly terrifying. "You've got some spunk in you! Good. Be sure to keep that. You'll need it."

Gwen had been tidying up the front of the bed and breakfast when Helen had emerged. It was a quiet afternoon. Most of the guests had gone off to do various activities for the day. Gwen wondered why Helen had stayed in.

"I think it's time for a break. Would you like to join me?" said Gwen.

"Only if it involves coffee," was Helen's reply.

The bed and breakfast had a small porch out front with a few chairs, where patrons could relax and watch passersby on Main Street. It was a crisp autumn day, the sky a sharp blue. Gwen cupped her hot mug of coffee, inhaling the steam. Helen perched on a chair next to her and began drinking the piping hot coffee so fast that Gwen marveled that the woman didn't burn her tongue off.

Helen finished her coffee before Gwen had barely made a dent in her own. "That was better, but still not great," she said. "Can't say I've found any real good coffee on this island."

"I'm sorry to hear that. I guess we can't compare with Seattle coffee."

"Seattle? Good lord, no. Can't stand the place. It's loud, dirty, and the traffic..." Helen shuddered. "I haven't been there in over ten years, besides passing by it on the way to the airport. Cities aren't for me."

"There is something nice about living on an island. Barely any traffic around here."

"I'm surprised, a young woman like you, wasting her life away in a place like this." At Gwen's surprised look, Helen added, "You aren't married, clearly. So that means you're single, and any eligible bachelors in this place are probably twice your age."

Gwen nearly choked on her coffee. "There are some guys my age." *And I rejected one of them already,* she thought glumly.

"The pool is very limited. Do you want to be a spinster with twenty cats? Because that's what you're going to be if you don't get out of here."

Gwen was torn between laughing and feeling offended. "My entire life is here. My business, my friends. All of it. I'm not going to abandon it just because I'm single. It's the twenty-first century, Helen. Women can be single. It's not a death sentence."

"Oh, men in general are worthless. I won't disagree with you there. But take it from someone who's a little bit older than you: hiding doesn't do anybody any good. And if you're burying your head in the sand in this place, you'll regret it."

"Is that what you did?" Gwen asked softly.

Helen snorted. "Whoever said I was talking about me? I'm speaking in generalities."

Gwen didn't press the issue. She wondered if Helen was right. Was Gwen just avoiding getting involved with someone to protect herself? She had moved here to get away from her old life. She'd known that the day she'd decided to come to Hazel Island.

But what was so bad starting anew? She wasn't hiding. She'd needed this place. It didn't hold all the memories of her marriage that now only served to sting her bruised heart.

Jack passed them by in his truck, stopping to let a couple

cross the street. His gaze caught Gwen's, and she had to remember how to breathe.

"Now, he's a fine specimen," said Helen slyly.

"Who is?"

"Don't try to play coy. That fisherman. I've seen him around. Is he single?"

"I think so."

Helen nodded. "I've seen him looking at you. He's interested. You should take him up on it."

"Are you trying to set me up?"

"If you're not going to do it, someone has to."

Gwen almost wanted to tell Helen about her failed marriage and the disaster that was her almost-kiss with Jack. But she didn't think Helen would be particularly sympathetic. She'd probably tell Gwen she was being a ninny.

And what would Jack say? Would he be sympathetic? The mere thought of revealing that to him made her anxiety rise. She couldn't bear the idea of him looking at her with pity. Even worse, she couldn't bear the thought that he'd decide she wasn't worth the trouble after all. What man wanted to deal with her baggage, with no guarantee that she'd ever be able to have sex with him?

She wasn't going to doom someone to that kind of relationship. Helen didn't understand. Gwen wasn't just protecting herself: she was protecting anyone foolish enough to get involved with her.

CHAPTER SEVEN

When Jack's phone beeped, he wished once again that he hadn't caved and bought a cell phone. He blamed his customers: too many had had last-minute changes to their orders, which he'd miss because he didn't have a cell phone. So he'd finally gotten a very basic flip phone that didn't have GPS or Internet or any of that nonsense.

It did, however, have texting capabilities. Which Luke Wright had been taking advantage of the moment Jack had let slip he'd gotten a cell phone.

Did you talk to Gwen yet? Luke wrote. *She hasn't contacted me yet.*

In the middle of his breakfast, Jack felt the eggs in his mouth turn to ash. How did he explain that Gwen was avoiding him still and that he didn't know how to get her to trust him again? *I almost kissed her, she flipped out.* Yeah, Luke would enjoy that text way too much.

Been busy, Jack replied.

Time is money, dude. Get on it.

Luke was right: Jack was wasting time. Grunting, he quickly finished his breakfast and headed into town. After a handful of errands for supplies, he parked his truck outside Gwen's apartment.

He knew she didn't work on Thursday mornings, every other week. Her car was still in her parking spot.

"Just fucking do it," he muttered to himself.

When Gwen opened her door, he said, "I need to talk to you. About Luke. Nothing else."

Gwen blinked. She was wearing glasses, something Jack had only seen a handful of times. It made her green eyes bigger. Her hair was in a messy bun that Jack wanted to sift his fingers through. And worst of all, she was wearing a see-through camisole and silk shorts that left little to the imagination.

"Um, okay. Do you want some coffee? I just made a pot."

Gwen hurried to the kitchen. Jack had only been to her place once, and he hadn't even stepped inside. As he'd expect of Gwen, her place was spotless. The only sign someone lived here was the used bowl and spoon next to the sink and the blanket left on the gray couch.

Gwen had gone to put on a robe, much to Jack's disappointment. She gestured for him to sit on one of the barstools in the kitchen. After they'd both gotten their coffees, Jack launched into what he'd needed to say.

He told her about his meeting with Luke. He explained how Luke was interested in Gwen's restaurant idea but that he wanted her to present him with a business plan first. Jack pulled out a business card of Luke's.

"This is great," said Gwen, staring at the business card. "I honestly didn't think he'd be interested."

"Why not?"

"Because..." She shrugged. "He's a Wright. They have lots of money to throw around. Why invest in some piddly island restaurant?"

"Luke himself isn't rich."

Gwen's smile was wry. "Okay, maybe not technically, but he will be. And I doubt he lacks for much. Regardless, thank you. You taking the time to talk to him means a lot to me. Not a lot of people would want to go to the trouble."

Jack just grunted. He didn't want her gratitude. He wanted...what? *Whatever it is, you aren't going to get it.*

Gwen was drumming her fingers against her coffee mug. She hadn't sat down next to Jack, instead standing on the other side of the counter, as if she needed something between them.

Jack finally broke the silence. "You've been avoiding me."

Gwen's fingers stopped their drumming. A blush crawled up her cheeks. "You noticed?"

"Yeah, I noticed. I don't know how to make things go back to the way they were."

"You didn't do anything wrong. Seriously. This is all me."

Jack couldn't help but snort at that assertion. "The 'it's not you, it's me' excuse? Come on, now, we both know that's bullshit. I tried to kiss you, but you don't think of me like that. I fucked it up."

Jack was rarely this forthright, at least with subjects like this, but he was desperate. He hated that Gwen couldn't be comfortable around him anymore. Mostly, he hated himself for screwing everything up.

"What? No. It's not like that," replied Gwen hurriedly.

Now Jack was getting irritated. "Then how about you explain it to me since I'm apparently too dense to understand?"

She bit her bottom lip. Not meeting his gaze, she said heavily, "My divorce messed me up."

Jack just waited.

"Well, not the divorce itself. That was necessary. I mean, my ex. Or rather, he made me realize something about myself that I'm not proud of."

She swallowed hard, meeting Jack's gaze now. "I'm not good at dating or relationships. My marriage failed mostly because of me. I don't want to repeat that mistake and make another man unhappy." She shook her head. "I'm keeping my distance because it's better for everyone in the long run."

Jack just gaped at her. "That's the biggest bunch of shit I've ever heard," he spat.

Gwen's blush deepened. "See? This is why I didn't want to tell you. Now you're telling me I'm lying—"

Getting up from the stool, Jack stalked to the other side of the counter, forcing Gwen to back up. "Lying? I don't think you're lying, except maybe to yourself. Do you really expect me to believe you ruined your marriage? Somebody like you?"

"For all you know, I cheated on my husband ten times over."

Jack snorted. "Did you? Is that what you're saying?"

Gwen had raised her chin, defiant, but she quickly

looked deflated. "No. I didn't cheat. Not in the usual way, I guess. But I betrayed my vows." Her lower lip started to tremble, tears sparkling in her eyes. "If you really want to know, I couldn't have sex. Okay? I'm broken. There's something wrong with me and I can't exactly be in a relationship or even date if I can't ever have sex."

Jack felt like the world was tipping on its axis. She couldn't have sex? He'd never heard of such a thing. Either you wanted sex, or you didn't.

Feeling decidedly uncomfortable now, he gave her a little more space. "You mean, it hurts, or—?"

"No. I mean, I freeze up when it starts." She gave a sad shrug. "It got to the point that my ex-husband just gave up trying. He said I was frigid, and he was right. I am. And I've tried dating again, but it keeps happening."

Gwen looked so sad, so defeated, that Jack couldn't stop himself from embracing her. She stiffened at first, but when she realized he was just offering a friendly hug, she let herself be comforted. Burying her face in his shoulder, she cried a bit, until she eventually stepped back and muttered an apology.

As he held her, Jack felt anger rising inside of him. *What kind of a man says that shit to his wife?* He wanted to find her ex and beat him black and blue.

Gwen forced a smile onto her face. "Ugh, I did not plan on crying this morning. And I'm sure you didn't plan on having to deal with me crying when you stopped by."

"It's fine." Jack had to shove his hands into his pockets to restrain himself from touching her again.

They stood like that in silence, Jack wondering what to say further. Thankfully, Gwen's phone ringing saved them.

"I have to take this," she said apologetically. "I'll talk to you later?"

He nodded.

Gwen gave him a short hug, then added, "I'm glad we're still friends."

Jack didn't have an answer to that.

GWEN THREW herself into her work, along with putting together a business plan for the restaurant. She'd somehow managed to avoid writing one when she'd started the bed and breakfast, as the majority of the funding coming from her own savings.

Forcing herself to construct a concrete plan versus a flimsy idea was harder than she'd expected. It also shone a bright light on the fact that she still needed to do more research if she wanted this venture to be successful.

She was glad for the distraction. Along with running the inn, she spent her evenings working on the business plan, which didn't give her much time to brood over Jack Benson.

After he'd left that morning, she'd instantly regretted telling him her secret. She hadn't been able to read his expression when she'd revealed it. Had he pitied her? Or had he acknowledged to himself that he'd dodged a bullet?

Considering she'd spoken all of ten words to him in the last week, she had a feeling it was the latter. And she had to admit, that hurt. A lot.

It was late on a Friday night when Gwen was jolted from her thoughts by a knock on her office door by Jocelyn.

"Burning the midnight oil, boss?" Jocelyn slid into the chair across from Gwen's desk. "It's nearly eight o'clock."

"It is?" Gwen groaned. "I lost track of time. I should probably go home." But then her mind moved back to the business plan in front of her, and she turned her monitor toward Jocelyn. "Want to help me with this?"

"Do I want to spend my Friday night putting together some report? I mean, how is that even a question?" joked Jocelyn.

"It's for the restaurant. And if you're going to be the head chef..."

Jocelyn snorted. "Fine, fine. What do you need from me?"

Despite Jocelyn's stubbornness and Gwen's need to appease, the two of them worked together well now. Jocelyn must've sensed that she needed to have a gentler approach with Gwen. Gwen had accepted that she needed to stick to her guns so Jocelyn didn't walk all over her. As a result, they spent two hours working, almost having fun in the process.

By ten o'clock, Jocelyn got up and stretched, yawning widely. "When did I turn into such an old lady? Once upon a time, I stayed out late and somehow managed to get to class on time in the morning."

"I'm sure you'll be signing up for AARP very soon," said Gwen, grinning.

"Oh God. Next I'll be carrying butterscotch candies in my bag and yelling at kids to get off my lawn."

Right before Gwen was going to shut off her computer, an email landed in her inbox. It was from Luke Wright. Heart pounding, she opened it.

It simply read, *I'm looking forward to seeing that business plan, Ms. Parker.*

"What's got you smiling like that?" said Jocelyn. Before Gwen could close the email window, Jocelyn read over her shoulder, "Luke Wright. He's the one you're writing this for?"

Gwen hadn't mentioned Luke because, quite frankly, she had no idea if he'd even give her funding. And looking at Jocelyn's stone-cold expression, Gwen knew she hadn't made a mistake in keeping that detail to herself.

Any time the Wrights were mentioned, Jocelyn bristled. Gwen had noticed it weeks ago. When she'd asked Alex about it, Alex had just shrugged. "I have no idea. She might just hate them because they're rich."

"He's interested, yes," said Gwen, trying to sound casual. "But who knows if he'll say yes. It's just one potential avenue for money."

"You could go to a bank."

"I did. They said no."

Jocelyn had returned to the other side of the desk. "You don't want to get tangled up with the Wrights."

"Why not? They have money. I need money. And Jack is friends with Luke—"

"Luke is the worst of them all!"

Gwen stared in surprise. Jocelyn was chewing the inside of her cheek, her arms crossed.

In a calmer voice, Jocelyn said, "Just, be careful. I don't want you to get screwed over."

"Well, who wants to get screwed over? And it's all legit, I promise you. I doubt Luke is going to send out a bunch of his minions to rough me up if I don't repay the loan."

"That's what you think," muttered Jocelyn.

"I might not know Luke well, but I trust Jack. If Jack trusts him, then I'm not worried."

"Just because he's been decent to one person doesn't mean he hasn't been shit to others."

Gwen desperately wanted to press Jocelyn for more information right then. To her consternation, Darla came into her office right then, interrupting them. "Room 205 has lost power. I flipped the circuit breaker for the room, but no dice," she said hurriedly.

"I have to take care of this. Are you all right going home by yourself?" asked Gwen.

Jocelyn snorted, some of the tension leaving her body. "It's Hazel Island. What's going to happen?"

CHAPTER EIGHT

After getting a latte from across the street—the inn didn't have an espresso machine at the moment—Gwen stopped to wave at Alex through the bookstore window. Alex gestured for her to come inside.

"I have the latest Lila White!" said Alex, holding up the book in question.

Gwen didn't need any more persuasion. She snagged the book from Alex, greedily reading the blurb and flipping through the pages. It was a big, fat novel; Gwen loved those kinds of books. Doorstoppers, the ones that completely engrossed you the moment you started reading.

"The reviews are pretty stellar," said Alex as she continued shelving. "I wasn't a big fan of her last one, though."

Gwen scoffed. "And you call yourself a bookseller. Her last book was *amazing*."

"I'm just not a big fan of the secret-baby thing. It only works in ye olden times, not in the twenty-first century."

"But Lila White can handle it. Come on, that grand gesture at the end—"

"Oh, it was great. I'll give you that."

Alex had worked in Hazel Island Books, or HIB as the locals called it, since she was a senior in high school. The owner and manager, Max, had been a single man with no children, and he'd taken Alex under his wing. Although Alex had left the island for various jaunts around the world, she'd always returned to HIB.

When Max had become ill and unable to run the business, Alex had stepped in. Now, she was the official owner.

Island folk had been skeptical someone as flighty as Alex Gray would be able to run a bookstore. She was also still young, and despite her quick mind and ambition, she'd been inexperienced with the finer aspects of owning a business.

It didn't help that so much of the book world had shifted to digital. Although many of HIB's patrons were loyal to buying and reading print books, the pool shrunk every year. And it wasn't uncommon for a previously loyal patron to return in the summer with a shiny new eReader in hand to read on the beach.

"How's everything going?" asked Gwen.

Alex hopped down from the ladder. "Good. We're having a reading for Lila White soon. Actually, I've been in contact with Lila's people to see if she'd do a reading here on the island."

"Seriously? Do you think she'd come?"

"No idea, but you'll never know if you don't ask."

Inside the store were only two customers, and as Gwen wandered the store with Alex, she didn't see any more come in. Then again, it was the morning. Business would probably pick up later.

"So business is good?" said Gwen after one of the customers left without purchasing anything.

"Good? I don't know about that." Alex laughed a little. "It's not terrible. Let's just say anyone making a profit from a bookstore must have magical powers."

Gwen stared in surprise. "How are you paying yourself? Are you getting a salary?"

"Oh, that one is so good." Alex pointed to the mystery novel the other patron had just pulled from the shelf. "I highly recommend it. The twist at the end!"

Gwen knew when she was being ignored. Although Alex had never outright said the business was struggling, Gwen had no idea if it was even paying Alex a salary. How was she paying for her apartment? Gwen worried that her friend had gotten in over her head.

Once the store was empty, Gwen said frankly, "If you need help, you know you can always ask me, right?"

Alex blushed a little. "Help? You mean you want to come work for me? Bonuses are free books."

"Alex, be serious."

"I am. About the bonuses, that is." Then her shoulders sagged. "Look, I can take care of myself. I'll figure it out. I always do."

Clearly, Alex wasn't going to unload her problems. She had too much pride, Gwen thought, to admit when she was stuck. It was both commendable and frustrating. Gwen had a feeling Alex's stubbornness could get in her own way far too easily.

Changing the subject, Gwen said, "Your sister said

something interesting last night, about Luke Wright. She seemed super hostile when I mentioned him."

Alex laughed. "If you're trying to get me to spill, I'll tell you right now, I know nothing." At Gwen's expression, she said, "No, really. Jocelyn has never told me why she hates the guy. Or the family. And you know I'm the best person to get someone to confess their secrets."

But you don't know mine, thought Gwen wryly. "She said I shouldn't trust Luke."

"Knowing Jocelyn, he was probably rude to her once in high school and she holds a grudge. She's like that. Once she decides she hates you—" Alex drew a line across her throat. "There's no coming back."

Alex peered more closely at Gwen. "Why should you trust Luke? I didn't think you two were friends." Her eyes widened. "Are you two dating?"

Gwen nearly choked on her latte. "Luke Wright? God, no." Not that he wasn't attractive, but he wasn't her type.

She couldn't help but think of Jack's dark eyes right then. No, Luke Wright was not a guy she'd want to date. He'd had life too easy, for one. What would Gwen do with a man who'd been born with the proverbial silver spoon in his mouth?

"Then why are you asking about him? Seems fishy." Alex poked Gwen in the shoulder. "What's going on?"

"Nothing. I just mentioned something offhand about the Wrights, and Jocelyn was there. That's all."

Alex didn't seem convinced but surprisingly, she didn't press the matter. "Well, I will say that if Jocelyn says he's shady, she probably has a good reason for it."

"You just said she could be holding a silly grudge!"

"She's my older sister. I have to roast her, duh."

Returning to work, Gwen couldn't help but mull over Alex's words. *She probably has a good reason for it.*

Did that mean Gwen should avoid getting a loan from Luke? But she was also confident that Jack wouldn't be friends with someone untrustworthy.

Jack might not know everything about his friend. Your friends don't know everything about you.

Gwen felt twisted up inside. Most of all, she wished people would just be transparent for once. But then she laughed at herself, because she'd been as opaque as anyone, what with her beating around the bush with Jack.

As if he'd heard her thoughts, Jack appeared next to her in the inn's kitchen. He looked like he'd been running, his breaths coming in pants.

"What in the world? Are you okay?" said Gwen.

"I need to talk to you."

Gwen looked around, but they were alone. But she still took him to her office for privacy's sake, closing the door behind him.

He started to pace, but her office was too small for pacing. Instead, he leaned over the single chair, gripping it hard. Gwen's anxiety shot up. Had something bad happened and he was trying to find the words to explain?

"I thought about what you told me, about your ex-husband." Jack said the word "ex-husband" like a curse, star-tling Gwen. "But most of all, I want to ask you one thing."

His eyes were blazing with fire. "Are you attracted to me? Because by God, I want you, Gwen. And I want to prove to you that you aren't broken."

To Jack's dismay, Gwen started laughing. "You're joking. Seriously? Who put you up to this?"

"No one put me up to anything."

Gwen just kept shaking her head. "You seriously came in here and would say that to me? Why? I told you that in confidence, but if you think it's all just a joke—"

Jack went around to her side of the desk and took her hands, squeezing them, forcing her to look him straight in the face.

"I'm not joking, Gwen." His voice was low, and he felt like his heart was going to explode out of his chest. "Why the fuck would you think I'd do something like that to you? Have I ever treated you like that?"

Her lower lip was trembling. "No," she whispered.

"Then tell me the truth: do you want me? Because when I almost kissed you that night, you wanted me. And don't try to lie to me. I can tell when you're lying."

That made Gwen scoff. "What, like you can read my mind? For all you know, I lie to you all the time."

"Any time you've tried, you get twitchy."

"I do not."

He moved closer. He could feel the curves of her body pressed against his own, the way she fit against him perfectly. Just being this close to her sent his senses into overdrive. It took everything in his power not to kiss her right then and there.

"Do you want me?" he repeated. "Tell me. If you say no, I'll never touch you again."

He could tell she was trying to find a way out of this. She was shaking now, but her cheeks were flushed, her nipples hard. Even if she wouldn't say it out loud, her body wanted him.

"I don't want you." Her fingers flexed against his hand as she said the words.

"I don't believe you. Why are you lying?" Jack tilted her chin up, brushing his thumb across her lip. "Try that again."

She didn't have the strength to keep lying. He could feel the fight go out of her in that moment. Her eyes pooling with tears, she said, "I do want you."

Jack dug his fingers into her hair and kissed her—hard. She moaned in surprise, but then she wrapped her arms around him. His tongue delved into her sweet mouth. He kissed her like he was starved for touch, and he was—he was starved for this woman.

Even if this is temporary, it'll be enough. It has to be enough.

Gwen dug her nails into his shoulders as he kissed her harder. But then she pulled away, panting, her entire face and chest red now.

"Jack."

"Give me a chance," he rasped.

She just shook her head. "Just because I want you—it won't work. I won't do that to you."

"You won't be doing anything to me. Even if this is all I get, this one kiss? Fine."

She stared at him. "You're seriously telling me that you'd want a relationship with no sex?"

"Want? No. But for you? I'd manage." He touched her cheek. "And I'm not talking about a relationship, Gwen. I'm just talking about having fun. No commitment. If you want to end it, you can. It doesn't have to be messy."

"You're saying we should become friends with benefits."

He tucked a stray curl behind her ear. "Sure. Call it that."

"I've never done that before. I don't think I'm that kind of person. I'd probably get all emotional and overly attached."

"Then just don't fall in love with me. And I'll do the same."

"Not fall in love with me? I'm not sure if I should take that as a compliment."

Jack reached down and squeezed her ass, pressing her pelvis against his semi-hard cock. "I want to bend you over this desk right now," he rumbled. "I want you every possible way a man can have a woman."

Gwen licked her lips, her lashes fluttering. "Let me think about it."

"Forty-eight hours. That's all the time you get." He wanted to kiss her again, but Gwen was starting to think again. He had a feeling pushing her too hard would end poorly for them both.

He forced himself to put space between them, even though his body screamed at the broken contact.

"Forty-eight hours? Okay," said Gwen, her voice husky. "I'll talk to you then."

"I'll be counting the hours."

CHAPTER NINE

I t was three hours until midnight. Jack hated that he'd been watching the clock, waiting for Gwen's answer. He'd even restarted his stupid flip phone to make sure it was really working.

He scoffed at himself as he made himself a late dinner: frozen lasagna with a beer. Jack's house was barely a house: it was one room, with a little kitchen nook, a rickety dining table and two chairs, along with a bed in the corner. There was a small bathroom with a shower. Jack had built it himself, mostly because he hadn't been able to afford anything else at the time.

Now, apparently "tiny homes" like his were all the rage. He'd even had a few random tourists showing up on his doorstep for a tour in the last year, like his place was some damn museum. He'd shot one black look at them, and they'd scurried off to their rented Priuses.

His lasagna was cold in the middle, but he couldn't find the energy to care. *Pathetic, Benson*, he told himself.

If Gwen didn't want him, fine. He'd find another

woman. There was plenty of fish in the sea, which as a fisherman, he could attest to personally.

Smile, Jack. You look so scary when you make that face.

Jack heard his mom's voice in his head. An old memory surfaced, of bringing home his school picture and his mom, Debra, hating it. How old had he been? Six? Seven? He couldn't remember.

He did remember that his mom had been high, and she'd taken one look at Jack's frowning, childish face in the photo and had started crying.

"Why do you look like this? Everyone will think you're unhappy." His mom sobbed, tears running down her face. She never bothered to get a tissue. She just let the tears, the snot, everything drip down her face and onto her shirt.

"I am smiling," protested Jack. And he was—kind of. Jack had been distracted by another student. The photographer had caught Jack in that moment, which resulted in the weird, lackluster smile on his face.

"You don't look good when you do that. It scares people. You're already so big for your age," said his mom.

She went to the kitchen. The counters were covered in clutter that included wine bottles, dirty cups, old magazines, prescription bottles, and dog food for the dog that had been hit by a car six months prior. Jack had never seen any surface in their apartment clean. When he'd gone to a friend's house and had seen the bare counters, he'd asked what had happened to all their stuff.

His mom knocked off two of the liquor bottles onto the floor. Although neither broke, she let out a wail like they had. She clutched one to her chest, the photos wrinkling in her grasp, as she cried hysterically.

Jack just stared at her. He was used to this. She'd get tired of crying eventually. More than likely, she'd drink and fall asleep on the kitchen floor or get high off the pills she had stashed around the house. Jack had stashed a blanket in one of the lower cabinets to drape over her when she fell asleep on the floor.

His little brother Danny, only four years old, hated when their mom cried. He went and snuggled next to her on the floor, but she eventually pushed him away because he was too warm. "Go play in the living room," she said tiredly.

"What are we having for dinner?" asked Jack.

"I'm going to bed," was all their mom said, leaving them to find their own meals.

Jack had had to grow up quickly. He'd been the one to watch out for Danny, to make sure he was fed, that he did his homework. Jack would forge their mom's signature on field trip forms when she was too drunk to hold a pen. Jack lent her money when she'd needed to buy booze. It had been easier than hearing her crying from the withdrawal.

Jack forced himself to shake off the memories. But despite his best efforts, they clung to him, wanting to pull him back to the past. He hadn't spoken to his mom in ages; he only talked to Danny once or twice a year. He'd distanced himself from his family because he'd gotten to a point where it was easier.

But the guilt still ate at him. Even now, he wondered if he'd just tried harder, he could've helped his mom. He'd left her, and his brother, to rot. He was the man of the family. It had been his responsibility to take care of them.

Jack had never been bothered by being alone. He'd had company when he'd needed it, female or otherwise. When he'd needed sex, he'd found it. He'd lived his life how he'd wanted to live it: unencumbered by other people.

Yet as the years had passed, the loneliness had crept in on him. Would he live in this tiny house until he was old and gray? Would he die here, all by himself, no one to care about his passing?

He growled under his breath. "What the hell is wrong with you?" he muttered to himself.

He thought of Gwen. He remembered how she'd felt under his hands, the way she'd felt pressing against him. Her warmth, her sweetness.

She made him long for something he hadn't known he'd wanted. And despite his best efforts, he checked his phone, hoping she'd give him the answer he wanted more than he cared to admit.

The sun had long since set, the night settling around him. Jack was surprised that Gwen hadn't given him any answer. That wasn't like her. She wasn't flaky. Had something happened?

Before his anxiety could reach panic levels, there was a knock on his front door. Who the hell was out here at this time of night? He just hoped it wasn't a tourist who'd gotten lost.

Opening the door, he braced himself to see a bunch of confused old ladies with maps. Instead, it was Gwen herself.

"Gwen," he said, staring at her.

She took a deep breath. "Yes, Jack. My answer is yes."

CHAPTER TEN

J ack wondered if he was dreaming. He must've fallen asleep at his kitchen table and was having a fever dream. There was no possible way that Gwen Parker was at his door, telling him what he thought he'd never hear.

But then he realized that it was misting outside, and Gwen was starting to shiver. He hustled her inside and grabbed one of the two blankets from his bed, wrapping it around her shoulders.

"Are you drunk?" he snapped.

Gwen blinked. "No."

"Are you high?"

"Um, also no."

"Then why the hell are you here?" He knew he sounded like a dick. But he wasn't capable of lowering his voice right now.

"I mean, if you want me to leave, I will. I don't want to bother you—"

Jack acted on instinct. Pulling her into his arms, he

kissed her. She made a little yelp of surprise, but a moment later, she melted against him. Jack sifted his fingers through her silky hair. She tasted like vanilla and sunshine.

"Are you sure?" His voice was hoarse.

"I think so." At his frown, she added quickly, "I just...I need to go slowly. If I want you to stop, you need to stop."

He furrowed his brows. "That's obvious."

"We should probably choose a safe word. Just to be, you know, safe."

Jack stepped away, his brain going a mile a minute. He also had no idea what Gwen was talking about. A safeword? Would they have to write out a contract for each of them to sign, too? Whatever happened to just enjoying each other without talking about every single detail?

"A safe word," he repeated, skeptical.

"It's a word you wouldn't normally say during sex that means 'stop.'"

"As opposed to saying the word 'stop?'"

Gwen chuckled. "You've never read or watched *Fifty Shades of Grey*, have you?"

"I don't even know what that is."

That made Gwen laugh harder, which Jack admittedly didn't appreciate.

"Have you been living under a rock?" asked Gwen.

"I don't have the Internet out here. So, pretty much."

"No Internet? Goodness, you really are an old man in a young man's body, aren't you? I'm surprised you didn't come to the door with a shotgun pointed at me while yelling at me to get off your lawn."

"I don't own a shotgun. I'm a fisherman. Guns aren't

much use for catching things that swim. And I don't have a lawn."

They stared at each other, the tension lengthening. Jack suddenly wished he didn't live in this tiny house with barely any furniture. Gwen had never been inside his house. Very few people, in fact, had come inside the place, besides a few women who'd come over for the night when they couldn't find a room in town.

"I think our safe word should be salmon," said Gwen, breaking through Jack's thoughts. "Nobody says salmon during sex."

"Clearly you've never slept with a fisherman," was his droll reply.

That response seemed to shatter the tension. Gwen laughed, a sound that went straight to Jack's groin. With her red hair tumbling down her shoulders, her cheeks pink and her mouth red from his kisses, she looked delicious. Seductive. Dangerous.

"Salmon it is." He approached her and touched a strand of hair. "We won't do anything you don't want to do," he said seriously.

Tears sprang to her eyes. "That means so much to me."

Jack didn't want to see her tears. It made him feel strangely guilty, like he was taking on something he knew would end in failure. But he couldn't resist the temptation she presented. He was only human, after all.

"This isn't a relationship, either. We're enjoying each other until we decide we're done," he said.

She nodded. "Does that mean we can date other people?"

The thought of Gwen with another man sent a stake

through his heart. Gritting his teeth, he replied, "Yeah, I guess it would."

"I'm kidding, by the way. I'm not interested in anyone else at the moment." Her pupils dilated. "Just you."

"Thank fucking God." He growled the words and kissed her.

She mewled, the sound sweet to his ears. Pushing the blanket to the floor, he pressed her against him, needing to feel her curves nestled against his hardness. It took all his self-control not to strip her naked and have her right here on the kitchen table like some animal.

This is just sex. Nothing else. He knew that. He knew this was temporary. He just had to keep telling himself that, or he'd lose himself letting Gwen burrow further into his heart.

When he slipped his tongue into her mouth, she stiffened. He broke the kiss to look into her eyes. "Too much?"

"Just surprised, that's all."

"Have you never been French kissed?"

"I have, it's just—" She sighed. "I've never liked it."

Jack realized that this wasn't going to be as easy as he'd thought. He'd assumed that with a little patience, he could shed Gwen's reservations within a night. Maybe two. Clearly, he'd been way over-confident.

He took her to his bed, glad that he'd recently washed his sheets. They sat together, facing each other, still fully clothed.

"Do you trust me?" he asked quietly.

She let out a shuddering breath. "I trust you."

"Then can you trust me that I want to make you feel good? This is all about you. Not me."

She nodded. "Okay. But if it gets too much, I'll use the safe word. Salmon."

"You can scream salmon into my ear if you need to."

That made her laugh a little. "That's not a sexy image at all."

"No, but you are." He twined her hair around his fingers. He wished it were daylight so he could see all the various colors in her hair. He inhaled the scent of the silky strands before kissing her softly on the side of her neck.

Gwen sighed. Jack kissed her neck, peppering soft touches of his mouth along her shoulder and then upward, to the sensitive place behind her ear. She shivered when he tugged lightly at her earlobe with his teeth.

"You're so soft," he marveled. "I want to touch every inch of your skin."

"I do, too."

He growled. His cock was hard and aching already and he'd barely touched her. If she touched him right now, he might explode in his boxers, he was that turned on.

He rubbed the back of her neck. Gwen tipped her head back, sighing. When he turned her around so he could massage her shoulders, she truly began to relax under his touch.

Jack had figured out long ago that a little bit of effort with women in the beginning yielded better results later on. Besides, he liked just enjoying a woman's body, from head to toe.

He pushed one of Gwen's bra straps down, and he waited. She didn't stiffen. Kissing the bare patch of skin, he kept running his hands along her spine, working out any knots he found.

"I had no idea you could give a massage like this," said Gwen. "I would've asked you to massage my shoulders years ago."

"I'm just good with my hands."

Her expression was flirtatious as she looked over her shoulder at him. "I can feel that."

He pushed her hair aside so he could kiss and lick the nape of her neck. When goosebumps rose on her skin, he knew he'd found a sensitive spot. He then reached under her shirt until he reached the hook of her bra.

"Can I take this off?" asked Jack.

"Um, not yet. Sorry." Gwen shot him a pleading look.

"Don't apologize. Nothing to be sorry for."

He removed his hand, instead focusing on making her relax. He eventually turned her back around and began kissing her again. As the kisses deepened and lengthened, Jack touched her bottom lip with his tongue. This time, she allowed him in. He felt triumph shoot through his veins.

It didn't take long for them to lie down on the bed, facing each other. Jack was touching Gwen's bare skin under her shirt, while Gwen was doing the same to him.

"I want to see you," he murmured.

Gwen inhaled deeply, as if gathering her courage. Then she nodded.

Jack slowly slipped her shirt off and then, reaching behind her, unfastened her bra. He didn't immediately reveal her bare breasts. Instead, he kept kissing her, tracing figure eights on the tops of her breasts, letting her get used to the sensations.

Gwen kept wiggling to get closer to him. When she began to tug off his shirt, Jack didn't hesitate.

"Let me see these beauties." He tugged at the center of her bra.

To his surprise, Gwen slipped the bra off herself, flashing him a wide grin. But her courage failed when she realized how hard he was staring at her breasts.

"They're kind of small." Gwen tried to cover herself now, but Jack peeled her arms away.

"They're perfect."

He kissed her, coaxing her, until she let him touch and caress her breasts. Her nipples were sensitive buds that made her gasp when he tweaked them.

Everything faded away for Jack. It was only Gwen, and this bed, and the taste, touch, and scent of her. He wanted to make her moan, beg, even scream. He wanted to kiss every crease, every secret part of her. He wanted her to let go of the fear that had been holding her back for so long.

When he began to palm her ass, rubbing her core through her jeans, he was so intent on kissing her that he didn't hear her at first.

Then Gwen was pinching his ear and saying repeatedly, "Salmon, salmon—Jack!"

He stopped. His brain screeched to a halt, and it felt like a bucket of ice water was dashed on top of him. He sat up, allowing Gwen to scramble away from the bed. She was holding her shirt in front of her and breathing fast.

"Gwen," he said, taking her hand. "Gwen, breathe. It's okay. I'm sorry I scared you."

He could've kicked himself for not hearing her. He should've been paying more attention, and now he'd probably made things worse.

Gwen took in a shuddering breath, then another. She

then shot him a wobbly smile. "I'm okay. Sorry. I was having a good time until—"

"Until it was too much."

She looked like she was trying not to cry, and it made his heart crack in two.

"I don't know if this is going to work. I'm probably too much of a mess." Gwen was staring at her hands.

"Gwen, look at me."

She did, finally.

"If you don't want me to touch you ever again, I won't. If you only want to cuddle with our clothes on, we can. I don't care. There's no agenda here."

She finally let him hug her. "Thank you," she whispered.

He didn't want her to go, but it seemed as though she needed some space. Jack kissed her goodbye, and she just said thank you for a second time.

Jack returned to his bed, the scent of Gwen still on the sheets. He was still hard as a rock. Unzipping his jeans, he stroked his cock, thinking of Gwen and hoping he'd get another chance to show her how good things could be between them.

CHAPTER ELEVEN

When Gwen got the text from Tim, she wondered if it was an omen.

Did you get my last text? Thinking about you lately.

Gwen stared at her phone, her brain seemingly trying to translate the message on the screen. Tim had been thinking about her?

When they'd first separated, Gwen would've done anything to receive a message like this from Tim. Despite everything he'd done, she'd wanted their marriage to work. She'd vowed *until death do us part.* And she'd loved her husband still.

Now, though, Gwen could only feel confusion. And a touch of anger. When she'd failed to respond to the first message, that should've been clear enough. Apparently she was going to have to be more transparent than that.

Please don't text me things like that, she replied.

She watched the three dots blink. Then: *We were good together. I miss you.*

"What happened?" said Jocelyn over Gwen's shoulder.

Gwen nearly threw her phone across the front desk of the inn. Instead, it fell from her hand, bounced from the counter to the floor, and was screen-side up when Jocelyn picked it up to hand it back to Gwen.

"Good lord, are you jumpy." Jocelyn eyed her. "Did you get bad news? Is it from Luke?"

It took Gwen a moment to remember who Luke was. She shook her head. "No, no. Nothing to do with the business."

"Then what is it?"

"It's personal." Gwen winced at how snippy she sounded. "Just something that I didn't need today. That's all."

"You've been out of it for the past few days. You were staring off into space yesterday. It took me saying your name three times for you to hear me."

Gwen blushed. Since her night with Jack that had ended so awkwardly, she'd been struggling to stay focused. If she didn't think about him during the day, she dreamed about him at night.

What was worse was that she'd gotten so twisted up inside, so sure that he wanted nothing to do with her now, that she was in a constant state of alert in case he stopped by.

It was Tuesday. He was due to drop off some salmon this morning. Gwen's heart sped up at the thought. She hadn't seen him since their last evening together.

When Gwen heard the sound of Jack's truck trundling up the road to the inn, she nearly dropped her phone a second time. She forced herself to take a deep breath. She couldn't act like a crazy woman just because the local fisherman was dropping off fish for them.

She didn't need Jocelyn speculating about their relationship, either.

As Gwen went to meet Jack, her shoulders slumped when she realized one of Jack's workers, Philip, was the one driving the truck.

"Where's Jack?" Gwen forced her voice to sound casual. She also pointedly ignored Jocelyn standing next to her, watching the exchange.

Philip, a young man in his early twenties, shrugged a shoulder. "Said he was too busy for drop-offs and asked me to do it. Where do you want all this?"

"I'll show you," offered Jocelyn.

Gwen felt her skin prickling with goosebumps. In the five years since she'd opened the bed and breakfast, Gwen could count on one hand how many times Jack hadn't been the one delivering. Once, he'd been sick with flu; the other, his truck had had a flat tire.

Both times, Gwen had been worried because it was so unlike Jack to be absent. And each time, whichever worker Jack had sent in his stead had a specific reason why Jack wasn't able to come.

Never once had Jack been "too busy."

You're freaking yourself out, Gwen told herself. *He probably is just busy.*

Or was he avoiding her? Shame, guilt, anger—it washed through her until she had to stagger to her office and close the door. She sat down in a chair and, realizing the world was spinning around her, put her head between her knees.

Her brain, awash with anxiety, seemed intent on

torturing her as memories surfaced. She saw the look on his face when he'd rolled off her. She relived the moment when Tim had stopped hugging her from behind when she'd been cooking. When she'd tried to cuddle next to him on the couch and he'd told her she was too warm.

She'd experienced the death of Tim's affection slowly until it'd been too late to revive it. When she'd called him on it, he'd been defensive. *It's your fault, not mine. You're the one with issues.*

Gwen was panting. She forced herself to take one slow, deep breath, and then another. Slowly but surely, the world stopped spinning.

But when she thought of Jack, that anxiety resurfaced. She didn't know if she could finish work today. The thought of leaving early for something so trivial made her want to hide under her desk.

Someone knocked on Gwen's office door. "Hey, Philip says your card's expired, and he needs a new one," said Jocelyn through the door.

When Gwen didn't immediately answer, Jocelyn opened the door, peeking in. "Sorry, are you busy?"

Gwen was trying to remember where she'd put the new card she'd gotten from the bank. Had she even activated it? Sighing, she began shuffling through the mail in the wire bin that hadn't been sorted in God knew how long.

When she found the card, she handed it to Jocelyn. "Can you take care of it for me?"

"Sure." Jocelyn gave her a concerned look but didn't press the issue, to Gwen's relief.

But Jocelyn being Jocelyn, she was soon back again, returning the card and asking Gwen what was wrong.

"Is it Philip? He definitely smells like fish. I'm pretty sure he hasn't washed his hands in at least three years," said Jocelyn jokingly.

Gwen tried to smile but failed. "I'm sure he's a fine young man."

Jocelyn leaned against the wall opposite to Gwen. "Then what is it? You looked like you were about to faint when Philip stepped out of the truck."

"Have I mentioned how annoying it is that you pay such close attention?"

Jocelyn nudged her with her foot. "You're stalling."

"I'm okay. No, really. I'm just dealing with some personal stuff right now. It has nothing to do with Philip."

"Is it connected to whoever texted you earlier?"

Gwen let out a breath. "Kind of. It's complicated." Feeling like Jocelyn was only going to keep hounding her, Gwen added, "You know I was married, right?"

Jocelyn nodded.

"My ex has started texting me lately. He says he misses me."

"And how do you feel about that?"

"Not great. It brings back a lot of bad memories."

"Then you should block him."

Gwen felt a little embarrassed that she hadn't done that already. She'd told herself that she didn't want to be that petty. Now, though, she had a good reason to block Tim: his very presence in her messages just sent her spiraling.

Would Jack care if he knew Tim was texting me? Or would he relieved that he could stop being involved with me?

Gwen's stomach twisted. "I'll block him," she said, more to herself than to Jocelyn. "I should've deleted him a long time ago, anyway." Gwen found Tim and blocked him, relief lifting some of the anxiety that had been pressing on her.

"So that's it? Your ex is just being annoying?" Jocelyn asked.

"Pretty much." Gwen was still staring at her phone because she knew she was a terrible liar.

"Well, I know it might not seem like it, but if you need to talk, you can. I might not be super sympathetic, and I might be too frank in what I think you should do..."

Gwen felt touched by Jocelyn's offer. "I appreciate that. But maybe not right now. I think I'm too messed up to hear any of your advice, anyway."

"Oh, don't worry. I'll save it for when you really need to hear it."

JACK NEVER FAILED to appreciate that he wasn't part of the Wright family. Oh, the money would sure be nice, of course. Considering everyone in the family were local celebrities, Jack was glad he wasn't wealthy. Even money couldn't make up for the lack of privacy.

"My mom is doing great, thanks for asking," said Luke for what felt like the thousandth time that day. "She had a cold a month ago, you're right. But it went away quickly. Oh no, it wasn't the flu. Nothing that serious."

Jack rolled his eyes. He'd run into Luke at the local grocery store and Luke had invited Jack to go to lunch. At this point, Jack had a feeling by the time they reached the restaurant it'd be time for dinner, not lunch.

The old biddies of Hazel Island loved Luke Wright. He was handsome, charming, rich, and single. More than one had done her level best to match him up with one of their granddaughters. Luke, though, had remained uncatchable.

Outside the grocery store, Jack folded his arms and waited. Three old ladies had surrounded Luke and weren't about to let him go.

Jack admired his friend's patience. Jack would've up and run from the onslaught of questions and inquiries.

"I have to get going. Yes, I'll tell Mom you said hi. I don't know when she'll be here in town. She doesn't like driving."

Luke gently parted the wave of ladies and gestured at Jack to follow him to his car. Although they could easily walk the four blocks to the Salty Shack, the car provided protection from overzealous islanders.

"The light is red," said Jack when Luke nearly ran over a man crossing the street. The man was about to say something rude when he recognized Luke. Then he just waved happily.

Luke groaned. "Is it me? Do I give off signals that I want them to talk to me?" He gave Jack a pleading look. "Seriously. Be honest."

"Well, you are polite. Be ruder and they'll leave you alone."

"I tried that. They just assumed I wasn't feeling well and plied me with their soup recipes and nasty herbal teas."

Jack laughed. Luke just glowered.

Luckily, the Salty Shack was too much of a dive bar—even during lunchtime—for the island's old-biddy population.

Luke never called them old biddies, of course. He was too polite, and Jack knew Luke would take offense if Jack said the term out loud.

Luke was like that. He tended to want to see the good in everyone. *Rather like Gwen*, Jack thought.

The thought of Gwen brought back memories of their night together. He hadn't seen Gwen since then. He'd been dealing with a busted pipe at home and hadn't delivered Tuesday's order. Had Gwen noticed? Or had she been relieved?

Luke snapped his fingers in Jack's face after they'd sat down at a sticky table. "Did you hear me?"

Now it was Jack's turn to glower. "No. And don't snap your fingers like I'm a damn dog."

"I said, have you talked to Gwen yet? She hasn't responded to my emails."

Jack frowned. That wasn't like Gwen. Had she gotten second thoughts about putting together the business plan for Luke?

"I haven't seen her in a few days," hedged Jack.

After he and Luke had ordered burgers and drinks, Luke said, "Well, I'm getting the vibe that she's not interested. It's fine if she's changed her mind. I just need to know so I don't waste my time."

"You could talk to her yourself, you know."

"I only have her email. Besides, I'm driving over to Seattle this weekend and will be gone for two weeks. I don't have time to track her down."

"I'll talk to her."

Luke grunted. Jack was grateful when their orders arrived, which put a pin in talking about Gwen.

He'd been racked with guilt since she'd shown up at his doorstep. He should never have touched her. But he'd been so sure that he could help to end her fear of sex. He'd been too sure of his own prowess, and now he didn't know if she'd ever talk to him again. His own ego might've destroyed their friendship, and it made his stomach turn to think about it.

"You know, every time I say Gwen's name, you get a look on your face," said Luke.

Jack didn't feel compelled to reply.

"I mean, if you're interested in her, you should ask her out. She's single, right?" Luke bit down on a French fry. "I might ask her if you don't."

That made Jack see red. The jealousy that burst through him surprised him in its intensity. Apparently, the jealousy showed on his face because Luke chuckled.

"Don't strangle me, dude. I'll leave her alone if it pisses you off."

Jack took a long drink of his beer. "She's too good for you."

"Oh, I'm sure she is. But we should always aim high, right?" Luke lifted his glass in a toast, which Jack grudgingly returned.

"Then again, she does smile a lot," said Luke. "I've only talked to her half a dozen times, but she was always smiling. It was kind of weird. Have you noticed that?"

Now Jack really had to restrain himself from decking his friend. "No, I hadn't noticed," he growled.

Luke raised an eyebrow. "Really? I doubt that. Everyone who I've talked to about her mentions it. That, and her red hair."

"Who are you talking to about Gwen?"

"I don't know. People? You know how small towns are. It's a circle jerk of gossip."

"Then I'd ask that you don't gossip about Gwen, especially if you're just going to talk shit about her."

Putting up his hands, Luke let out a little laugh. "Whoa, whoa. I'm not talking shit about her."

"You were just criticizing her."

"Fine, I was. A little. I won't do it again." Luke gave Jack a speculative look. "I've never heard you get this defensive over a woman before. It's interesting."

"Just shut the hell up, Wright, before I break your pretty face."

Luke only laughed. By the time they left the Salty Shack, Luke had managed to apologize enough to satisfy Jack.

When they stepped into the sunshine, Luke nearly collided with a woman. She dropped the bags she was holding, Luke apologizing and helping her.

It was Jocelyn Gray, Gwen's cook.

"It's fine," Jocelyn was saying to Luke.

Luke, though, wasn't listening. He was putting the groceries back into the bags, but based on Jocelyn's expression, she wasn't happy about it. It didn't help that Luke was putting the bread at the bottom, then a carton of eggs, and then heavy cans on top of it all.

"Look, it's fine," Jocelyn repeated. When Luke didn't stop, she said sharply, "Will you stop already? You're screwing everything up." She grabbed the bag away from Luke.

Luke stood and dusted off his pants. "I was just trying to help," was his mulish reply.

"Maybe not everyone wants your help." Jocelyn grabbed the rest of her groceries and headed off without another word.

Luke eventually turned back toward Jack. "What are you smiling about?"

"You really fucked that up."

"And that makes you smile?"

"The exalted Luke Wright getting put in his place? That'll always make me smile."

CHAPTER TWELVE

I t was a cold, blustery day. Jack always wore his rain gear during this time of year. Despite the heavy cloud cover, though, no rain appeared as he pulled nets from the depths of the ocean.

But with every catch he pulled in, Jack almost wanted to toss all of it back into the water. The salmon were small and pathetic-looking. The percentage of his catch that he could actually sell seemed to dwindle with every net he pulled in.

He was sweating by the time he'd finished. Stripping out of his raincoat, he let himself enjoy the brisk wind that would make anyone else shiver. The Pacific wasn't exactly warm and inviting. It was easily twenty degrees cooler on the water than on land.

Jack felt a few raindrops hit his head. When the deluge began, he couldn't bring himself to put his coat back on. He let the rain soak him to the skin. Maybe, deep down, he hoped that he could cleanse himself of whatever bad karma had infected all his catches.

What the hell am I going to do? His savings were dwindling

—fast. He'd thought he'd saved enough of a nest egg. But between house repairs, multiple poor seasons of salmon and crab, and then stupidly committing to finance Gwen's restaurant, Jack knew he was screwed. Even a man who lived off the grid had some bills to pay.

He returned to the harbor slowly, not just because of the rain but because he didn't want to see the looks of concern from his workers or fellow fishermen. Several of the fishermen and -women who worked on the island worked for large businesses that could afford these lean times. Only a handful was like Jack's, a mostly one-man enterprise.

Jack hated the thought of no longer being his own boss. He'd have quotas, expectations. He'd have to heed whatever stupid rules the owners felt like imposing. And for what? Lower pay and the possibility of shitty health insurance? It didn't appeal to Jack in the slightest.

"Looking a little damp!" said Lyle after Jack had docked. Lyle, a red-faced, pleasant sort of guy, guffawed at Jack. "You'd think after all of these years you'd remember to bring an umbrella with you."

Jack wasn't in the mood for Lyle's jokes. Pushing his wet hair out of his face, he replied, "The rain doesn't bother me."

"You know, when I was your age, it didn't bother me, either. But as I got older, I realized that wearing wet denim sucks balls."

Jack barely heard Lyle's random chatter. It was only when he heard Lyle mention Gwen's name that Jack's head whipped up.

"What was that?" said Jack.

Lyle chuckled. "Now you're listening to me. I was just asking if you two were an item."

Jack had the strongest urge to push the man into the water. Mostly it was because Lyle was smirking at him like he knew what he was asking was ridiculous.

"We're friends," growled Jack.

"You don't sound like you're happy about that. Did she friend-zone you?" Lyle slapped Jack's shoulder. "Bummer, man."

Another defensive remark was on Jack's tongue, but he held it back. Why did he care what Lyle Hutchins thought? Lyle just liked to rile people for his own amusement. He was also one of the worst gossips on Hazel Island. Jack didn't know how the man had time to winnow out information when he had his own fish to catch.

Both luckily and unluckily, Lyle's comments about Gwen ended when he noticed how dismal Jack's catches were. "Shit, is that from this morning?"

Jack snorted. "No, they're from two years ago, Lyle. Just a bunch of live salmon I've had stored on my boat."

Lyle poked at one of the salmon, clearly ignoring Jack's sarcastic comment. "It might be time for me to retire. The missus won't be pleased, but what's a man to do when the fish are this bad?"

Lyle's gaze was sympathetic now. "You gonna be okay, Benson?"

God, Jack hated pity. His jaw tight, he managed to say in a rough voice, "I'll manage."

"If you need money—"

"I'm not taking your fucking money." Jack shook his head. "Not in this life or the next."

But some hours later, the single bin of salmon in the back of his truck, Jack wondered. If he needed money, the one person who would say yes was Luke. And the thought of being in Luke's debt was unbearable.

It would mean admitting that Jack had failed. That he'd have to go begging for funds. And although Luke wouldn't lord it over him, the blow to Jack's pride would be enough to make Jack want to end the friendship. How could he look Luke in the eye as an equal after that?

No, he wouldn't ask Luke for a dime. Not for himself, at least. For Gwen, though, he would.

The thought of Gwen made Jack's stomach twist. In all honesty, he didn't know if he could still afford to give her the money that he'd promised her. But the thought of going back on his promise made him want to rage at himself.

What if Gwen took it personally? Or worse, that he was breaking his word because his idea to have an affair with her had already backfired spectacularly?

Jack pressed his forehead to the steering wheel at a stop-light. It was only when someone honked behind him that he realized the light had turned green. Considering that it was once in a blue moon that anyone on the island actually used their horn, he must've been sitting at the green light for a decent amount of time.

When Jack arrived at the bed and breakfast, he couldn't find Gwen. The entrance and dining room were empty. The kitchen was also deserted. It was only when Jack went upstairs that he heard Gwen's voice and her laughter.

At the end of the long hallway, Gwen was standing in front of an open doorway. Jack hurried toward her until he heard a man's voice replying to Gwen's.

Jack stopped. The hairs on the back of his neck rose when Gwen laughed again. Who was she talking to?

The green beast of jealousy made him clench his fists. Gwen's cheeks were pink, her hair tumbling about her shoulders. Based on the way she was smiling, she was clearly enjoying her conversation.

"Gwen," said Jack, only a few feet away now.

Gwen turned, surprise clear on her face. "Jack! Oh, I must've lost track of time." She then turned back to the open doorway. "I hope you have a good morning."

The man answered in the affirmative before Gwen shut the door. "Were you looking around for me? I'm sorry. I wasn't paying attention to the time," she said.

"You were busy," said Jack dully.

"Just welcoming a new guest, that's all. He came all the way from Los Angeles. He'd seen the great reviews and decided to stay here after he'd spent some time in Seattle." She peered more closely at Jack's face. "Are you okay?"

Jack didn't know how to respond to that question. It felt like everything around him was crumbling. He wanted to toss Gwen over his shoulder and take them far, far away from this damn island.

"My catch was shit this morning," he found himself admitting.

"Wait, do you not have any fish for me today?"

"I have fish for you. Just not as much as usual."

"Oh. That's a shame. Why was it bad?"

Jack leaned against the wall, sighing deeply. "Things have been shit for a while. Each year, it gets worse, it seems like. It used to be that you'd get one bad season but bounce back the next." He shrugged. "Not sure what I'll do."

"This has been happening for a while? Why didn't you tell me?"

Jack was surprised at the hurt in her voice. "Because it's my problem, not yours."

"Maybe, but friends tell each other things they're worried about. I've told you about plenty of things. You could, for once, let your guard down and talk to someone."

Jack didn't know what to say to that. He'd never even considered talking about this subject with Gwen or anyone else. He'd always taken care of his own problems. He'd only ever relied on himself, and it had been like that since he'd been young.

"I can't necessarily do anything about it," Gwen was saying, "but it's nice to have a shoulder to lean on."

Jack's throat felt dry. He didn't know what to say to that.

"You look like I just told you I'm a vampire who wants to suck your blood," joked Gwen.

That remark knocked him out of his stupor. Shaking his head, he replied, "Nobody's said something like that to me."

"Really? No one?"

"Weren't we talking about fish?" He desperately did not want to have this conversation. He felt like he should be lying down on a couch while some shrink asked him why he had commitment issues. *I'd rather swallow knives*, he thought sourly.

"Are you going to be okay? Be honest." Gwen raised her chin.

"Of course I'll be fine. Don't worry. I can take care of myself."

He stepped closer to her. He could smell her sweet scent, and he was fascinated as he watched the pulse in her throat flutter. The memory of how soft she'd been, the sounds she'd made, made desire sweep through him.

She seemed to know what he was thinking about. Gwen was chewing on her bottom lip, which made Jack want to haul her into his arms and kiss her. But then something crossed her face, and she took a step back from him.

He hated that. He hated that she seemed intent on avoiding him.

Sighing, he pushed his fingers through his still-damp hair. "Look, we can forget that night ever happened. I shouldn't have suggested it. It's my fault."

"I don't want to forget it!"

She seemed as surprised by the admittance as he was. She added in a sad voice, "I'm a mess. I'm sorry."

"Will you stop apologizing?"

Her eyes widened, a blush creeping into her cheeks.

Jack knew he was probably being too harsh, but he'd run out of patience today. "You've got your issues. I have mine. Whatever. I don't care. Either you want this or you don't. That's all that matters."

"It's not that simple. Come on, even you know that."

Now he gave in to the urge to haul her into his arms. She let out a gasp of surprise. "Kissing you, touching you, making you feel good? Yeah, baby, it's fucking as simple as that."

Gwen was breathing fast, her breasts pushing against her emerald-green sweater. The color made her eyes seem even greener. Jack also noticed for the first time that her lashes were tipped with blond. It was such an intimate detail that it made his own heart stutter.

"But if you've moved on," he said, his voice rough, "that's fine. Just tell me, for the love of God."

"Moved on? To who?"

His fingers were digging into the flesh of her upper arms, and he forced himself to loosen his hold. "That man down the hallway. I heard you flirting with him."

"Flirting? What?"

Jack growled. When he leaned down to kiss her, though, a door opened down the hallway. Before Jack could react, she'd squirmed from his embrace.

And then the guest who Gwen had been flirting with earlier appeared.

Instead of the rival Jack had imagined, a tiny old man tottered out of the room. He was completely bald, his glasses taking up half of his face. Despite his stooped posture and obvious age, he still managed to walk at a fair clip. After a quick hello and goodbye to Gwen, he just as quickly went down the stairs.

Gwen didn't say anything for a long moment. Neither did Jack. Her lower lip was trembling, and then her chin, and then her entire body was shaking with soundless laughter.

Jack glared at her. "It's not funny."

"You thought I was flirting with Jerry—" Gwen let out another peal of laughter.

Jack just crossed his arms and waited for her to stop. She giggled, snorted, and then when she looked into his face, started the routine all over again.

"You sounded flirtatious." Even Jack knew how stupid he sounded.

"I was being courteous, you weirdo. And anyway, you

never know. Maybe Jerry is my type." She grinned. "He is very nice, after all. He's already invited me to play checkers with him later tonight. Who knows what we'll get up to after that. Maybe we'll watch reruns of *Murder, She Wrote* and go to bed by eight o'clock."

"Are you done?"

Gwen patted him on the chest. "Am I done teasing you? Never." Her expression turned more serious. "You don't have to be jealous. I'm not interested in playing checkers with anyone but you."

Cupping the back of her neck, Jack tilted her head up. "Are you being honest? Or just trying to spare my feelings?"

"I don't care that much about your feelings," was her wry response.

That made him kiss her. He knew he should've warned her, but the urge was too great to ignore. When she responded, though, he let himself kiss her for a few seconds longer before breaking their embrace.

"You want to try again?" Her words were a whisper.

"Yeah. I do."

She beamed at him. He almost looked away, because he knew he didn't deserve that kind of look from a woman like Gwen. But being the selfish asshole he was, he didn't tell her no, either.

"My place or yours?" he rasped.

"Mine. Your place is too far. How about Saturday night?"

"It's a deal." He brushed his thumb across her lip. "I'll be counting down the days."

CHAPTER THIRTEEN

G wen usually didn't mind living on an island. Sure, you couldn't get some things as quickly as you could in a bigger city. It took sometimes up to two weeks to get packages from online retailers, depending on the weather.

But today, Gwen wished she lived in a bigger city. Even a decent-sized town would suffice. But here on Hazel Island, she had nowhere to go to buy new lingerie for her upcoming night with Jack.

At the general store, Gwen perused the pathetically bare racks of oversized nightgowns. Most of them either had fish on them or the Seattle Seahawks logo. Hardly the sexy type of stuff she wanted to buy. Just the thought of her opening the door to Jack, while she wore a huge nightgown with a gaping salmon on it, made her giggle.

The store had a few packs of underwear that Gwen couldn't tell if they were for men or women. Maybe they were unisex. Sighing, she gave up looking, only nearly to run into Helen.

"Watch where you're going! Oh, it's you." Helen pursed her mouth. "You nearly ran me over, you know."

"Sorry. I was just distracted."

"Hmm. That seems to be a theme with you lately. Yesterday I saw you stepping into your car, and you didn't even hear me call your name. Or maybe you were just ignoring an annoying old lady."

Gwen felt her face heat. "I wasn't ignoring you."

Helen didn't seem convinced. She glanced over at the packs of underwear, picking up one of them.

"I appreciate that this place just has the essentials. Small, to the point. But a shame they don't have more vegan things. When I asked an employee if they had vegan cheese, she looked like her head was about to explode."

Gwen had to restrain herself from tapping her foot. Normally, she didn't mind having these short chats with guests and island residents. It was simply the nature of where she lived.

But now, she needed to figure out what the hell she was going to wear tomorrow night when Jack came over. Did she have time to take the ferry down to one of the suburbs outside of Seattle? Or would she need to go into the city itself? She needed to figure out what she was looking for...

"Now I know you're ignoring me." Helen clucked her tongue. "Did you hear a word I just said?"

Gwen considered lying. Instead, she admitted sheepishly, "No, I didn't. I just have a lot going on."

Before Gwen could make her exit, who should appear but Jack Benson himself? He didn't see Gwen or Helen, as his attention was on something in the next aisle over. But

Gwen would recognize that dark hair and broad shoulders anywhere.

Helen looked over to where Gwen was staring. She raised her eyebrows. "He is quite a snack. I don't blame you there."

Reaching over to the rack of nightgowns, Helen pulled out a white one with lace edging. It looked like it had come straight out of an episode of *Little House on the Prairie*. The cherry on top, though, was the huge fish plastered on the front with the slogan Gone Fishin' below it.

Helen held the nightgown up, assessing how Gwen would look wearing it.

"You need something to get that man's attention. Go over to his place wearing this, and he'll lose his mind," said Helen sagely.

Gwen struggled to contain her laughter. When Jack turned and spotted her, Helen still holding up the nightgown, he raised an eyebrow in question.

Gwen took the nightgown from Helen, stuffing it into her basket, blushing to the roots of her hair. The last thing she needed was Jack to think she was going to wear something as unsexy as this stupid nightgown!

"I have to go," said Gwen. She waved at Jack as she passed, not wanting to have a chat with him. He just gave her another confused look and waved back, frowning.

Gwen was too nice to stuff the nightgown in some random spot for an employee to find later. Sighing internally, she paid for the monstrous thing while ignoring the smirk on the teenage cashier's face.

~

THE UNIVERSE SEEMED intent on not allowing Gwen to buy pretty lingerie. One thing after another snagged her attention, and by Saturday morning, she knew she didn't have time to go buy something.

She'd just have to make do with her boring cotton bra and panties. Jack hadn't seemed to mind them when she'd come to his before. Then again, that night she hadn't been thinking about something as mundane as her underwear.

By the time seven o'clock rolled around, she knew she'd probably gone overboard. She had stew in the crockpot along with an assortment of bread, cheeses, meats, and fruits. She had three different kinds of wine. She'd even bought an entire cheesecake that was defrosting in the fridge. Even a guy like Jack would struggle to eat all this food.

She'd done her hair and her makeup, vacillating between a glamorous look or something more natural. She realized as she was trying to tame her curls that she didn't know what Jack himself preferred.

She was touching up her eye makeup when the doorbell rang. Her heart pounding, Gwen hurried to open the door, forcing herself to pause a moment to take a deep breath.

Jack held a bouquet of flowers and was wearing a button-up shirt. Gwen didn't know if she'd ever seen him wear a shirt like that. She would've assumed he didn't own one.

By the time Jack was sitting on her couch, Gwen moved the platters of bread and cheese to the living room. "Do you want anything to drink? Do you want a bowl of stew? I wasn't sure if you were going to eat before you came over—"

As Gwen was setting down a bowl of grapes, Jack said, "Gwen. Sit."

She sat down.

"Are you nervous?" he asked.

Considering she was about to tear her skirt in half, she had to stop from laughing hysterically. "How can you tell?"

"You haven't stopped moving since I got here, for one." He moved so his knee was touching hers. "There's nothing to be nervous about. We can take this as slowly as you want. If you still want it."

Gwen's head shot up. "I do. I really do. I just get too inside my head. I'm also worried it'll be a repeat of last time."

Jack snagged the glass of wine and handed it to her before picking up his own. "Don't think about the what-ifs. Just enjoy what's happening right now."

Gwen nodded. He was right. She needed to stop spiraling inside her head. If she weren't careful, she'd scare Jack away. It was a miracle that she hadn't done that already.

The wine soon made her nerves less jangled. Warmth spread through her limbs. She ate a little bit, but by the second glass of wine, Gwen was feeling like all her worries had faded into the background.

Jack smiled at her. "Your face is flushed," he said.

"Is it? Oh, it's warm. Wine does that to me. It's annoying."

"It's cute."

He brushed his fingers across her cheek, making her shiver. Soon, he'd entwined his hand with hers, and then he was kissing her.

Her heart nearly burst at the touch of his lips. Why was it that each time they kissed, it felt like the first time? It was like he had some magician's spell that enthralled her. Or maybe it was simply that Jack Benson was a hell of a kisser.

He seduced her with his lips, his tongue, even his teeth. His hands wandered down her back, but always above her clothes. He kept kissing her at a steady pace, like he would be content kissing her for the entire night.

Gwen, though, wanted more. Squirming, she climbed into his lap, wrapping her arms around his neck. In this position, she couldn't deny the hardness pressing against her ass.

Jack's eyes were stormy. "Keep wiggling like that and this night will be over soon."

She giggled. Giggled! She couldn't remember the last time she'd laughed during sex. She realized that she'd never thought of sex as something fun.

"I want you to touch me," she breathed.

"I am touching you."

"No. I want more."

Jack kissed the tip of her nose. "You're in control of this, baby. If you want something, you have to say it."

"I want you to touch me under my shirt."

He smiled, lifting the hem of her blouse and tracing a finger down her spine. "Like this?"

"More. Higher."

He just chuckled, which made her want to grab his hands and put them where she ached the most. Her breasts; her core. Even her skin felt like it was ablaze wherever he touched her.

Gwen soon found the courage to ask him to touch her

breasts. He teased her nipples through her bra. Then she was unhooking her bra herself and taking her shirt off completely.

"Touch me. Here." She lifted his hands to her breasts. "Like you did that night at your place. Do you remember?"

"How could I ever forget?"

He played with her breasts until Gwen was mindless with pleasure. She barely noticed how she was pressing herself against his hardness, or how his grip had tightened on her hair as he sucked on her nipples.

"I want to kiss you," he said, raspy.

"Isn't that what you're doing?"

He slanted her a look. He cupped her center. "Here. Will you let me?"

Gwen trembled. Did she dare? She'd never enjoyed oral with Tim. Then again, Tim hadn't really given her oral more than three times in total. It had always been an awkward, lackluster experience.

Jack traced her furrowed brow. "Stop thinking. Just feel."

Gwen forced back her doubts. "Okay."

"What's the safe word?"

That question made her laugh because it reminded her of the ugly nightgown she'd been forced to buy. "Salmon."

"Good girl."

Soon enough, Gwen was lying down on the couch while Jack stripped her out of her jeans and panties. She'd already forgotten about how boring her panties were. All she cared about was Jack and the way he made her feel.

She closed her eyes when she felt his heated breath against her pelvis. When he gently parted her folds, she wanted to squirm away, but she knew that was her anxiety talking. She was tired of it wanting to control the show.

For once, Gwen wanted to enjoy sex without fear.

"Doing okay?" Jack asked.

She nodded. "Keep going."

Jack didn't need to be told twice. He was gentle, almost too gentle, as he kissed and licked her. When she responded to one stroke more than another, Jack made sure to repeat the movement.

Gwen could feel her sheath tightening around Jack's fingers. When he fastened his lips around her clit, the breath whooshed out of her. Her toes curling, her body bowing, it was only a few more moments before she burst into flames.

She barely heard herself scream as her orgasm crashed like a wave into her. It surprised her with its strength. It seemed to go on and on until Gwen opened her eyes and saw Jack just looking at her with heavy lids.

"Oh my God," she croaked.

His smile was lazy. "My thoughts exactly."

CHAPTER FOURTEEN

Gwen felt boneless, languid. It took all her effort to raise her head and sit up. When she saw Jack just staring at her, she grabbed a nearby blanket and laughed into it.

"Don't cover yourself," said Jack, gently taking the blanket from her. "There's nothing to be embarrassed about."

Gwen wasn't embarrassed. She just felt giddy, and maybe a little overwhelmed. If she thought too much about what she felt right in this moment, that giddiness would disappear like a puff of smoke.

Forcing herself to be brave, she pulled Jack's face down to kiss him. She caressed his chest and moved to the bulge that was all too noticeable.

"Gwen." Jack's voice was a rumble she felt throughout her body. "What are you doing?"

"Touching you." Gwen traced a figure-eight around his cock; she felt his entire body stiffen. "I think you want me to touch you."

"It's not a matter of want."

She suddenly felt self-conscious. Pulling her hand away, she waited for the inevitable blow to hit. *I'm not really feeling it. It's not you, it's me. I should go. It's getting late.*

But the ax didn't fall. Instead, Jack kissed her quickly and then stood up. "Let's eat," was all he said by way of explanation.

She didn't protest, as her own stomach was rumbling ominously. While Jack got them both some stew, Gwen put her clothes back on.

She probably would never be the type to lounge around the house completely nude. Besides, eating hot stew naked was a recipe for burns in awkward places.

Jack sat down next to her. He ate his stew in silence, which Gwen found maddening. She wanted to press him for answers, or explanations. She wanted to know what he wanted to do next. Were they just supposed to act like he hadn't been eating *her* out not even twenty minutes ago?

She blushed as she remembered. She was still tingling from her orgasm. She was also still sweaty, and the hot bowl in her hands didn't help cool her down, either.

"This is good," said Jack, pointing to his own bowl. He'd already eaten half of it. "Is it okay if I have a second bowl?"

Gwen's lips twitched. "Go for it."

They finished their meals in relative silence. Jack seemed at ease. Gwen tried her best not to stare at him from the corner of her eye, trying to gauge what he was feeling. If he got up after eating and said he needed to get home, she'd probably throw the cheese platter at his head. She was that wound up.

"Jack," said Gwen, watching him continue to eat. How

much could this man put away? Her worry about finishing all this food had disappeared watching him.

"Yeah?" He swallowed a slice of brie.

"Are you seriously just going to sit there and eat and say nothing?"

He was now popping grapes into his mouth. Based on how slowly he was chewing, she realized he was messing with her, the jerk. When he smiled, looking mischievous, she picked up a pillow and hit him with it.

"Hey, hey! What's with the hitting?"

He put up his hands, but it was no use. Gwen went on a rampage of pillow hitting that only resulted in Jack laughing loudly.

"You. Are. The. Worst." She punctuated each word with a smack of the pillow. "I'm over here dying and you're just eating every bit of food in my place!"

"I didn't even open your fridge, so I doubt that."

Gwen just stuck out her tongue, but she couldn't stop herself from smiling, either.

"Feel better?" Jack popped one last grape into his mouth.

"Sort of." Gwen sighed. "Not really." Steeling herself, her back straight, she asked, "Why did you reject me? I wanted to return the favor. Why did you say no?"

Jack's expression turned somber. He rubbed the back of his neck, like he didn't know how to answer her question. "It didn't seem like a good idea," he rumbled.

"Me touching you is a bad idea?"

"Going too fast is what messed us up last time." He glared at her now. "I'm trying to go slow, but you're making it very hard."

Where she was expecting more rejection, she realized that she'd been silly. And defensive. Mortified, she grimaced.

"Now I feel like a complete asshole," she admitted. "I was afraid you'd changed your mind."

"Gwen, look at me." She did. "I want you to touch me. I want your hands on my cock, your mouth. I want to be inside you more than words can explain. But you're testing every bit of my self-control."

To Gwen's horror, she felt tears prick her eyes. Relief poured through every limb. Scrubbing at her eyes, she sniffled, forcing the tears down. She was not going to burst into tears. Not with Jack looking at her like she'd just handed him a severed limb.

"Shit, why are you crying? Please don't cry." He looked almost panicked.

"I don't know why I'm crying. I mean, I'm trying not to. I guess I just have a lot of feelings right now."

How did she explain it to Jack? That she was still so afraid of him reacting like Tim that hearing the opposite was almost a painful kind of relief? That she hadn't realized how much she'd been expecting the blow to occur?

"Baby, talk to me." Jack took her hand in his.

"My head is all screwed up. My marriage did a number on me."

"Your ex." Jack spat the word.

"I already told you what happened. Things between us just got worse and worse. Eventually, I couldn't have sex with him anymore. I still don't know why. I can't even blame him for calling me frigid, since that's what I was."

"He was an asshole."

"Yeah, he was. But I was at fault, too. I accept that. I stopped trying altogether."

"How many times did he make you feel good? In bed?"

Gwen blinked. Jack looked pained. She knew he didn't like talking about things like this. He probably wanted to run for the hills, she thought in despair.

"Tim? He tried. But it was a lot of work to get me there. Then I got inside my head and then I just...couldn't. It's hard to explain."

"Work? It's not fucking work to make your woman feel good. It's the best feeling in the world. If it took me all day and all night, I'd get a woman to come if she wanted me to."

Gwen smiled a little. "Good thing it didn't take you that long this time."

"Because I give a shit. Sounds like your ex didn't. It's as simple as that."

Gwen didn't know how to reply to that. For so long, she'd blamed herself for her marriage failing. Oh, Tim had been at fault, too, but she'd never placed the blame solely on his shoulders. Strangely, thinking that it was due to Tim's selfishness meant admitting that she'd had no control of the situation.

She hadn't failed. Tim had failed her.

"You don't look like you believe me," said Jack quietly.

Gwen shook her head. "I don't. I think I will eventually. Why is it so much harder to forgive yourself than others?"

"Because you're a good person, that's why. I knew it the first moment I met you."

She cuddled up next to him, enjoying the warmth of his body and how he stroked her hair absently.

"You're way more of a softie than you let on," she said eventually, smiling.

Jack looked embarrassed. He muttered something under his breath, and Gwen could almost see his face turning red under his tan. Had Jack Benson ever blushed in his entire life? It was difficult for her to imagine.

"You are. Underneath all of the growling and scowling, you're squishy." Gwen poked his stomach. "Well, not literally. Do you have an eight-pack under there?" She lifted his shirt to inspect further.

"You've already seen me with my shirt off." He raised a single eyebrow. "Actually, I distinctly remember catching you staring at me when I was naked."

Gwen had never mentioned that event to Jack since it'd happened, and he'd called her out on it later in the day. She'd just been too mortified to talk about it. Covering her face with her hands, she tried to squirm away from him.

Soon after they'd met five years ago, Gwen had stumbled upon a naked man swimming in the ocean. She'd been transfixed; he'd been like something out of a movie. She'd soon realized who it was, but that hadn't been enough for her to tear her gaze away. It had only been later that Jack had given her some binoculars, telling her it had seemed like she'd needed some.

"Do you still have those binoculars?" mused Jack, laughter in his voice.

"Oh, they're in a closet somewhere. I was too embarrassed to use them."

"Why?" He sounded genuinely surprised.

"Because if you'd seen me using them, it'd just make you

remember how much of a creep I'd been." She grimaced. "I shouldn't have stared. It was rude."

"Rude? Gwen, baby, do you think I've been offended all these years?" He took her hands from her face. "I was flattered. Besides, I was out in public. It's not like you were lurking in the bushes outside my house to catch a peek."

"Do you even have bushes around your house?"

He grinned. "No. Helps keep peeping toms away, though."

Gwen wanted to die. It didn't help that Jack kept laughing, either. Eventually, she just rolled her eyes at him. She was glad he was laughing. He didn't do it nearly enough.

"Where are the binoculars?" said Jack suddenly.

"Um, in my coat closet. I think. Why?" Gwen pointed at a door near the entrance.

Jack rose and after asking if it was okay for him to look, he began to search in the closet for said binoculars. It was only when he said, "What the hell is this?" that Gwen remembered she'd stashed the ugly nightgown in there.

Jack held up the offending article of clothing. "What the hell is this?"

"What are you talking about?" Gwen went to him and took the nightgown from him. "I bought it for you. Isn't it sexy?" She held it up, the fish on its front as open-mouthed as Jack was currently.

"Seriously?" he said.

"I mean, you're a fisherman. It's a nightgown with a fish on it. What's not to love?"

He looked so confounded that Gwen couldn't help but laugh at him. Realizing she was teasing, he growled at her.

"You brat." He took the nightgown from her and then

tossed it into some dark corner of the closet. "I really thought you were serious."

"I know. Your face—" She giggled. Her giggles only ended when he kissed her, hard. The giggles soon turned into a moan of surprise.

"Your bedroom," he rasped. "Now."

JACK LAY in Gwen's bed, gazing at the ceiling. They were naked, and Gwen was dozing next to him.

Normally, he felt frustrated if he hadn't gotten sex yet. But for some reason, he was content to show Gwen how good sex could be with a partner who gave a shit.

When he made a little noise, his heart contracted. He didn't want to examine these feelings too closely, though. If anything, he should get up, get dressed, and go home.

But he stayed where he was, watching Gwen sleep.

Eventually, her lashes fluttered, and yawning, she asked, "What time is it?"

"Late. Early. Dunno."

"Well, that's helpful." She stretched, their legs hooking together. "Why are you still awake?"

"Just couldn't sleep. I usually sleep alone."

Gwen blinked in surprise. "You've dated other women, though."

"They usually leave that night."

"Oh." She wouldn't look at him now. "You can go if you want."

"I don't. Want to go, that is."

The smile she gave him was blinding. *Do you really think you can end this without her getting hurt?*

He told himself that Gwen knew the rules. She knew this was temporary. If she caught feelings, it'd be her own fault.

But even as he told himself that, the guilt for something that hadn't even happened made it difficult to speak.

"Have you never had a long-term relationship?" said Gwen, breaking through his thoughts.

"This is why I don't let women stay over," he rumbled, "because then they start asking questions."

Gwen wasn't deterred. She just waited patiently for his answer.

"I've never had a relationship that lasted longer than a few months. It's been years since I've had a girlfriend. Not since I was in my twenties."

"That sounds kind of lonely."

"It never bothered me."

"No man is an island. Even you, I'm sure. Everybody gets lonely."

"Not me."

If he sounded less than convincing, Gwen was smart enough not to comment on it.

"Sometimes it's nice to be single," she said, "but then other times, you want a person you can cuddle with. That person who you can eat meals with, who asks you about your day and vice versa. That you can rely on if you need anyone."

"I've never had that." Jack's voice was just a murmur.

"What about your parents?"

He hated this. But at the same time, he didn't sense any

judgment in Gwen's tone. Merely curiosity, and concern. There was no one he trusted more than Gwen Parker.

"My dad ran off when I was a kid. I don't remember him. My mom..." How did he explain that to Gwen? "She had issues."

"Do you talk to her at all? My mom passed a while ago. My dad moved to Florida three years ago, so I really only see him for the holidays. So I kind of get not being close to your parents. Well, parent singular. I was close to my mom."

"When did she pass?"

"When I was in high school. She had breast cancer. It was already stage three by the time she was diagnosed, and it spread quickly." Gwen sighed. "I miss her every day."

"I'm sorry." And he was because if Gwen's mom was anything like Gwen, she must've been a hell of a woman.

"Thank you. I guess I get weird about people talking to their parents because you never know when they'll be gone."

Guilt nipped at Jack. Even as he'd distanced himself from his own mom for his mental health, there was still a part of him that had wanted to fix her.

"My mom was an addict. Still is, although she denies it. She was addicted to all kinds of things when I was a kid." He lifted one shoulder in a shrug. "So my childhood wasn't great."

"Oh, Jack. That makes me so sad." Gwen took his hand and squeezed it. "No wonder you've kept to yourself."

He hated the way she could see inside him so easily. The feeling of being vulnerable was almost physically painful.

"I don't need you to be my armchair shrink," he said, rather harshly. "I'm alive. I'm working. I'm okay."

Gwen, being Gwen, didn't take offense. She just kissed

his fingers, laid her head back onto his shoulder, and eventually returned to sleep.

Jack, though, couldn't sleep. He stayed up most of the night, listening to Gwen breathe, wondering if he should be the one afraid of getting hurt.

CHAPTER FIFTEEN

October moved into November. The crisp days of autumn turned into the rainy days of winter. The few days of sunshine meant that all the residents of Hazel Island got outside, including Gwen.

Sometimes Jack joined her. Other times, he was working, or Gwen was working, too. But they found a rhythm to their friendship that they'd never experienced before.

They still hadn't had sex. At least, not sex-sex, as Alex would've described it. Gwen had tried to bring it up, but Jack had always told her there wasn't any hurry. Besides, their work schedules didn't lend to them being with each other all that often. Sometimes an entire week would pass before they could find time to spend together.

It was on one of those misty, gray days that Hazel Island hosted its annual Cider Festival. Gwen had never understood why they didn't hold it in September or October. Then again, there was something cozy about drinking hot cider on damp, cloudy days.

Given the crowd, Gwen couldn't deny they were right.

The festival was packed despite the depressing weather. The clouds overhead seemed to warn that a deluge could happen at any moment. But the locals knew that deluges of rain were rare. Instead, it was a steady drip of light rain or mist that permeated the island until springtime.

The festival featured booths serving all kinds of cider—such as apple, pear, and marionberry—with foods to match. Cider doughnuts, cider cookies, cider cotton candy. Displays and signs were covered in colorful apple graphics. A poor high school student who'd agreed to dress up as Cid the Cider Apple was constantly bumping into people due to the bulk of his costume.

"I want some doughnuts. Oh, wait, are those kolaches?" Alex handed her cup of cider to Felicity. "Do you guys want some?"

"Yes," Gwen and Felicity said at the same time.

Alex pushed through the crowd, determination on her face. No one could come between Alex and doughnuts. Gwen had learned that a long time ago.

"How many do you think she'll buy this time?" asked Felicity.

"If she comes back with fewer than a dozen, I'll buy you a drink," replied Gwen.

Felicity grinned. "Deal."

Alex eventually returned with two dozen doughnuts, along with three kolaches. "They'd already run out of most of the kolaches. Sorry, guys."

"How are we going to eat two dozen doughnuts?" Gwen shook her head at her friend.

"Oh, we can do it. I have faith in us," said Alex before biting into one of the doughnuts.

Felicity leaned over to Gwen and murmured, "You owe me a drink."

Despite the cold weather, Gwen felt warm and toasty as she and her two good friends enjoyed the festival. It helped that they didn't skimp on spiking the cider.

But as she wandered down Main Street, Gwen stopped in her tracks when she saw a dark head of hair. Her heart in her throat, she wondered how she should react if Jack were to approach them.

The man turned out to be a stranger, though, and Gwen let out a relieved sigh. Although she'd confided in Felicity about her relationship with Jack, she'd yet to disclose anything to Alex.

"Gwen, are you listening?" said Alex.

"What? Sorry, did you say something?"

"Well, it's too late now." Alex shrugged. "Cid nearly knocked a kid over. It was hilarious."

Felicity lightly elbowed Alex. "Alex, seriously."

"What? The kid's fine." She took a big bite of her second doughnut.

The trio eventually found an open bench and began to people-watch while eating all their goodies. Gwen sat in the middle between Alex and Felicity. Felicity seemed to content merely to watch the passersby, while Alex chattered about everything and nothing.

"Did I tell you about the dude who came into the store and was upset that we didn't have some random German book in stock?" said Alex. "He got super offended. I was like, dude, why would we have some book written in German that was published over fifty years ago? We can barely keep books in English that were released this year."

"Did you order it for him?" said Gwen, only half-listening.

"I couldn't. It wasn't available." Alex shrugged. "I think he might've cursed me and my descendants in German when he left."

"Oh, look, people I know." Jocelyn approached the trio, a cup of cider in her hand. "I didn't know you were coming to this thing."

Gwen felt a bite of guilt that she hadn't invited Alex's sister. It wasn't that she didn't like Jocelyn's company. It was more that Jocelyn and Alex tended to get snippy with each other over the silliest things. They weren't exactly the closest of sisters.

"We didn't think you'd want to come," said Alex.

Jocelyn took a sip of her cider. "Based on what, exactly?"

Alex shrugged. "You get all weird about food. Like you always have to make comments about it. Not everything has to be a Yelp review. It's weird."

Felicity was looking at her shoes. Gwen could feel the tension in the air already.

"You haven't been to this festival, have you? How do you like the cider?" said Gwen, trying to keep the conversation from going off the rails.

"It's good. At least the one I bought." She held out her hand. "Can I have one?"

Alex had closed the box a moment before Jocelyn had approached. "They're all gone. Sorry."

Gwen knew there were at least three still in the box. She opened her mouth, but Alex reached over to pinch her —hard.

"You already ate them all? You're going to get fat, you know." Jocelyn reached down and pinched Alex's cheek.

Gwen grimaced. Felicity looked like she was about to run for the hills. Alex, for her part, scowled and slapped her sister's hand away.

"The menu for Monday looks great," said Gwen hurriedly. "The crab cakes sound amazing."

"Well, the Dungeness crab here is so good, I like to use it as often I can. It helps that that fisherman of yours is so good at catching them," said Jocelyn.

Gwen's cheeks flushed. "He doesn't go crabbing much anymore," she stammered.

"Oh, Jack Benson, he's delicious." Alex licked her fingers. "I'd eat him up if he'd let me."

"I think he's already taken," said Jocelyn.

Jocelyn was looking at Gwen when she said that, and Gwen wished both of the Gray sisters were in the deepest parts of the Pacific Ocean.

"I always thought he was into you, Gwen. You should get on that horse and ride it," said Alex.

"Pretty sure that horse has already been ridden," was Jocelyn's quiet murmur.

Gwen stood up, surprising Jocelyn and nearly causing her to spill her cider. "I don't know what the hell you two are pissed at each other about, but I'm not going to be caught in the middle of it."

"What did Jocelyn mean? About you and Jack?" demanded Alex.

Jocelyn was looking pale. "Shit, Gwen—"

"What are you not telling me?" said Alex.

"Jack and I are..." Gwen struggled to find the right words. "Having fun with each other."

Now Alex looked pale, her eyes wide with shock. "And you told my sister before you told me?"

"I didn't tell her, not exactly—"

Alex's eyes filled with tears. She shoved the box of doughnuts into her sister's hands. "Eat the stupid doughnuts. You guys suck."

Gwen sighed. Felicity looked distraught, while Jocelyn just looked annoyed.

This is the exact reason why I didn't invite both sisters, thought Gwen.

Jocelyn opened the box. She shut it without comment and set it back down on the bench.

"Is anyone going to go after her?" said Felicity softly. She'd already stood up, but Gwen stopped her from walking after Alex.

"I'll do it," said Gwen.

She found Alex sitting under a tree near one of the parks at the north end of town. Some people meandered here, but compared to the festival, it was nearly deserted.

Alex had her arms wrapped around her knees, her chin resting on top. She didn't even notice Gwen coming up to her.

"Can I sit?" said Gwen quietly.

Alex just shrugged a shoulder.

Gwen fought against a sharp retort, knowing that it would only make Alex defensive. Sometimes it was hard to remember that Alex was five years her junior. But right now, Alex seemed painfully young to Gwen.

"Why didn't you tell me about Jack?" said Alex.

Gwen had struggled to come up with a response as she'd followed after Alex. But now she was all out of patience for both sisters.

"Because I wasn't sure you'd keep it to yourself," said Gwen bluntly.

Alex flinched. "That's not fair."

"The last time I told you something in confidence, you ended up telling your cousin, if I remember correctly—"

"It was an accident! I'd had too much to drink!"

"And I believe another time you told multiple people about the time I got sick on that rollercoaster because you thought it was so hilarious. Even though I begged you not to say anything."

Alex scowled. "That was a long time ago."

"It was like a year ago!"

"Fine. But to tell Jocelyn instead? Are you guys friends now?" The disgust in Alex's voice was obvious.

"Yeah, I think we are. But I didn't tell her everything about Jack. It just happened."

Alex didn't say anything for a long moment. Gwen watched as Alex's lower lip trembled; she swiped away a few stray tears.

"What is it with you and your sister, anyway?" Gwen asked.

"It's complicated."

"Everyone's relationship with their sibling is complicated."

"Ours is on another level."

Gwen gently poked Alex in the shoulder. "You can tell me, you know."

"Can I?" Alex sounded angry now. "Because you won't

trust me. Yeah, I've done some stupid things before. But to tell Jocelyn and not me, one of your best friends, because you can't trust me... That's shitty. Really shitty."

"Why does it have to be a competition between you and Jocelyn? Can't I be friends with the both of you?"

"No. Because my sister has always tried to take everything I've had."

Gwen gaped at Alex. "Now you're being overdramatic."

"Really? You should ask Jocelyn about it. See if I'm being overdramatic. But there are things you don't know about. Maybe consider that before you judge me."

Gwen felt like the world had turned upside down. What in the world had Jocelyn done to make Alex this angry? It made no sense. Gwen had assumed their rivalry was some childish thing that they'd yet to shed upon reaching adulthood.

Now Gwen wondered. Alex was normally more than happy to give all the juicy details about her life. But to find out that she'd been hiding something like this from Gwen...

Pot, meet kettle, she thought sadly.

"I'm sorry I didn't tell you about Jack. I've just been so out of sorts with the whole thing that I haven't been thinking clearly," said Gwen.

"Does Felicity know?"

Gwen sighed. "Yeah."

That just made Alex clench her jaw and look away from Gwen.

"I know I can be a pain in the ass sometimes," whispered Alex. "But I want to be a good friend to you. I want you to feel like you can tell me things."

"I know you do. And you have been a good friend."

Alex wiped her nose on her sleeve. "Ugh, I'm a mess. I'm sorry for all of this. I guess I'm just a drama llama today."

"I can't disagree with that."

Alex elbowed her. "Tell me about Jack. Are you guys doing the dirty or what?"

Gwen told Alex everything, although it took a second since Alex kept interrupting to ask questions. Gwen didn't disclose everything about her marriage and anxiety about sex, though. That subject still felt too raw, and Gwen was half-afraid she'd start sobbing like a crazy person right here in the park.

By the end of Gwen's story, Alex was looking at her like she didn't recognize her.

"What a little slut you are now," marveled Alex. "I'm so proud of you."

"He's only the second guy I've ever slept with," replied Gwen wryly. "Well, mostly slept-with. We haven't officially gone all the way."

"I always thought he had a thing for you. What guy delivers you fish and gives you a discount for five years straight?"

Gwen stared at Alex. "Discount?"

"You didn't know? I thought you did. Jocelyn mentioned it. She noticed that Jack always charged you something like 30% market value. I can't remember the exact number. But it was a lot."

Gwen felt her heart stutter. How had she not known this? Then again, she'd never thought to ask. She'd always assumed Jack was charging her what was fair.

"You didn't know." Alex blew out a breath. "Shit."

"I think I might be falling for him," whispered Gwen.

Alex took her hand and squeezed it. "You sound like that's the worst thing ever."

"It might be."

"Nah. It'll be all right. You'll see. He's totally crazy about you. Everybody on the island knows it."

Except me, thought Gwen. *Apparently I've been blind this entire time.*

Later that evening, Gwen went to her office to retrieve a handful of the receipts from Jack. She texted Jay, the owner of the fancy island restaurant Verity, asking him what he was charged for his local salmon.

$15-17 per pound. Depends on the catch and the season. Why? Somebody cheating you? he replied an hour later.

Gwen glanced at the number on her receipt. *$8 per pound.*

Alex had been right. Jack had been giving her a significant discount. The question was: why? And how would she ever repay him?

CHAPTER SIXTEEN

Jack woke up to the text from his mom.

I'm sick, call me.

Jack sighed. He was tempted to go back to sleep. Or better yet, delete the text and forget his mom had sent it in the first place.

Debra hadn't texted him since he'd gotten his new phone. The last time he'd talked to her on the phone had been...he had to think a moment. Five years ago? Jack had only kept her number in case of emergency.

Instead of replying to his mom's text, Jack called his brother Danny. Their relationship was distant at this point; they spoke maybe once a year.

Jack felt guilt, thinking how he'd abandoned his family all those years ago. He'd been young and dumb. But what excuse did he have now?

"Who died?" was Danny's greeting.

Jack grunted. "Nobody died. And most people answer the phone with a 'hello.'"

"Why are you calling me, then? I'm busy."

Jack couldn't help but feel stung at his brother's complete disinterest in talking to him. Then again, it'd been this way for as long as Jack could remember. He had a feeling Danny had never forgiven him for leaving him with their mom when he was still a kid.

"Mom texted me out of the blue. Do you know why? She said she's sick." said Jack.

"I haven't talked to her in months. The last time I saw her, she was asking me for money to pay for a deposit on a new place." Danny scoffed. "The last time I gave her money, she spent it in three days on booze. Really doubt she's actually sick."

"She might be. She hasn't tried talking to me in years."

"Look, dude. I have to go to work. Call her and ask her what's up."

Before Danny hung up on him, Jack said in a rush, "How are you doing? Doing okay out in the big city?"

Danny was quiet a long moment before responding. "Not sure why you care."

"The fuck does that mean? Of course I care."

"Well, you're not so great at showing it." There was another pause before Danny gave a hurried goodbye and hung up.

Jack stared down at his phone. He'd tried to keep in contact with Danny when he'd first moved to the island, but he'd been so busy that he hadn't tried very hard, either. And then Danny had reached adulthood and hadn't wanted much to do with his big brother.

Jack then stared down at his mom's text. Guilt filled him. He wondered if their mom was really sick, or even in the hospital. Or was she just sick because she'd run out of money for booze or drugs?

The thought that he'd ignored her when she genuinely needed help ate at him. No matter how much he told himself she'd made her own bed, he'd never been fully convinced of it.

He called her number, hoping against hope that she wouldn't pick up. But after four rings, she did.

"Thank God. Jack, I need your help. Where are you? Can you come to my place this afternoon?" said his mom in a rush.

Jack pinched the bridge of his nose. "I'm still living on Hazel Island. I have work this afternoon. What's wrong?"

"I'm sick and tired of this fucking apartment. I need to get into a new one, but my credit is shit. Not my fault. George stole my identity, remember? He fucked it all up, and now it's impossible to get a place."

Jack couldn't remember who George was. Probably one of the many boyfriends that had come and gone from his mom's life.

"What do you need?" said Jack.

"I need money. That's what I need. If I can pay double the deposit, I can get this nice little studio close to downtown. It's right by the bus stop. I can't drive anymore, you know. My license was suspended again. Did I tell you that?"

Before Jack could reply, Debra added, "And I know what you're gonna say. 'I can't give you money.' Just know that where I'm living now is a hell hole. Mold everywhere, my neighbors are selling crack. The guy across from me threatened to kill me. I have to get out of here."

The desperation in Debra's voice made Jack's heart

crack a little. He couldn't stand that his mom lived in a place like that. How could he stand by when she needed help?

"How much?" His voice was quiet.

"Twenty-five hundred." Debra paused. "I also need money for food. I just lost my job."

"What did you do this time?"

"Nothing! They got rid of me because I'm old. That happens all the time around here. They want young kids who can do twice the work. So they fired me while saying I wasn't putting in the effort. Buncha bullshit."

Jack felt a headache coming on. "I can lend you three thousand. That's the limit," said Jack.

"Thirty-five hundred."

"Three thousand or nothing."

His mom made an annoyed sound, but she finally agreed. After providing him with her bank information, she told him she had to go and hung up. There was no thank you. Jack hadn't expected one, if he were honest. His mom had always assumed that, as her son, he had a duty to provide for her. If she wanted money, he needed to give her money and not wonder where it would actually go.

Jack's tiny house suddenly felt oppressive. Grabbing his raincoat and keys, he got into his truck and drove into town without any destination in mind.

His own bank account was dwindling with every passing day. With his mom needing money now, he knew he wouldn't be able to help Gwen like he'd promised. The thought of letting her down, though, made him want to drive his truck off the nearest cliff.

Gwen would understand, of course. She always did. She

was too good for this world. But Jack had his pride, and to admit that he didn't have the money when he'd said he did was a fierce blow. Even worse, he'd have to tell Luke.

Would Luke still be interested in financing the restaurant if Jack backed out? Jack groaned at the thought, the headache that had been building reaching epic proportions by the time he'd gotten into town.

It was raining softly, as it usually was this time of year. Despite that, there were still people meandering about, wearing raincoats or, if they weren't from around here, using umbrellas. Those folks would eventually learn how useless umbrellas were on the island. One windy day would set them straight.

He went to the bed and breakfast, not sure why he needed to see Gwen right then. Maybe he just needed to confess that he was letting her down. Maybe he wanted to tell somebody about his family, or lack thereof.

He found Gwen in her office. She was busy typing, but when she saw him, her face lit up.

How has she gotten under my skin so easily? he thought, a little terrified at the realization. *I'd do anything to keep that look on her face.*

Gwen must've sensed something was wrong because the smile faded from her face. "What's wrong?"

"I just—" He didn't know what to say, or how to explain. Instead, he pulled her into his arms and kissed her.

GWEN FROZE, taken aback by Jack's ardor. But then her body soon responded, and her brain shut off. She just let herself feel. His hands roved over her body, caressing, as his mouth claimed hers.

She knew something was bothering him. She could feel it in the way he clutched at her, the way the kiss deepened until she felt dizzy.

She was about to break the kiss to try to get him to talk, but apparently he had other plans. He pushed her papers off her desk and, setting her on top, he stepped between her legs.

"You're so sweet," Jack said, husky. He sucked on the side of her neck. "I just can't stop wanting you."

"I feel the same."

He groaned, delving into her hair, pulling her so close that their bodies were aligned. She could feel his hardness, and her own core heated in response. When he touched her breasts and licked at her collarbone, she felt like she was going to burst out of her skin.

The heat of his hands against her inner thighs made her jump in surprise. He pressed the heel of his hand against her, and pleasure bloomed behind her eyelids.

"Did you lock the door?" Gwen whispered.

Jack stopped. He thought for a moment before going to the door and locking it. "I wouldn't be too loud, though. Unless you want everyone to hear you."

Gwen blushed scarlet. The last thing she needed was a patron or employee hearing her moaning Jack's name! She nearly told him that she needed a rain check, but then he was kissing her again.

Gwen was helpless against Jack's kisses. He was just too damn good at it.

"I'm glad you're wearing a dress," said Jack.

"You are?"

"Gives me easy access."

That made her laugh. Although she was wearing a dress, she was also wearing tights due to the cold. As Jack trailed his hands up her torso, he soon discovered that getting the tights off her wasn't going to be a simple task. He grunted in frustration as he tried to find the top of the tights.

"Where the hell do they start?" He flipped the skirt of her dress up.

His frustration only made Gwen giggle. "Are you having trouble? Do you need help?"

He squeezed her waist. Then he tore her tights down the middle, making her gasp.

"That's better," he growled.

"You ripped my tights!"

He cupped her sex again, the contact against her clit making her moan. "I'll buy you ten new pairs," he said.

Gwen soon forgot all about the ripped tights. She could only focus on Jack stroking her as he kissed her. Her toes curled, and her body was on fire. He played her like an instrument. Soon, she was gasping and biting the inside of her cheek to keep herself from being too loud.

"You're gorgeous. I love seeing you like this." His breath was hot on her cheek. "You drive me insane."

"You're the one driving me insane—" Gwen let out a mewl when he pushed a finger inside her tight sheath. She felt herself clench around him.

"Gwen—" He growled something she couldn't hear. "I need you."

Gwen floated on a haze of ecstasy, her body still taut

with the orgasm that was just within reach. She watched, heavy-lidded, as Jack took out his cock, stroking its length.

"Touch me. Christ, touch me, please." He took her hands; she didn't need any more encouragement than that to squeeze and fondle him.

He was already iron-hard. As they kissed, she reveled in how she could make him shake and beg. She suddenly felt empty, desperate for him to fill her.

Then he was hitching her legs up around his hips and pressing the tip of his cock inside her.

He was big—bigger than Tim, that was for sure. When he met some resistance that included a bite of pain, Gwen froze. Suddenly, the pleasure collided with fear.

It was all too much right then: Jack, pressing into her, his large body keeping her captive. The way he made her feel split open. Vulnerable.

"Stop." Her voice wouldn't work. Why was she so quiet? Why couldn't she get his attention? "Stop. Jack. Stop—salmon!" She yelled the safe word nearly in Jack's ear.

Jack's entire body stilled. Then he was climbing off her and zipping himself into his jeans with clumsy fingers.

Gwen hugged her knees to her chest. She wanted to cry, but no tears came. Mostly, she felt defeated, exhausted, and hopeless.

"Jesus, Gwen." Jack was shaking his head. "What's wrong? What happened?"

Gwen felt a lump in her throat. "I don't know," she whispered.

When Jack reached out to touch her, she flinched. His expression instantly turned stony.

"I shouldn't have come here. This was a mistake," he said.

Gwen wanted to fall into the deepest, darkest hole. "I'm sorry."

Clearly frustrated, Jack just kept shaking his head. "I'm an idiot. Stupid fucking idiot. Christ, I should've known better."

He didn't offer any further explanation for that statement. But then he was handing Gwen her shredded tights and placing the jacket he'd been wearing on her shoulders.

"Do you want me to go?" he said quietly.

"I think it'd be best."

She hated how hurt he looked. Mostly she hated herself. When he hesitated, she nearly broke and begged him to stay. But at the same time, she wanted to be alone, to collect her thoughts.

"I'll talk to you later." He looked like he wanted to touch her, but then he stopped himself. That made Gwen's heart sink into her toes.

He left without another word. Gwen eventually sank to the floor and hugged his jacket, letting the scent of him calm her pounding heart.

CHAPTER SEVENTEEN

J ack stood at the edge of a cliff, gazing at the ocean.
Normally, he found the sound of the waves calming.
But he wasn't in the mood to be calmed.

He'd fucked up. Badly. He should never have pushed
Gwen like he had today in her office. He'd been mindless
with wanting her and it'd made him stupid. If he would've
just used his brain for one millisecond, this entire cata-
strophe could've been avoided.

Jack had hated leaving Gwen. He'd only done it because
she'd asked him to. In his mind's eye, he saw her with her
arms wrapped around her, her eyes filled with fear.

Fear. She'd been afraid of him. It made Jack loathe
himself for making her feel that way.

He'd texted her an hour ago, but she hadn't replied.
He'd almost called her; he resisted the urge. Even as he
wanted to take her into his arms and make that fear in her
eyes melt away, he knew that she'd need to initiate next
time.

Jack went home when it got dark. He ate some tasteless

frozen dinner. He drank more than he knew he should. He even considered calling Luke again, just to hear another human voice.

But the thought of telling his friend everything made Jack hesitate. The thought of spilling his guts to Luke made Jack want to drink another glass of whiskey. Probably the only way he would tell Luke about all this shit was if he were raging drunk.

When Jack heard a knock on his door, it was so faint that he assumed it was the wind. When it happened a second time, Jack lurched to his feet, frowning.

And on his doorstep was Gwen Parker. It wasn't raining this time, fortunately.

Jack wondered if he'd drunk so much that he was hallucinating.

"Are you real?" he said.

Gwen looked down at herself. "I think so. Do I look not real?"

"You look like an angel and a demon all in one."

Gwen let out a startled laugh. She stepped inside, undeterred that Jack hadn't invited her in.

"A demon? That's not a very nice thing to say to your friend." She wagged a finger.

"Because you haunt me. No matter what I do. I need an exorcism."

"I think ghosts haunt people, not demons." Gwen went over and touched Jack's cheek. "I'm sorry, for today. For everything."

He closed his eyes, leaning into her touch. Pressing her hand that lay on his cheek, he said, "I'm the one who should be apologizing. I scared you." He opened his eyes to see her face. "I never, ever, want to see that look on your face again. If I vow anything, it's that you will never have cause to be afraid of me."

"You stopped, Jack. You did exactly what I needed."

"Not soon enough."

She brushed her fingers across his jaw, feeling the stubble. Then she traced a line down his throat.

He'd been wrong: she wasn't a demon. She was a siren, and he knew he'd happily crash his ship into the rocks just to hear her sweet voice.

"You stopped," she repeated firmly. "I just freaked out. It was a lot of things all at once."

"Again, my fault."

"Then we're both idiots. Will that work?"

That remark made him smile. "I won't commit to calling you an idiot."

Gwen turned away. She gazed at the bare walls of Jack's house, at the basic furniture, the simplicity of it all. Of course, she found the one framed photo he had on a table and picked it up.

"This must be your mom," she said. "And apparently, you were already good at scowling even as a kid."

Jack looked at the photo over Gwen's shoulder. It was one of the few family photos of Debra, Danny, and Jack together. Jack would've been five or so; Danny, just a baby. Their mom had had periods of sobriety, and this had been one of them.

Jack had remembered his mom waking him up and getting him dressed in an itchy shirt and slacks. She'd been excited, telling him that they were going to get their pictures taken at Sears. "I even bought you a bow tie!" she'd said, clipping on the little red tie that Jack had played with throughout the photoshoot.

"That's my brother, Danny," said Jack, pointing to the plump baby in his mom's arms.

"You don't talk about him much."

Jack lifted his shoulder in a shrug. "We aren't close."

Returning the photo frame to the table, Gwen turned so she faced Jack. "My brother and I are pretty close, but not super close. I think we're like any other brother and sister. Since Elliot moved away and got married, though, he's been too busy to pay much attention to his little sister."

"You miss him."

Now it was time for Gwen to shrug. "I miss him; I miss our dad. I miss my mom, of course. It's hard not having family close by. When I was young, I didn't realize how much I depended on them. When Elliot moved, then our dad a few years later, I'll admit a part of me felt kind of abandoned."

Jack brushed a stray curl from her forehead. "I'm still here," he rumbled.

"You've been a good friend to me. Better than I deserved, probably."

"You deserve everything, Gwen. You deserve all the good in this world. Don't ever think otherwise."

She looked away, her lip trembling. Jack turned her back toward him. He kissed her gently.

It wasn't a kiss of seduction: it was a kiss of promises. A kiss that said, *I'm here, and I'll always be here*. Even if Gwen decided tomorrow that she wanted nothing to do with him, he'd watch over her.

"I want us to pick up where we left off," said Gwen softly.

Jack stilled. "You're going to have to be very clear what you mean."

"I mean, I want to have sex with you. Tonight."

A blush climbed up her cheeks, which was so charming that Jack's chest ached. And then he thought of today in her office, and his cock began to harden. He'd been so close to paradise already. He didn't know if he could survive getting so close again, only to be denied.

"Are you sure?"

She touched his chest. "Completely sure."

Gwen felt her nerves disappear. Maybe it was because she was entirely in control of the situation. Or maybe it was because she knew she'd always be safe with Jack.

His eyes were dark, his nostrils flared, as she caressed his chest. She remembered how it'd felt, pressed against him in her office, and she wanted to strip out of her clothes so there was nothing between them.

Jack cupped her cheek. "What's the safe word?"

"Salmon." She wrinkled her nose. "I won't use it this time, though."

"You don't know that for sure."

Strangely, it seemed like Jack was hesitating more than she was. Not wanting to argue with him, she began to unbutton his shirt, pushing it aside to reveal a white under-shirt underneath. His chest was rising and falling in quick breaths.

Gwen kissed him over his heart.

"You're killing me," he growled, sifting his fingers through her hair.

"Then take me to bed."

Jack glanced at his bed: it was probably no bigger than a full, and Gwen wondered if they'd both fit. She hadn't thought about those kinds of logistics when she'd decided to drive over here.

"How do you have sex with anyone in your bed?" Gwen mused aloud.

Jack let out a startled laugh. "Because I'm usually on top. Don't need a big bed for that." He grinned. "Or we can have sex on the table, in front of the fireplace, outside—"

"Okay, okay, I get it. You're a sex fiend."

"And you love it."

She couldn't disagree. They undressed each other in between kisses, laughing when Jack struggled to unhook Gwen's bra. They laughed when Gwen began to take off Jack's jeans, only to remember he was still wearing his shoes.

They finally tumbled into Jack's bed, naked and glorious, and Gwen couldn't stop kissing him. She felt like she was going to burst out of her skin from sheer happiness. Had sex ever been this exciting for her? Not even when she and Tim had been newly married had she felt like this.

Jack soon made sure she was under him, just like he'd described. He kissed her as his hands traveled the length of her body. He cupped her breasts, flicking her nipples, before kissing and licking seemingly every inch of her skin.

When he sucked a nipple into his mouth, Gwen arched

and moaned. When he swirled his tongue inside her belly button, she giggled.

But it was when he parted her legs and licked her already wet core that made her want to scream. She bit her lip, pleasure bursting like fireworks inside her veins, as he played her body like a musical instrument.

"I want to hear you moan," he said, his voice guttural, as he looked up at her. "Don't try to stay quiet. There's no one around to hear you, anyway."

Gwen had always tried to keep any noises soft during sex. It'd been embarrassing, and the one time she'd been too loud, Tim had teased her about it for weeks.

But that memory faded as Jack pressed one finger, then a second, inside her tight sheath. Her orgasm hovered at the edge of her consciousness. Her entire body tightened.

Jack let her hang at the edge until she whined. He just laughed softly at her.

"I want you to come around my cock." His heated whisper made her shiver. He gave one last soft lick of her clit before crawling up her body.

He kissed her as he riffled through his drawer. Eventually, he had to stop kissing her to find a condom. He swore when he struggled to find one.

"You clearly weren't prepared," said Gwen.

"I'll keep them in a jar by my bed next time," he quipped.

Her near-orgasm had faded somewhat, and she watched with heavily lidded eyes as Jack rolled a condom down his length.

Then he was on top of her, pushing her legs apart, his

breath on her face. He watched her intently as he pushed inside her.

Gwen gasped at the fullness. Where she expected pain, there was none. Only some pressure, then a feeling that made her tremble. She clenched herself around him, which made Jack's eyes close.

"Gwen," he whispered.

Then he started moving. Gently, slowly, never breaking eye contact with her. Gwen reached up and took his face to bring him down for a kiss.

The bed squeaked with every thrust; Gwen's toes curled from the pleasure. She could feel that lovely orgasm returning, like the sound of a train soon approaching.

"You're so tight, so wet." Jack kissed her harder as he picked up the pace. "Are you going to come for me, baby? It feels like you're nearly there."

Gwen could only nod. She moaned loudly as he thrust, faster and faster, his pelvis hitting her clit just enough that it didn't take long for her to reach her peak.

When her release hit her, she cried out. Jack caught the sound, kissing her, as Gwen's orgasm swelled and burst. She felt like she was caught in a tidal wave, except it was glorious and warm and she never wanted to return to shore.

In the throes of her own climax, she felt Jack's cock twitch. He groaned as he came. The sound made Gwen feel powerful. When he collapsed next to her, she felt like she could conquer the world.

Jack pulled her into his arms. Pressing her face against his shoulder, she took in a shuddering breath. She felt like she could either start laughing or crying. Maybe a little bit of both.

"How are feeling?" said Jack, looking into her eyes. His cheeks were still flushed.

Gwen took stock of her body: she felt boneless. Weightless. A sheen of sweat covered her skin, and she was probably flushed from cheeks to chest.

"I feel awesome," she replied.

Jack kissed her forehead. "Same."

Sighing happily, Gwen snuggled into his embrace. He was so warm and strong; she wanted to stay with him, in this bed, and never leave it.

"Go to sleep," Jack murmured. "I'll watch over you."

CHAPTER EIGHTEEN

Weeks passed. Jack spent his nights with Gwen, while his days were spent trying to keep the dam over-flowing financially. It didn't help that the universe seemed to be against Jack being happy. Not even two days after that magical night with Gwen, Jack returned home to find a huge hole in his roof, rain pouring inside.

A huge tree branch had fallen while he'd been gone. It'd been so windy that it hadn't taken much to snap the branch —nearly twenty feet long—like a tiny twig. It'd fallen directly on top of Jack's house, puncturing the roof that he'd been meaning to replace but hadn't had the time. He'd cursed his procrastination. He hurriedly cleaned up the rainwater that'd drenched his makeshift kitchen. The water damage had already ruined both the stovetop and microwave.

But before the cleanup, Jack had had to climb to the roof and cover the hole with a tarp as best he could. He'd nearly broken his neck in the process, it'd been so rainy and windy.

Now it was morning, and Jack found himself without hot water. Swearing, he discovered that his hot water heater was shot. He'd need to replace it entirely.

"Fuck me," he said to himself. He raised a fist. "Can you cool it with the house breaking down?"

No voice replied, of course. Inside Jack's head, he was calculating how much money he still had left in his bank account, and how much all these repairs would cost. He wondered if he could forgo hot water for a while. But the thought of ice-cold showers in the middle of winter made his bones hurt.

The bad luck continued. That evening, Jack answered a call from Danny. At first, Jack felt hopeful, that Danny was trying to reach out this time.

Jack's hopes were quickly dashed. "You need to take care of Mom," said Danny without so much as a question as to how Jack was doing.

"I already told her I'd give her the money."

"How much?"

"Three thousand."

Danny laughed, but there was no mirth in it. "Dude, she does not need three thousand dollars. Come on now."

"She needed it for the deposit."

"Look, the city is expensive, but she can find a cheaper place. She probably already has. She's just using you like she always does."

Jack's shoulders felt heavy. He couldn't even feel outraged at Danny's pronouncement. He'd expected it if he were honest.

"So how am I supposed to take care of her? Give her even more money?" Jack said hollowly.

"Fuck no. I haven't given her a dime in years. But she's always coming around my work, begging me, making a scene. Last night my boss had to throw her out. I was fucking embarrassing."

"I still don't get what you want me to do."

"Have her move in with you. You can keep an eye on her."

Now Jack was the one who was laughing. That hollow feeling had left him, only to be filled with anger. "That's your solution? Put her on my doorstep like a lost puppy and then wash your hands of her? Jesus Christ."

"Hey, I've done my part. I've looked after her, given her money, helped her out all these years while you hid out on your island. You haven't been around. So how about you put in the effort this round? Because I'm fucking done."

Jack couldn't refute Danny's words. Even though every cell in Jack's body rebelled at bringing their mom to Hazel Island, there was some merit to the idea. Maybe if Jack watched over her, helped her get into treatment, made sure she had employment...

"She can't live with me," said Jack. "My house is too small."

"Then get a new place."

"That costs money. You want to pay for that?"

Danny sighed. "Look, I'm willing to help some, money-wise. I just can't do all the other stuff."

Jack could hear the frustration, the exhaustion, in Danny's voice. He understood that all too well because they were the same feelings he'd had when he'd left his family behind all those years ago.

"If you want to make up for everything, do this for me," said Danny.

"Let me think about it."

Jack wanted to go to Gwen right then. He wanted her to tell him what he should do, but at the same time, he hated how weak he felt. The thought of Gwen pitying him made him want to punch something.

All he had now was an old mug that he threw at the wall. But it didn't even have the grace to shatter. It just thumped to the floor and rolled under the bed, as if saying to Jack, *get it the fuck together, dude.*

Jack didn't have much time to think about Danny's idea. Their mom began blowing up his phone, to the point that Jack nearly blocked her number. Instead, he texted her a terse, *I'll call you when I can. Stop hassling me.*

That resulted in a five-minute voicemail where Debra called him ungrateful, cruel, selfish, and a whole host of other unsavory adjectives. Despite her guilt trip, Jack couldn't feel guilty.

At least not about his mom. But Danny? He could feel guilty about that for ages.

But as Jack pondered Danny's idea that he should have their mom come to live on Hazel Island, Jack knew he couldn't have her here. The thought of Gwen meeting her —sweet, innocent Gwen—and then trying to bilk money out of her was an unbearable thought. The entire island would soon know what kind of a person Debra Benson was. And they'd whisper about it, the gossip flowing like a river, until Jack was certain the islanders would soon be looking at him and wondering if the apple didn't fall far from the tree.

It would probably cost more money to keep Debra in

Seattle. Jack knew that. And along with his house falling apart, and the continually terrible salmon catches, he wouldn't have much left over. Certainly not enough to fund Gwen's restaurant.

Jack was supposed to go to Gwen's that evening. He considered canceling, but he was too weak. He needed her. He didn't know if he'd talk about everything that was happening. There was so much shame wrapped up in it, as if his mom had infected him with her madness.

But before he drove to Gwen's, he called his mom finally.

"I'll give you the money," said Jack. "But only if you agree to go to treatment first."

GWEN COULDN'T HIDE her excitement when Jack arrived. Not just because he was coming over, but because she and Jocelyn had finished the business plan for the restaurant.

"I want you to look over it," she said, handing Jack a stack of papers that were still warm from the printer.

"I'm not a writer." He took the papers but didn't seem inclined to look at them.

Jack had seemed subdued since he'd stepped inside her doorway. Despite asking him more than once if something was bothering him, he'd said he was fine. Just tired.

"Well, you still might see something we missed. At the very least, it'd be nice to hear if you think the concept makes sense," said Gwen.

"It's a restaurant. What's there to explain?"

Gwen was in the middle of pouring them both some hot

cider she'd purchased at the festival a few weeks ago. She nearly spilled some of it on her hand when she looked up at Jack in surprise.

"What crawled up your butt and died?" Gwen shot back.

"I told you: I'm tired."

Now they were both staring at each other, both annoyed with the other person. This was not how Gwen envisioned this evening. She expected Jack to look through the business plan, exclaim over what an amazing idea it was, and then he'd make love to her all night long.

So much for that fantasy, thought Gwen.

"What is going on with you? You've been a total grump since you walked in," said Gwen.

Jack's jaw tightened. He still held the papers and ended up crumpling them in the middle, probably not even realizing he was doing it.

Instead of answering her question, he went and sat down on her couch and began reading. She stared at the back of his head, halfway tempted to throw something at him. But she quelled the childish impulse and instead brought him a mug of cider.

If she refrained from adding whipped cream to his, well, he could get that himself if he wanted it.

Jack didn't comment on the lack of whipped cream. He barely even touched the cider, letting it go cold as he read through the business plan.

Gwen's heart pounded in anticipation. It'd been a lot of work to put the plan together, especially with Jocelyn feeling the need to edit every little detail. Gwen had appreciated the input, especially the nitty-gritty of how a restaurant worked. Jocelyn, though, tended to refuse to compromise on the small things if she was certain she was right.

When Gwen hadn't included a ten-year forecast for potential profits, instead sticking with a five-year forecast, Jocelyn had balked. When Gwen had written that the restaurant would be "American comfort food with a twist," Jocelyn had told Gwen point-blank that the description basically meant that they were opening an expensive Denny's.

Jack said nothing as he read. When he turned over the last page, he leaned back, his forehead furrowed.

"The menu is too large," he said finally.

"It's only twenty items."

Jack shook his head. "It's all over the place. Pizzas, pasta, tacos, and then risotto and..." He found the page with the menu on it. "Arugula salad with Ahi tuna, crumbled chèvre, and roasted dates." His expression was wry now. "Are you seriously going to be roasting dates?"

Gwen took the page from Jack. "I didn't push back on the menu. Jocelyn is the chef, after all."

"Sure, but she's not going to be the owner. You are. You get the final say on everything. Even the menu."

"Jocelyn isn't going to like hearing that."

"She'll live. If she wants to keep the gig, she'll get over it."

Gwen smiled, shaking her head. "I already had some ideas about the menu. I'll talk to Jocelyn about them tomorrow."

"How pissed is she gonna be?"

"Oh, she'll probably tell me to go to hell. I'm not looking forward to it." Gwen sighed deeply. "She and Alex have been butting heads lately. Alex was upset with me because she thought Jocelyn was stealing me."

Jack looked bewildered. "Stealing you? Like kidnapping you?"

"No, stealing me as a friend."

"You can't have more than one friend?" Now he really sounded confused.

Gwen laughed at his expression. "I can. It's just that these two sisters don't get along so well. Alex has been my friend for longer. It was a whole thing during the cider festival. I think Alex is still waiting for me to start picking Jocelyn over her."

"Sounds fucking stupid."

"I know! It's middle-school stuff. I'm way too old for this. And Alex knows it, too. She said she knows she's been stupid but there's a history there. Then when I try to get her to explain, she clams up."

"Stupid," was Jack's only response.

Gwen knew the situation between the Gray sisters had more nuance to it. Alex could be flighty and impulsive, but she was loyal and thoughtful, too. If she couldn't explain why she felt so triggered by Jocelyn becoming Gwen's friend, there must be a good reason for it.

"Now you're going to think we're all just a bunch of silly women," said Gwen.

Jack raised a dark eyebrow. "Why should I?"

"Because that's what it sounds like."

Shrugging, he replied, "Everybody has their shit. Some people are better at hiding it than others."

His gaze seemed to go to a faraway place. Gwen once again wondered what was hanging over him. Weren't they friends, too? Why did he feel like he couldn't be honest with her?

She couldn't help but feel hurt at his lack of trust in her. Did he think she'd judge him? Or worse, that she wouldn't keep his secrets?

"Do guys ever have these kinds of fights?" said Gwen.

"Nah. We just punch each other." Jack drank some of his cider finally. "Way healthier."

Gwen giggled. She put her arms around his neck and kissed him. He tasted of apples and cinnamon. When he deepened the kiss, she let herself float away, releasing all the jumbled thoughts inside her head.

They kissed for a long time. The cider was soon forgotten entirely, Gwen's whipped cream melting into the drink a while ago.

"This affair or whatever it is that we're doing," said Gwen during a moment between kisses, "has probably been the best thing in my life right now. You make me happy, Jack Benson."

Jack looked like she'd slapped him. His gaze skirted away, which made her wish she'd kept her mouth shut.

"Not sure I deserve a compliment like that," he admitted.

"Even if you don't deserve it, I'm giving it to you anyway. So take it and enjoy it."

He placed a stray curl behind her ear. "I wish I could give you everything you deserve."

"Then you better start kissing me again."

～

JACK SHOULD TELL HER NO. He should end this thing, right then and there, and let Gwen get on with her life.

He knew what he should do. But he didn't have the strength to do the right thing. Not with Gwen gazing up at him, like she believed he could do anything.

No one had ever looked at him like that. It humbled him, and it terrified him. It reminded him that he'd let her down. If not now, then someday.

She was too tempting, with her smile and her red hair, her green eyes bright with desire. She'd blossomed so much since they'd started this thing, whatever it was.

Affair. Fling. Friends with benefits.

Jack marveled over the silk of her skin as he caressed her cheek. Her throat. The shadow inside her collarbone. Her eyelashes, tipped in blond, fluttered as he touched her.

"You're addictive," he admitted. He let his fingers roam across her back. "I can't get enough of you."

"I feel the same way."

When she pulled his head down for a kiss, he didn't resist. He couldn't. Not with how soft her lips were, or how she tried her hardest to get as close to him as she could, like she wanted to meld their bodies together.

He licked inside her mouth, tasting the cider she'd drunk, and she giggled when he nipped at her bottom lip. The kiss was lazy, sensual, as Jack rubbed the bare skin of her lower back before lifting her into his lap.

It didn't take long for him to slip her out of her shirt or her bra. He played with her breasts, still kissing her, loving the way she wiggled on his lap. His cock was already hard as iron.

"I want to do something different tonight," said Gwen, her eyes glassy.

"Like what?"

She just smiled, shaking her head, before going on her knees in front of him. He didn't need her to explain what she was thinking about. As she began to unzip his jeans, he tensed.

"You don't have to." Even as he said the words, he knew he'd die if she stopped.

Gwen cupped his cock through his boxers. "I want to." She freed his length, gently stroking it, her touch so light that it was almost painful.

Jack groaned when she began tasting him. She was tentative at first, licking at the tip, swirling her tongue around to see his reaction.

"Do you like this?" she asked.

He licked his dry lips. "Squeeze me at the base when you lick the tip or suck it."

When she immediately took him inside her mouth, he nearly came right then and there. The heat, the wetness, the flush on her cheeks, the redness of her lips around his cock were nearly his undoing.

"Fuck, Gwen." He touched her hair. "You're amazing."

She just winked at him. Then she was squeezing and sucking at the same time. She'd lost that hesitation and instead seemed to revel in making him writhe.

He could feel himself getting close. He'd never gotten this close, this fast, and especially not from a blowjob.

"Gwen." Jack gently lifted her away and brought her up for a deep kiss.

"Why'd you stop?"

"Because I want to be inside you when I come."

He pulled out a condom that he'd put in his wallet just in case, all the while knowing he should let Gwen go. But as she shimmied out of her pants and underwear, all his doubts disappeared.

Once he had the condom on, Gwen sat on his lap, his cock rubbing against her dripping core. They both moaned when he nearly sheathed himself inside of her but missed.

Gwen took his cock and notched the tip at her entrance before slowly sliding down his length. Jack gripped her hips, not sure if he wanted her to go faster or slower.

"Gwen. Shit, Gwen." He was incoherent as she began to bounce on top of him.

Gwen titled her head back, her hair trailing down, her eyes closed. She rode him in quick strokes. Jack had to restrain himself from making her go faster. He squeezed the globes of her ass, which made her quicken her pace.

"Oh my God." Gwen was going faster, faster. She was breathing hard. "Oh my God—Jack!"

She squealed. As her sheath gripped him and her release burst through her, Jack's exploded, too. He shouted as he came. His entire body was wracked with convulsions.

He was barely aware of Gwen kissing his face and rubbing his chest. He was panting. He felt like his heart had exploded and then had come back together again somehow.

"That was fun," said Gwen breathlessly. She pushed sweaty strands of hair from his forehead. "How about you?"

He couldn't speak. He knew that he'd have to let her go, but it was unbearable.

Don't look too closely. Don't think about the future just yet. Let yourself enjoy this one last time.

He pressed his forehead to hers. "I think you broke me," he admitted with a sad laugh.

"I hope not. Because I'm not done with you tonight."

And Jack, not being a complete idiot, wasn't about to deny her a second round.

CHAPTER NINETEEN

A week before Thanksgiving, Gwen and Jocelyn headed to Luke Wright's place. They planned to present their business plan for the restaurant they would call Lyn's Eatery. The name was a play on Gwendo*lyn* and Joce*lyn*'s names. Jack would also meet the two of them at Luke's for the presentation.

Gwen's palms were sweaty as she drove the winding roads up to the Wright house. She'd never been there. She'd heard about it—everyone on Hazel Island knew how huge it was—but she'd never had a reason to be invited. When she'd asked Jack what it was like, he'd only said, "It's big."

It didn't help that the roads were narrow, and it was raining. And there were no guard rails, either. Everyone had heard horror stories of tourists driving too fast and careening off the roads.

Gwen slowed down further. The car behind her honked impatiently.

"You know we need to get there before noon," said Jocelyn, her tone joking.

Gwen shot her a glare. It was currently only ten AM. "You want to switch places?"

"Not particularly."

Gwen returned her focus to driving. The car behind her eventually passed her, flipping her off in the process. Great. That was surely a good omen for this presentation this morning.

"Then again, it might be preferable to end up on the side of a cliff instead of going to the Wright's," muttered Jocelyn.

Gwen ignored that comment. She didn't much care that Jocelyn disliked Luke Wright. Gwen had asked Jocelyn to keep any snarky comments to herself when they arrived. Jocelyn had looked offended, replying sarcastically that she'd keep things completely professional.

They arrived to see Jack parking his truck. They hustled into the house, the rain coming down harder now. The housekeeper ushered them to the mudroom, where they could hang up their coats. They were then given slippers to wear in the house.

No outside shoes in the house said a large sign inside the mudroom.

"I wonder if they throw you in the dungeon if you track mud inside," joked Jocelyn as she slipped on some house slippers.

"They just toss you into the ocean," was Jack's deadpan reply.

Gwen shot them both glares. "Behave yourselves. We're trying to get money here, aren't we?"

Jack and Jocelyn just looked at each other, as if wordlessly agreeing that Gwen was in a strange mood.

Gwen forced herself to take a deep breath. She wiped her hands on her pants, wishing she'd brought something to put her hair up. Whenever she got nervous, she got sweaty. She hated the thought of getting all red and sweaty in front of Luke Wright.

Jack passed by Gwen as he left the mudroom with Jocelyn behind him. Gwen caught his eye, but he didn't stop to say anything. She'd expected him to at least give her a pep talk, in his stoic way.

Then she heard a voice that she assumed was Luke's. Taking another deep breath, she went to face the music.

LUKE SAT BACK in his leather office chair, considering Gwen and Jocelyn. Gwen's heart was still pounding, even though they'd officially finished the presentation.

Finally, Luke glanced at Jack, then said, "I like it. I'm in."

Gwen gaped at him. "What?" She'd expected he'd grill her with all kinds of questions.

"I'm in. Like you pointed out, every year we get more tourists. The more attractions the island has, the better. We have all of ten restaurants currently and having yours linked to the bed and breakfast is brilliant. Your clientele already exists, too. I'm only surprised you hadn't opened something before now," said Luke.

Jack had been silent for the entire presentation. He'd paid attention, of course, but now he sat in continued silence.

He'd been strangely aloof the last week, Gwen had

noticed. When she'd asked about spending time together, he'd always had an excuse to decline. They hadn't been together in two weeks.

Gwen felt her stomach turn with anxiety. Was she just overthinking Jack's behavior? Or was he starting to pull away already?

Jocelyn, for her part, had presented the menu and everything food-related with the utmost professionalism. If she didn't look Luke directly in the eye, well, Gwen decided that that had just been nerves.

"As I mentioned before," Luke was saying, "I'm funding a handful of new ventures here on the island. I currently can offer you ten thousand in seed money. The rest you'll need to procure via a bank loan or through friends and family." He looked at Jack. "Jack? Your thoughts?"

With both Luke and Jack giving her twenty thousand combined, that money would be a huge help getting the building remodeled. The ten thousand alone, though, she knew wouldn't be enough.

"I don't have any questions," said Jack. "I would like to discuss the funding with Luke. In private."

Gwen glanced at Jocelyn. Jocelyn's eyes narrowed. But Luke showed them to another room across the hallway, a smaller office.

He said cheerily, "Just a second, ladies. If you'd like anything to drink, there's a mini-fridge in the corner." He gave them his most winning smile and shut the door.

Jocelyn immediately went to the tray of liquor, picking up one bottle after another. "Want a drink?" she said.

"It's eleven AM," said Gwen.

"Eh, it's five o'clock somewhere. Besides, I think you could use it."

Jocelyn made them a quick gin and tonic, with tonic water she pilfered from the fridge. Gwen drank hers without tasting it. The alcohol did calm her anxiety to some extent. She hadn't realized how on edge she was until that moment.

She and Jocelyn waited in silence. Any attempt at speculating about the guys' conversation ended quickly. Gwen wondered if she and Jocelyn were afraid that they'd jinx things. Or maybe Gwen was simply all out of words. Her throat had been dry from talking so much. After she finished her gin and tonic, she found herself sucking on the ice cubes just for something to do.

Luke returned ten minutes later. He saw the empty glasses and smiled wryly. "Drinking already?"

"Are you judging us, Wright?" said Jocelyn, her hands on her hips.

"I'd never judge you for anything. You're spotless." He spoke solely to Jocelyn, who blushed a little and looked away.

When they returned to Luke's office, Jack was standing up and looking out the large window at the rain. It pattered against the glass, the rhythm of it soothing to Gwen.

Luke gestured for Gwen and Jocelyn to sit down. They did, reluctantly. Luke followed them, but Jack remained standing, his back to them.

"Jack, can you stop brooding and come and talk?" Luke rolled his eyes. "And he claims I'm dramatic."

That remark made Gwen smile. Jack grunted and sat down across from Gwen. He wouldn't look at her.

"I'm sorry for keeping you waiting. I'm withdrawing

funding for your venture. It has nothing to do with you or your presentation, however," said Jack in hollow tones.

Gwen felt her earlier anxiety return. Jocelyn's mouth fell open. It was Gwen reaching over and squeezing her hand that kept her from saying anything she'd regret.

"May I ask why?" said Gwen.

Jack finally looked at her. "It's private." Then, more quietly, "I'm sorry."

Gwen felt like someone had cut her off at the knees. *Why hadn't he told me before this morning?*

Luke cleared his throat. "The unfortunate side effect of Jack withdrawing funding means that I'll have to put this venture lower on the list."

Spreading his hands, Luke explained, "It simply makes more sense to give money to ventures that have individuals or firms willing to match this seed money. It's mostly about getting the best return on investment. As Jack said, your restaurant is a great idea. But I have to balance between what seems great and what seems likely to succeed. Does that make sense?"

"So this entire thing was a waste of time," said Jocelyn.

Gwen didn't have the energy to stop Jocelyn this time. She couldn't help but agree, too. Why had Jack had them come up here if he was just going to change his mind?

Luke steepled his fingers. "I can't agree with that assessment. It's been very useful for me—"

"Oh great. As long as it was useful for *you*." Jocelyn shook her head. "You brought us up here, getting our hopes up, and then you tell us to go to hell. Typical. I should never have let Gwen talk me into this."

Now Gwen was flushing to the roots of her hair. "Jocelyn," she hissed.

Jocelyn at least had the grace to look embarrassed. "Sorry. It's not your fault. If it's anyone's, it's Jack's." She tipped her chin up. "What the hell happened, Benson?"

Gwen wanted to know the same thing. What had happened? She felt tears prick her eyes, but she refused to cry in front of everyone.

"Can I talk to you in private?" was all Jack said to Gwen.

"This seems to be a theme," muttered Jocelyn.

Gwen nodded and then she found herself back in the same room she and Jocelyn had been in. This time, though, Gwen was seriously considering making herself another gin and tonic. If not to drink, then to splash in Jack's face.

"Why?" was all she could get past her lips.

Jack began to pace like a restless, wild animal. Back and forth, back and forth. The room was small enough that his movements made Gwen a little dizzy.

"This isn't going to work," said Jack.

"You're going to have to be more specific."

He spread his hands. "Us, Gwen. I'm stepping aside. I realized that I was getting in too deep. I never should've offered to fund your restaurant. It was idiotic. For that, I'm sorry. I've let you down."

Gwen licked her dry lips. "Why didn't you tell me before today?"

"I should have. I hoped that Luke would still offer you funding. In fact, I assumed he would." Jack gripped the edge of the wooden desk, his knuckles turning white. "I fucked up."

"Okay. Okay." Gwen had to sit down. Her brain was going a mile a minute. "It's your money. I'm not entitled to it. I'm not going to blame you if you needed to change your mind."

"You should blame me," he growled.

"I do for not telling me sooner. For not talking to Luke, too." She sighed. "Honestly, I don't care about the money."

He turned so he was gazing straight at her. He looked stunned. "But this is your dream."

"I have a lot of dreams. But I've realized, in the weeks we've spent together, that spending the rest of my life with you is what's most important."

Jack just stared at her, motionless.

"I love you. I do." She let out a sob. "I know we agreed to avoid 'catching feelings' for each other, but I have to be honest with you. I probably fell in love with you before we even kissed. I just didn't want to admit it to myself."

"Christ, Gwen..."

"Restaurant or not, you're what matters to me." She stood up and took his hands. "And I think you feel the same. I know it's not just my imagination. No man who didn't care deeply would've done what you've done for me. Would've waited for me. Tell me I'm wrong."

He said nothing for a long moment. The only sounds in the room were the rain falling against the glass of the windows and the wind whistling.

Jack hadn't squeezed her hands or intertwined his fingers with hers like he usually would. His hands were limp against her own. When he let go of her, she felt ice drip down her spine.

"This isn't going to work," he repeated.

Gwen felt her heart disintegrate into a million pieces. Tears fell down her cheeks. "You don't love me."

"I told you this was only a fling." He sounded almost apologetic.

She nearly hated him right then. She knew he was lying. He wouldn't look into her eyes, and he wouldn't let her touch him.

"I never took you for a coward, Jack Benson," she snapped. "But I guess I was wrong about that. You want to walk out that door and destroy what we could have together? That's your choice. But I know you'll regret it."

That stubbornness of his she knew all too well crossed his face. His jaw was tight, his nostrils flared.

"I'm doing this because I know it's right," he rasped.

"I'm not going to convince you otherwise." She hastily wiped away the tears that wouldn't stop. "And I still love you, anyway."

"I don't deserve that."

"That's not for you to decide. For too long, I've let fear dictate my entire life. I'm not going to keep being that girl who's too afraid to take a chance. So even if you can't love me back, well, at least I tried."

Suddenly the tears were too much. She couldn't talk anymore, only sob. Jack reached out, like he wanted to embrace her, but then he stopped himself.

"What is going on?" Jocelyn burst into the room. "What did you do?" She whirled on Jack, and Gwen half-expected her to deck him.

"We had a discussion," was Jack's numb reply.

"That made her cry? Your discussion skills suck."

Jocelyn took Gwen's arm. "Come on. We're going home. I'm tired of this stupid place."

Gwen couldn't disagree. As Jocelyn led her away like a mother hen, Gwen let herself glance back at Jack.

His back was turned. And Gwen knew that they were over.

CHAPTER TWENTY

G wen felt as though time came to a standstill. Colors seemed duller; the silliest things brought her to tears. Yet even as she grieved the relationship that was doomed from the start, everyone around her carried on. It was as if her broken heart wasn't enough to stop the world in its tracks for just a moment.

Gwen had called Jack more than once. She'd texted him for days after their fight, asking to talk. When he ignored all her overtures, she realized it was over.

And she had enough pride not to keep going to Jack, begging him to love her.

When she lay in her bed at night, staring at the ceiling, sleep elusive, she wondered if she was cursed. Maybe she'd done something terrible in a previous life, and this was karma. Her marriage had failed because she hadn't been enough. Now she'd fallen in love with her best friend, but he'd rejected her.

Gwen wondered if she was just unlovable. The thought

ate at her, a gnawing pain that she couldn't shake. Even as she reminded herself that Jack's rejection wasn't necessarily a reflection on her, it didn't feel that way.

It felt like Tim had been right all along, and that thought alone made her so angry she could scream.

To drive the stake further into her heart, Tim had begun texting her again. He'd left her alone after that first random text.

She almost wondered if he could sense she was lonely, like he knew she was vulnerable to him sneaking back into her life.

I still have feelings for you, the text read.

Gwen stared at her phone, trembling. She didn't know if it was from rage or despair.

I told you not to text me anymore, she replied.

I just needed you to know.

Gwen called him right then. He picked up on the second ring.

"Gwen—"

"No, don't say anything. This isn't about you, Tim. For once in your life, maybe think about someone other than yourself."

Tim was silent now.

"We're over. Our marriage ended five years ago when you cheated on me, when you made me feel like I was worthless. I never told you how much you hurt me because it seemed pointless. But you did.

"You probably won't apologize. I don't need an apology. I just want you to know that I'm okay on my own and I don't care how you feel about me still. Understand?"

Tim was silent for so long that Gwen wondered if he'd already hung up. Then she heard him inhale a deep breath.

"Fine," he ground out, "I won't contact you again."

When the call disconnected, Gwen couldn't feel anything except relief.

Her love life might currently be in shambles, but at least she'd finally been honest with her ex.

The staff of the bed and breakfast noticed her strange moods. They seemed to be walking on eggshells, afraid that they'd cause Gwen to burst into tears at any moment.

I've only started crying over something stupid once, thought Gwen irritably. She was decorating the inn for Christmastime. Normally she preferred to hire people to hang lights, but she wanted a reason to avoid talking to anyone.

Jack would've helped me with these, she thought, but that thought only made her cry. "I'm losing my mind," she said to herself. "Get it together, Gwen."

She worked until it was too dark to see safely, and it was so cold that her fingers felt numb. Although Hazel Island didn't get much snow, it got cold, especially after sunset. It didn't help that the sun tended to set before five PM, either.

Gwen was in her office when Jocelyn walked inside. She'd been giving Gwen a lot of space after the disaster that was the meeting at Luke Wright's. Jocelyn wasn't exactly the warmest and fuzziest person, but Gwen could tell Jocelyn was worried about her. She seemed to choose her words more carefully. When she thought Gwen wasn't looking, her eyebrows would furrow, her teeth chewing on her bottom lip.

Luke had emailed Gwen shortly after their meeting to reaffirm what he'd already told them. He wouldn't be able to offer her funding at this time without finding someone else to match it. He apologized and once again told her that her business plan was a solid idea.

Ideas weren't enough to get a restaurant started, though. And Gwen didn't know where she'd find someone to replace Jack. She'd once again considered asking her brother Elliot, but he and Bekah had just closed on a house. Gwen doubted they had a lot of extra money lying around.

"How are you doing?" said Jocelyn, breaking through Gwen's thoughts.

Gwen shrugged a shoulder. "I got about half of the lights hung up. I didn't think it'd take me as long as it did. I probably should've started earlier in the day—"

"You know that's not what I'm asking about."

Gwen shot her friend a wry look. "If you're worried that I'm going to throw myself off the nearest cliff, don't worry. I'm not. The water's too cold, anyway."

"Well, if you can make jokes, I guess you're feeling a little better." Jocelyn leaned against the wall, her arms crossed. "Have you talked to Jack at all?"

"No." That was all Gwen had the strength to say about that. It still hurt to hear his name spoken.

Jocelyn blew out a breath. "I'm worried about you. You've lost weight. You don't smile much anymore. It's like you're walking around like a zombie."

"I told a man I loved him, and he didn't feel the same. And then he cut me off completely. I didn't just lose a lover, I lost a friend." Gwen's voice trembled. "So, yeah, I'm a zombie right now. I'm just hoping this feeling won't last forever."

"It won't. Take it from me. You'll get over it eventually."

That made Gwen blink in surprise. "Are you telling me someone broke your heart? I don't believe it."

"That I have a heart? Surprise, I do." Jocelyn's mouth twisted. "And apparently it can break, too. Even robots can be destroyed, you know."

"Are you saying you're a robot?"

"Pretty sure everyone thinks I'm one. That I'm heartless."

"I've never thought that."

"You'd be the first one." Jocelyn hugged herself. "My sister thinks I am."

Gwen desperately wanted to ask more about that situation, but she also knew she couldn't press her luck. Jocelyn was rather like a feral cat that was slowly getting used to people. The cat might let you pet it once, but the next time, it might bite that same hand just as a reminder not to get too close to it.

"I think you try to get keep people at arm's length because that makes things easier," said Gwen quietly. "But if you didn't care, you wouldn't be here in my office right now."

Jocelyn said nothing. Gwen thought she saw a tear on her friend's face, but a second later, she wondered if it was just a trick of the light.

"I actually came here to give you news. Jack's left the island," said Jocelyn.

Gwen felt the earth shift under her feet. Gripping the edge of her desk, it took her a while to reply, "What? When?"

"Yesterday. I heard it from Alex, who'd talked to Trevor, the guy who works on the ferry? He saw Jack getting on it."

"Maybe he was just going for a trip."

Jocelyn's expression was sad. "Trevor said Jack was driving a moving truck."

Gwen had to sit down. She stared at nothing, wondering if she was dreaming all of this. Jack had left, had *moved*, and he'd said nothing to her.

"I can't believe it," said Gwen, her mouth dry.

"His boat is gone, too."

That statement made Gwen close her eyes. Then it was true: Jack had left. Gwen had destroyed their friendship in one fell swoop. If she'd just kept her mouth shut, none of this would've happened.

She could've pined for him in silence, but at least he would've still been on Hazel Island. She could still hear his gruff laugh, see the rare smile cross his lips.

Gwen felt a touch. Jocelyn was standing over her desk now. "I'm sorry. I really am. He's an asshole, Gwen. You're better off."

"Am I? I don't feel like it."

"He'll regret all of this for the rest of his life. And then he'll die, all alone, wondering why he let someone like you go."

"I never took you for somebody who liked giving pep talks," said Gwen, her eyes watering.

Jocelyn shrugged. "It happens every once in a blue moon. Just don't get used to it."

That made Gwen smile, at least for a moment.

But something kept nagging at her, like a tap on a window that wouldn't go away. "You said Jack's boat was gone?"

"Alex said it was. I haven't confirmed it for myself."

"How would Alex know? She's not a boat person."

"No, but she's a terrible gossip, and everyone loves to tell her things for some strange reason."

Gwen drummed her fingers against her desk. "Did Trevor say Jack had taken the boat on the ferry?"

"I don't think so. Can you do that?"

Gwen's mind began turning. Jack's boat was everything to him. It didn't make sense that he'd just get rid of it if he had moved away. But if it was no longer in the harbor and he hadn't taken it with him...

"I need to talk to Luke," said Gwen.

IT TOOK five days before Gwen could meet with Luke. She only had his email address. Based on how he answered her email almost a week after she'd sent it, he didn't seem particularly inclined to see her soon. Then again, she hadn't mentioned Jack in her email. She'd made it sound like she wanted to talk about her business plan again.

After some back and forth, Luke finally agreed to meet with her at her apartment. He eventually arrived twenty minutes late, apologizing but seemingly unaware of how on edge Gwen was.

"Where is Jack?" said Gwen, hardly allowing Luke to sit down before she began to interrogate him.

Luke unbuttoned his jacket and folded his hands. "Is that your new business plan? It's a strange one, I have to say."

"I'm sorry I lied to you. I didn't think you'd talk to me if I said why I really wanted to see you."

"Not sure why you'd think that." Despite his words, Luke looked decidedly uncomfortable.

"I know Jack is gone. I know his boat is gone, too, and he didn't take it with him. You're his friend. He would've told you why he left, where he went."

"Again, I don't know why you think I know anything. Jack is hardly good about giving me the details of his life."

Gwen felt her heart sink into her toes. She'd been so sure Luke would have information that she truly hadn't considered the opposite.

"He won't answer my calls or my texts." Her voice was barely above a whisper. "I need to know he's okay. That's all. I'm not trying to stalk him. I'm just worried about him."

Luke sighed. He ran his fingers through his perfectly styled hair, and Gwen could see the tension in his expression.

"Look, I don't know what happened between the two of you," began Luke, "and I don't need to know. But Jack asked me not to tell anyone where he was going."

"You do know." Gwen leaned forward. "Why would he not want anyone to know, though?"

"Who the fuck knows. It's Jack. He keeps to himself. He doesn't like to ask for help. It was like pulling teeth to get him to tell me anything. He just shows up at my place, telling me he wants me to buy his boat—"

"His boat? He sold his boat?"

"He did. Not to me, though. I don't need a fishing boat. The hell am I going to do with that? But I gave him some names of people who I knew would want it. But before I did, I made him tell me why he was selling it in the first place."

Gwen wanted to cry. Jack had sold his beloved boat, the thing he needed to make a living, and she couldn't figure out why. It also told her that he had zero intention of returning to Hazel Island.

"Did he tell you, then?" she asked.

"All he'd say was that he needed to get off the island. Some kind of family issue. That was it."

"You're telling me everything? You're not keeping something else secret?"

Luke spread his hands. "I know nothing else. I wasn't supposed to tell you especially. He made me swear it." Luke looked heavenward. "If he finds out I blabbed, he'd kill me."

"Where did he go?"

"He didn't say, but I do remember him mentioning that he had family in Seattle. Make of that what you will."

Gwen's palms were sweaty. But as she thought about all of this, she realized that it didn't really matter. At least, not as it related to their friendship. Jack had essentially cut all ties with Hazel Island with one fell swoop.

If that wasn't a sign that he didn't want to see her ever again, she didn't know what it was.

"You know," said Luke slowly, "I don't think I've ever seen Jack as agitated as he was when he wanted to sell his boat. He just kept saying, 'don't tell Gwen.' It was strange."

"It's because I ruined everything." Gwen's voice was hollow. "I told him I loved him, but he didn't feel the same. Then he left."

Luke looked at her as if she'd sprouted horns. "You said that to him?"

"Yeah. You don't have to look so horrified."

Suddenly getting up from his chair, Luke began to pace. "I'm such an idiot," he was muttering to himself. "I should've known."

"What? You should've known what?"

Luke turned to face her. "Before he left, he made sure to give me a check for ten thousand dollars. He specified it was to match the funding he'd promised you." Luke pulled out an envelope that he'd folded and placed in his jacket pocket. "Actually, I was planning to tell you when I got here, but then you distracted me."

Gwen couldn't breathe. "He sold his boat for me," she whispered.

"Looks that way."

"But why would he leave without telling me? I don't understand."

Luke pulled at his collar. If Gwen weren't so confused and distressed, she'd laugh at how awkward he seemed. "Look, I'm not about to give you any relationship advice. That's not my area of expertise. But anybody with eyeballs could see that Jack cared—cares—about you. Probably more than he'll ever admit."

"You really mean that?" Gwen felt tears well up in her eyes.

"Wouldn't have said it otherwise." Luke handed her the envelope with the check. "I told Jack he should give this to you himself, but he's a stubborn bastard. You know that well."

She couldn't help but inhale the scent of the envelope, as if she could catch a hint of Jack on it. She then held it to her heart.

"I need to find Jack," she said. "Will you help me?"

Luke sighed. "I was afraid you were going to ask me that."

CHAPTER TWENTY-ONE

Jack stared up at the Christmas tree covered in lights. It was a cold, but clear night. It'd snowed about an inch earlier in the day, and it still covered the ground under the tree. It almost made Jack feel festive, if he were the type of person to celebrate holidays.

Jack liked coming to this park. It wasn't usually very busy despite being in the middle of Seattle. Usually only old folks from the assisted living complex down the street would be in the park. Occasionally, Jack would see moms pushing strollers, or singletons dragging their tiny dogs on a leash.

But in the evenings, after the sun had set, were the best times to come here. Hardly anyone was around, except for a few homeless people who slept on benches. Jack sometimes gave them cash, or food, if they wanted some. Most of the people sleeping in the park he only saw once or twice before they moved on to another spot.

One of the regulars nodded at Jack when he passed by. Ronny was his name. Jack had asked him if he'd wanted coffee, and he'd replied that he'd rather have some cigarettes. "Don't need anything to keep me awake any longer than I need to be," Ronny had said with a toothy smile.

"You have any smokes?" Ronny called out.

"I don't smoke," said Jack, approaching the man.

Ronny clucked his tongue, pulling a ratty blanket around himself. "Forgot about that. I smoked that entire pack you gave me in two days. Told myself I'd let it last." Ronny shrugged. "Told myself the same thing last week when I bought myself a twelve-pack of beers. Whoops."

"You need anything else? Are you hungry?" said Jack.

"Nah. I'm good, man." Ronny peered up at Jack, assessing him. "You come here a lot, don't you?"

"I think you're here more than I am."

Ronny chuckled. "True. Been here for a few months now. I'm a regular, practically."

Jack had offered to take Ronny to a shelter or even put him up in a hotel room, but Ronny had refused. Ronny didn't like charity—at least not beyond getting a packet of cigarettes. Jack hated the thought of him spending the night outside in the cold. But he couldn't force Ronny inside.

Besides, Ronny had told him that staying in the shelters was worse than sleeping outside. "It's like a fucking prison," Ronny had spat. "Never going back to one of those."

Jack had been in Seattle for a few weeks now. After he'd packed up and left Hazel Island, he'd gone to his mom's place and had helped her find a new place to live. He'd gotten his own place a few blocks away from her. Despite getting a decent job down at the shipyards, Jack knew it'd take him years to rebuild the savings he'd burned through in the last few months.

"You're not from around here, are you?" asked Ronny.

"I grew up in the city, but I haven't lived here in years. I was living on Hazel Island."

"Never been there. Heard it's nice. Why'd you leave?"

I left a woman behind because I wasn't good enough for her. I broke a promise. I'm a failure.

Jack wasn't sure which explanation he should go with. So instead, he replied, "I moved back because of family."

"A girl?" Ronny looked him up and down. "Or for a boy. Dunno what you're into."

Jack's lips twitched. "No, it wasn't because of a woman. I'm helping out my mom."

"You single?"

"Why? You interested?"

Ronny guffawed. "Don't flatter yourself. You're not my type."

Jack wasn't sure whether he should be relieved or insulted. Shaking his head, he sat down on the bench next to Ronny and stretched out his legs. "There was a woman, actually."

"Huh, thought so. I could tell by the look on your face."

"What look is that?"

Ronny crossed his arms. "I've been on the streets for ten years now. I've seen things that would make you cry like a baby. I've seen the look on somebody's face when they don't have anything else. Like they've been sucked dry by a vampire." Ronny glanced at him. "Same thing in your look."

Jack stared straight ahead. "I don't think my situation is as bad as being homeless," he finally said.

"I don't know. Maybe you've got other problems. We all have demons." Ronny pulled out a cigarette and lit it.

"Anyway, whatever's eating at you will kill you if you let it."

Jack frowned. "I thought you didn't have any more cigarettes."

"This is my last one." Ronny blew out a cloud of smoke.

As Jack walked home, he thought about what Ronny had said. He wanted to deny it, tell himself that Ronny was crazy and had no idea what he was talking about.

But that didn't mitigate the sting that Jack felt from Ronny's statement. If he were being honest, he felt like he was wasting away every day that passed without seeing Gwen.

He missed her, plain and simple. He'd hoped that with distance and time, he'd forget about her. But the opposite seemed to be happening: he couldn't stop thinking about her.

He wondered how she'd reacted to discovering he'd moved away. Guilt made him wonder if he'd made a mistake, leaving like that, without saying goodbye.

But he'd told her they were over. He'd been honest. Why make things harder with a painful goodbye?

Jack arrived home to his bare studio apartment. Currently, the furnishings included a rickety futon and a cardboard box for a table. He could've gotten more furniture, but it'd seemed pointless. He wasn't planning on staying here for that long.

Where will you go, then? You can't go back to Hazel Island.

A text message made his phone light up. His mom texted him often. Although she'd reluctantly agreed to go to outpatient treatment in return for his help, Jack had soon discovered it wasn't that simple.

Neither he nor his mom had the money to pay for a spot at a private treatment center. He'd also learned that it'd take months, even years, before there would be a spot available at a place that offered financial aid.

At first, his mom had been texting him to help her with something in her new apartment, like hanging a picture, putting together a bookshelf, or unclogging a drain. Then it had been requests for more money. Twenty dollars here, twenty dollars there. Jack had at first told her no, because he wasn't sure what she'd be spending it on.

When she'd fought him on it, he'd relented. He just didn't have the energy anymore to fight his mom, especially when she would lay on the guilt so skillfully, making him doubt himself and his reasons for denying her.

Can you send me money for groceries? his mom's text read.

Jack stared at it, anger rising within him. There was never any gratitude, never any attempt to pay him back. He only got endless demands, draining just as surely as a vampire drained its victims.

I just gave you money, Jack replied.

When he didn't receive a response, he naively thought that was the end of things. But not even fifteen minutes later, his front door jiggled, his mom's voice echoing in the hallway outside. "Jack, let me in! I want to talk to you!"

Jack considered ignoring her. But it was also freezing outside, and the last time he'd tried that stunt, she'd threatened to call the cops. The last thing Jack wanted was a scene.

He opened the door to find his mom not wearing a coat or jacket, her cheeks flushed. He wondered if she'd walked here without one.

"It's freezing," she complained. She shivered, wrapping her arms around herself.

Close to sixty, Debra Benson was a slight woman, almost frail-looking. But underneath the frailty was a stubborn streak that no one could match.

Her hair was newly bleached blond, her acrylic nails a startling shade of bright red with crystals glued to the tips. Jack didn't want to know how she'd gotten the money to pay for either.

"Are you gonna let me in?" she said in a whiny voice.

Jack stepped aside.

"You still haven't bought any furniture? This place looks like a serial killer lives here." Debra laughed, but it turned into a hoarse cough quickly enough. She didn't sit down: instead, she began to rummage around in Jack's fridge.

"What are you doing?" Jack asked.

"Making food. I'm starving." Debra pulled out a few random ingredients and began to assemble them on Jack's counter. "Do you even have pots or pans?"

"In the drawer under the oven."

Jack watched his mom as she practically ransacked his kitchen. Debra was hardly a cook; Jack was certain she didn't even know how to boil water for pasta.

"I don't need you to cook for me," said Jack quietly.

"Yet here I am. Aren't I a good mother? I'm always here for you, Jack." Debra filled a pot with water and then liberally poured olive oil in the water, which made Jack wince. "Which is why I'm heartbroken that I have to beg you for money constantly. A mother should never have to beg. If you needed money, I wouldn't do that to *you*."

His mom fiddled with the knobs on the stovetop until Jack wanted to scream.

"I'm never going to be good enough for you, am I?" he said, almost to himself.

Debra barely glanced up. "How do you work this stupid thing? God, what a piece of shit this place is. You'd think you could find something better than this."

"*Mom*." He nearly shouted the words.

Debra finally looked at him.

"I can't keep doing this. You can't keep doing this."

"Sorry for touching your stove, I didn't know it was important to you." Her words dripped sarcasm.

"This isn't about the fucking stove." Jack's fists clenched. "Do you know why I left all those years ago?"

Debra's expression shuttered. "I don't want to talk about that."

"Well, I do. I left because of you. I left because you're an addict who refuses to get help and because you drive everyone away. I left because I had no choice. You forced me to leave."

Her eyes filled with tears. For a second, Jack felt guilty, but he knew that his mom was talented at using tears as a weapon.

"How can you speak to your mother like that? I clothed you, fed you, loved you. Who gave you a roof over your head? Who stayed up late, helping you with your home-work? Not your dad. Me. I did it all by myself. And this is the thanks I get?"

"You don't get a fucking trophy for doing the bare minimum as a parent!"

The words burst forth, Jack hardly understanding what

he was saying. But then, he realized that for almost his entire life, he'd waited for his mom to get sober and then admit that she'd hurt him and Danny. She'd apologize, she'd say she loved him, and then they'd live happily ever after.

He'd twisted himself into knots to please her, to make her happy. If he was the perfect son, maybe she'd get better.

But it didn't matter. He could give her mountains of cash, a brand-new house, a shiny car. He could tell her she'd been the perfect mother, but she'd never change because she had no reason to.

Debra was crying now. Her shoulders were hunched over, her hands on her face. Despite his anger, Jack still felt guilty.

Sighing, he wrapped his arms around her. She tried to push him away, but it was a feeble attempt.

"Why are you so mean to me?" she was saying in between sobs. "I've tried and tried and it's never good enough."

Jack said nothing. He said nothing because there was no point.

He offered to walk his mom home, but she refused. He could only get her to wear his coat so she didn't freeze to death.

"I'm sorry, Mom," he said. He meant it.

"I don't accept your apology." She slammed the door behind her so hard it rattled the walls.

Soon after she'd left, Jack gave in and followed her. He only wanted to make sure she got home all right. There was no telling what his mom would do in this state. She could go to some bar, get drunk, and then pass out in some alley. Or she might hurt herself. Jack couldn't bear the thought that he'd cause her to do either.

He followed her without her realizing it. When she finally buzzed herself into her building, he let out a sigh of relief.

He wandered the streets for a while with no destination in mind. Why go home? That dump of an apartment wasn't his home.

He thought of Gwen, and it made his heart ache. And as he sifted through so many memories he had of Gwen Parker, he realized that she'd never treated him like his mom had. She'd never demanded anything from him. Even when she'd told him she loved him, it'd been offered as a gift.

And he, the greatest fool of all time, had thrown that magnificent gift back into her face.

Groaning, he sat down on a bench, his knees suddenly wobbly. *I love her. I love Gwen. And she'll probably never want to see my face again.*

"You back again?"

Jack looked up to see Ronny lounging on the bench across from him. He hadn't even realized he'd returned to the park.

"I guess I can't stay away," he said.

"I'm really not interested in you in that way."

That made Jack smile a little. "Noted."

They sat in silence for a while, Ronny gazing up at the sky, Jack wondering if there was any possible way to get Gwen back. If he had to beg, borrow, steal...he'd do it.

"Ronny, have you ever fucked up with a woman so badly that she wouldn't take you back?" Jack asked.

"Only once, when I was just a kid. I cheated on a girl. It

was the stupidest thing I could've done." Ronny peered at Jack. "You cheat on your girl?"

Jack shook his head. "She said she loved me. I told her it wouldn't work."

Ronny let out a low whistle. "Shit, that might be worse. I'm surprised you're still alive."

"So it's hopeless?"

"Hopeless? Fuck me, I don't know. I'm not your shrink. But you gotta at least try. Otherwise, you'll always wonder and that's the worst feeling. I didn't try with my girl. I had too much pride. And then she married some other guy and well, here you see me." He flashed Jack a grim smile. "She made the better choice in the end."

Jack sat on the bench and listened to Ronny snore. He watched people pass by as he thought. Eventually, he got up and bought a pack of cigarettes. He then set them on the bench next to Ronny's feet, covered them with the blanket, and headed home.

CHAPTER TWENTY-TWO

When Jack showed up at the Wright place, Jack found himself being politely told to get lost.

"Mr. Luke isn't available for visitors," the housekeeper said for the second time.

"I need to see him. It's an emergency."

The housekeeper didn't seem all that dismayed. She just raised one supercilious eyebrow and asked, "Are you bleeding, sir?"

"No."

"Is someone else bleeding?"

Jack clenched his jaw. "No."

"Then this is not an emergency. Please schedule an appointment at a later time—"

Jack pushed the front door open, causing the woman to gasp in outrage. He then yelled, "Luke! Luke, you bastard, I know you're in here!"

A few other people came around various corners to stare at the crazy man yelling up the stairs. The housekeeper fluttered around Jack before hurrying to pick up one of the phones.

Jack wondered if she'd call the police. It'd take a half an hour just to get out here, and by then, he would've found Luke.

Despite having been in the house before, Jack got lost more than once, losing valuable time. But then he recognized the hallway that Luke had led him down when he'd met with him that first time to talk about Gwen.

Jack walked into Luke's office to find his friend with a woman. Her back was turned, so Jack couldn't see her face. Luke had his arm around her waist. His expression was so intent on her that he didn't even notice his office door opening.

But the woman noticed. She looked over her shoulder, her eyes wide. It was then that Jack recognized her: it was Jocelyn Gray.

The trio stared at each other for a long moment. There was no noise except the sound of Jack shifting his weight and making the floorboards creak.

"Oh!" Jocelyn practically sprang from Luke's grasp. "Jack! You're here. On Hazel Island. In Luke's house." She was speaking so quickly Jack could barely understand her. "You're here. Why are you here?"

Luke shot her a look. She shut up after that.

"Yeah, Jack, why are you here?" said Luke. "This is sudden."

"I needed to talk with you."

"You have my number. You have a phone."

"In person."

Right then, the housekeeper rushed into the office,

panting like she'd been running. "Mr. Luke! I'm so sorry! He wouldn't leave. I called the police, they're on their way—"

Luke raised an eyebrow. "Did you accost the staff?" he said to Jack.

Jack crossed his arms. "They wouldn't let me inside."

"I wonder why." To the housekeeper, he said, "Maggie, it's fine. Jack here is just rough around the edges. I'm sorry he was rude. Please let the police know they aren't needed."

Maggie narrowed her eyes at Jack, unconvinced. Based on her expression, he was half-convinced she'd happily place a curse on him for his behavior.

"I guess I should go, too," said Jocelyn uneasily. She swallowed hard. "Nice to see you, Jack."

"Likewise."

Jocelyn glanced over her shoulder at Luke, but he was looking at papers on his desk. Jack saw her shoulders slump as she followed Maggie down the hallway.

"Close the door, will you? And maybe lock it for good measure. You're not the first surprise guest I've had today."

Although Jack was curious about Jocelyn and Luke, he had more pressing matters. "I need your help," he said after shutting the door.

"I thought you were leaving the island for good? I'm pretty sure you told me you were never coming back." Luke sat down, putting his feet up on his desk.

Jack didn't sit. "I fucked up."

"Keep going."

Jack scowled. "I left because I thought it was better for everyone. I sold my boat; I'm renting my house to Lyle now, too."

"So you came here to tell me that you're homeless and unemployed?"

"I came here to ask you for a job." Jack felt like his teeth would crumble in his mouth, he was gritting them so hard.

Luke stared at him. Putting his feet down, he peered up at his friend. "You, Jack Benson? Are you asking for my *help?*"

"If you're going to be a dick about it, I'll go somewhere else. I have my pride too. Asshole."

"Calling me an asshole is giving me less of a reason to help you."

Jack wanted to deck his friend. Did Luke want him to go on his knees and beg? He refused. He'd find work elsewhere. He'd ask Lyle if he needed a hand. Surely there were enough odd jobs on the island he could support himself.

"I don't need this. I came here asking for help, and all you can do is mock me," said Jack.

Luke sighed. "I'm not trying to mock you. I'm just pissed off at you. Pissed that it took you this long to ask. Christ, man, I thought I was your friend."

Jack stared. His anger melted away in a flash, and all he could feel in that moment was confusion.

"You decided to leave the island without talking to anyone, not even me. You sold your boat when I refused to buy it. I kept waiting for you to ask, or to even tell me what was going on.

"But you didn't. Jack Benson is an island, a man unto himself. He doesn't need anyone else in his life," said Luke sadly.

Jack sat down. His knees felt wobbly. He suddenly felt very, very tired. "I didn't realize."

"And worst of all, have you seen Gwen? She's a ghost. She was heartbroken when you left. I thought of anyone in the world, you would've told her. But I guess not."

Jack put his face in his hands. Groaning, he just said, "Fuck me."

"I can give you a job, Jack. Or help you find one. I can even put you up in one of my apartments. That's not a problem."

Luke came around the other side of the desk and put his hand on Jack's shoulder. "That's what friends do. I just wish you would've asked me sooner."

Jack hated feeling weak. Vulnerable. Yet at the same time, he felt almost peaceful, like a weight had been lifted from his shoulders.

"I need to find Gwen," he said, his voice hoarse. "I can at least apologize to her. Even if she hates me forever."

Luke was smiling sadly. "I doubt she hates you. If she'll trust you again, well, that's another matter."

As Jack thought over Luke's words, one question nagged at him. Since when did Luke Wright know so much about Gwen Parker?

"How do you know about Gwen?" Jack tried to sound casual, but suspicion laced his voice anyway.

Luke just laughed at him. "Jealous? It's a small town. Besides, I've seen her more than once to talk about her restaurant. Which is happening, you know. I'm funding her. Since you gave her the ten grand even though you're jobless, homeless, and honestly, you could use a shower, too."

Jack snorted. "Fuck off." But after he gave himself a whiff, he grimaced. "Can I use your shower?"

"Which one? We have ten to choose from."

Even as Jack muttered, "Eat shit," he still gave his friend a hug.

GWEN WAS in one of the rooms upstairs, wiping down the bathroom counters. Three of the housekeeping staff had called in sick with the flu. Gwen had been vacuuming rooms and cleaning bathrooms all morning. Even Jocelyn had pitched in, stripping the beds and doing the laundry.

When they'd been cleaning the room that had just been vacated by a newly married couple, Jocelyn had screeched, "Rat! Oh my God, it's a rat!" at the top of her lungs. Gwen had come running, only to discover that the rat was, in fact, a pair of gray boxer briefs. Gwen had laughed so hard that she'd nearly peed her pants. Jocelyn had not found it so amusing.

When Gwen heard footsteps in the room, she assumed it was Jocelyn. "Jocelyn, can you get me more bathroom cleaner?" she called. "I'm almost out."

But a voice that was decidedly not Jocelyn's answered, "Where do you keep it?"

Gwen whirled around. Jack stood there, his hands in his pockets, his expression unsure. His hair had grown out, and he was even sporting a bit of a beard.

"Do you want me to get you another bottle?" he said.

Gwen just shook her head. Her heart was pounding so hard that she felt dizzy. "What are you doing here?"

"I came back. I missed you, Gwen."

Setting down her microfiber cloth and cleaner, Gwen

washed her hands, trying to calm her swirling thoughts. Jack had returned. He'd come back and he'd missed her.

Don't get your hopes up. He's probably just saying hello.

"You missed me," she repeated as she dried her hands.

"Yeah."

She gazed at him, standing there, looking so handsome in the morning sunlight that her chest hurt. She wanted to throw her arms around him. But she held back because he'd already told her that they couldn't be anything but friends.

"Gwen."

She looked up, and now he was only a few inches away from her.

"I should never have left like I did. Without telling you." He reached out to touch her, but then his arm fell. "I thought it'd be better for everyone. I was trying to do the right thing."

Her lower lip trembled. "The right thing would've been telling me instead of letting me find out about it."

"I know. Shit, I know. I don't know what I was thinking. I guess I thought you'd get over it."

She gaped at him. Now she wanted to wallop him upside his head. "I'd just get over it? Jesus, Jack! I tell you I love you, and you assume it's just some fleeting emotion? That I'll move on with some other guy soon enough? I don't know whether to be insulted that you think so badly of me or sad that you think so badly of yourself."

"I wanted to protect you from me. My family—my mom has been calling me, needing money. She does this periodically. I didn't want to put all of that on you."

"Oh, Jack." Gwen sighed. "Everyone has baggage. You know I have some of my own!"

"I was ashamed." His voice was a whisper. "Or maybe I was afraid I'd turn into her."

Gwen's heart broke. "No matter what your mom did or has done, you are your own person. You make your choices. You aren't your parents. Nobody is."

Jack took her hand, brushing his thumb across her palm. Then he was pulling her into his arms, hugging her so tightly she was breathless. But she didn't care. Burying her face in his shoulder, she inhaled his scent and reveled in his strength and warmth.

"I don't deserve you," he was saying, "but I'll do whatever it takes to earn you."

"Earn me? I'm not a candy bar you save up for."

That made him smile a little. "No, you're better. You showed me that I don't have to be alone for my entire life, that there are people worth loving. You make me want to be a better man."

"Loving? Are you saying you love me?"

He touched her cheek. "Love you? I adore you. You're everything I never knew I needed, Gwen Parker."

Then he finally, *finally*, kissed her. It was a kiss that Gwen could feel from the top of her head all the way to her toes. It was a kiss that calmed all her fears, explained away all her doubts.

When Jack broke the kiss, he pressed his forehead to hers. "Luke is helping me find a job."

"You can't return to fishing?"

"I want to, but it won't pay the bills. Not like it did."

"I hate that you sold your boat. I know you did it for me. You shouldn't have. I could've found the money somewhere else."

"I promised you that money. I want you to open your restaurant. I'd do anything to make you happy." His eyes were dark now. "Anything."

Gwen had to kiss him again for that remark. They were so wrapped up in each other that they didn't hear Jocelyn enter the room. She finally had to clear her throat loudly at them.

"I take it you two made up?" she said, a smile on her face.

Gwen's cheeks were red. "Yes. Jack's back for good."

"Excellent. He can help us clean." Jocelyn shoved a bucket of supplies into Jack's hands. "Make yourself useful, Benson."

After Jocelyn left, he laughed a little. "She's terrifying," he said.

"Oh, I know it."

"Did I mention that she was at Luke's earlier today?"

Gwen's eyes widened. "What? Tell me everything. Right now."

And because he loved her and would do anything for her, Jack did as he was asked.

EPILOGUE

The grand opening of Lyn's Eatery brought the entire island, tourists, and media together to celebrate. Shortly after Gwen had gotten funding, she, Jocelyn, Jack, and a handful of hired contractors began renovating the house next door. They'd worked rain or shine, aiming to have the diner open by summertime for tourist season.

Standing outside the restaurant, Gwen felt such immense pride that she felt near to bursting.

Jack slung an arm around her. "Amazing job, baby," he murmured in her ear. "It looks like a real restaurant."

Gwen laughed. "Don't look too closely. Pretty sure the paper towel holder in the restroom is about to fall off the wall."

"Nobody cares about those things. I don't. They just see that you've worked your ass off." He then squeezed her ass, which made her roll her eyes.

Jocelyn was inside, cooking away, probably barking out orders to her sous chef, a young culinary graduate named

Kelly. Kelly, though, had quickly figured out how best to handle Jocelyn. The girl had balls, that was for sure. Gwen was just thankful they'd found her and convinced her to take a job on the island when she could've gotten a job anywhere.

"Don't you want to go inside?" asked Jack, cutting through Gwen's thoughts.

"I will. I just want to admire it some more. This is the first time it's been filled with customers." She sighed happily then turned to Jack. "I couldn't have done this without you. Thank you, for everything."

He kissed her forehead. "I feel the exact same way."

She and Jack went inside Lyn's eventually, going from table to table, talking to customers. The reviews so far had been glowing. Despite her initial resistance to changing the menu, Jocelyn had eventually realized that Jack's suggestions had been prudent ones.

"Elliot!" Gwen found her older brother, his wife Bekah, and their two-year-old daughter Lola at one of the booths. "How is everything?"

"Awesome job, Sis." He grinned up at her. "Can I get a discount for being the brother of the owner?"

"God, you're so cheap." Bekah shook her head. "Don't listen to him. He's just trying to save a buck."

"Yeah, because we're going to have another mouth to feed soon!"

Gwen's eyes widened. "What? You guys are having a second one?"

"I just found out last week," said Bekah. Then she watched as Lola begun throwing her French fries, then a dish of ketchup, onto the floor, laughing at her own antics.

"Not sure we thought this through, to be honest," added Bekah as she began to clean up Lola's mess.

Elliot looked a little pale now, which just made Gwen laugh at him. She squeezed his shoulder. "Good luck."

"Thanks," he muttered.

After Gwen and Jack had done the rounds and eaten their own meals, Jack asked Gwen to go for a walk. A clear summer evening, they found themselves down at the beach to watch the sunset. Gwen snuggled up to him, neither of them needing to say anything.

The past year had been sheer bliss for the two of them. They'd found a small house to rent—courtesy of Luke— and moved in together earlier that year. Jack, for his part, had decided to gain more experience as a general contractor as he'd helped with the renovation. He'd recently gotten his license and, with help from Luke, had begun work on a variety of projects on the island. Hazel Island was growing, and there was high demand to build more houses, offices, and stores.

"I heard from my mom today," said Jack quietly.

Gwen looked up at him. As far as she knew, he hadn't spoken to Debra in months. "And?"

"She wants to see me. And meet you. She says she's finished a ninety-day program and is now in sober living."

"Oh, Jack, that's amazing. I'm so happy for you and her."

His expression remained serious, though. "I'm not sure about you meeting her, yet. Besides, she could relapse again. She's never stayed sober for very long."

"That's true, but celebrate the good that's happening

right now. Your mom clearly wants to have a relationship with you."

"Or she just wants more money," he said darkly.

"Maybe. But give her a chance. Maybe she'll prove you wrong."

"You always like to see the good in people."

"You mean I'm not a grumpy old man like you?"

He growled, tickling her, which made her start laughing like a crazy woman. Soon enough, the tickling turned into kissing. It was only the lack of privacy that kept them from going further.

Jack shook his head. "You drive me crazy, woman," he said, even as he squeezed her ass for the second time that night. "I can't believe you're really mine."

"Believe it."

She was now staring out onto the horizon, and she didn't see Jack reach inside his pocket. He had to clear his throat to regain her attention.

In the palm of his hand was a ring box. Gwen stared at it, her brain taking a long moment to understand what she was looking at.

"Jack," she whispered.

"Gwen Parker," he said, slowly going down on one knee as he opened the ring box. "The first day I met you, I knew you were special. I also knew that no matter what, I'd watch over you. I just never thought you could love me as much as I love you."

Gwen was crying now. She was sniffling and trying to wipe away the tears as Jack took her hand.

"Will you marry me? I'll never stop trying to make you happy," he said.

She was nodding because her voice didn't seem to be working anymore.

"Is that a yes?" he asked.

"Yes—yes!" She nearly shouted the word. "Of course I'll marry you!"

He grinned. "No need to yell, sweetheart. I think the entire island heard you." He placed the ring on her left hand.

"It's beautiful. I love it," she said, looking at the ring. Then to Jack, "I love you. I would be honored to be your wife."

Then she launched herself into his arms, and they fell onto the sand together, laughing like love-drunk fools.

Luke Wright sat at the bar at Lyn's Eatery, seriously considering having a fourth beer. He didn't need another one, of course. He hadn't eaten much, so after the three he'd already drunk, he was rather tipsy. Not drunk. Luke didn't like to get drunk. Being out of control was one of the things he hated most in life.

He'd considered skipping out on the grand opening of the latest Hazel Island restaurant. But he had a stake in its success, so he didn't have much of an excuse to stay home. Besides, he didn't really like staying at his parents' place. He could stay in any of the rental properties he owned, but it was easier to stay at home right now.

Luke heard Jocelyn Gray's voice, even over the sounds of the diners. She was shouting something about a burnt rib-eye. When he heard another voice tell her that she was wrong, he raised an eyebrow.

Few people told Jocelyn Gray she was wrong. He'd done it once, and he had the scars to show for it. The woman was a terror.

Jocelyn, her blond hair coming undone from its usual ponytail, came huffing out of the kitchen. She instantly went to mix herself a drink from the bar. The bartender just blinked at her and gave her a wide berth.

"Having a good night?" said Luke lazily.

"I'm surprised you're still here," she said as she began pouring various liquids into a cocktail mixer. After mashing up fruit and tossing some mint leaves into the mixer, she shook it.

"What are you making?" Luke asked.

"A mojito. It's a guilty pleasure." Jocelyn poured the cocktail into a tall glass and took a long drink. "I love these things."

"I didn't take you for a fruity, cocktail kind of girl."

"What did you take me for?"

Luke shrugged. "Maybe a tumbler of whiskey. Or scotch. Maybe with a cigar to go along with the drink."

Jocelyn snorted. "So you imagine me sitting around in a smoking jacket like Hugh Hefner? How flattering."

The thought of Jocelyn wearing a smoking jacket made Luke imagine her wearing *only* a smoking jacket. He was glad he was sitting down because his body reacted instantly to the image.

He didn't know why this lingering attraction to Jocelyn wouldn't go away. He had a feeling the only way for it to disappear would be to fuck her. Then he'd get bored, and he'd move on.

That was how it usually went with women, at least.

But then he remembered his conversation with his father just yesterday, and his gut clenched. Those three beers he'd drunk didn't seem nearly enough.

"Can you get me another Pale Ale?" said Luke to Jocelyn.

"I'm not the bartender."

The poor bartender was drying some glasses and trying to act like he didn't mind Jocelyn in his space.

"No, but you're closer to where the bottles are." Luke gave her a winning smile. "Come on, baby, get me a drink."

"I'm not your baby." But she still reached down and, after taking off the cap, handed the beer to him. "That's twenty dollars."

"For one beer?"

"No, that's just for my tip." Now she was smiling.

Luke snorted. Taking out his wallet, he handed her a one-hundred-dollar bill. "Keep the change."

"Luke, I can't take this—"

"Too late. You already took it. Use it to buy yourself something nice."

"I don't need anything nice."

Luke nearly growled under his breath. This woman— she drove him *insane*. She never let anyone just do something nice for her.

"How about you get yourself something to wear?" In a joking tone, he added, "Maybe get rid of those ugly shoes you always wear. Not a good look when a woman looks as mannish as you dress."

"You're an asshole, you know that?"

Then she tossed the crumpled one-hundred-dollar bill in his face and walked off, nearly colliding with the bartender as she left.

Luke sat in silence, moping, as he nursed his beer. The bartender eventually said to him with wide, amazed eyes, "I can't believe you poked the beast and survived."

"We'll see how long until she actually kills me." Luke then downed the rest of his beer in one gulp.

ONE PERFECT SUMMER

A HAZEL ISLAND NOVELLA

CHAPTER ONE

B ekah Matthews gaped at her boyfriend of three years.
"You know we were never meant to go the
distance," Sam was saying. "We're just not compatible. You
know that, too."

Bekah did *not* know that. She and Sam had been dating
for three years now. Sam had given her a key to his place,
and vice versa. They'd discussed moving into their own
place together just two weeks ago.

"How is everything?" asked the waiter.

Bekah had barely started eating her linguine, and now,
she was seriously considering tossing it in Sam's face.

"It's great, thanks." Sam barely glanced at the waiter,
his tone dismissive.

As a scientist, Bekah had always prided herself on being
logical and practical. When she and Sam had first started
seeing each other, she'd written down a list of pros and cons
about him. One of the biggest pros was that he was ambitious in his career as a lawyer. It was also one of his biggest
cons, Bekah had eventually realized.

"Well? Do you have anything you want to say?" said Sam.

Bekah felt as though the English language had exited the building that was her brain. She took a long drink of water, then an even longer one of the wine she'd ordered.

"I never thought..." She swallowed. "I'm in shock."

If she were being honest, she'd honestly thought Sam taking her to the fanciest restaurant on Hazel Island meant he might be proposing.

Well, he was proposing: proposing to end their relationship. That thought made Bekah return to her glass of wine.

"We've hardly seen each other in the last few months," said Sam. "I've been busy with work, you with your research. The spark is gone." He leaned forward, his voice lowering. "There hasn't been a spark for a while now."

Bekah felt her cheeks turn red. "No, I don't think that's true. I think you can create sparks, if you want to," she said, rather sharply.

"Don't drag this out when we both know it's already dead." Sam then reached under his chair and pulled out a gift bag. He plopped the bag in front of Bekah, but she didn't reach out to take it.

"It's a gift," he said lamely.

"You got me a 'I'm dumping you' gift." She just looked at him.

Now he finally looked self-conscious. "Now I'm wondering if that was a bad idea. I just thought..." He shrugged. "I didn't want us to end on bad terms. I do care about you. You're a good person."

Bekah pulled out the tissue paper to discover a small screwdriver set inside. Screwdrivers. Bekah glanced around, wondering where the hidden cameras were, because surely this entire debacle was a prank.

A receipt fluttered out of the bag. "In case you want to return it," said Sam.

At this point, Bekah had merely been in shock, dismayed. But when she looked at the receipt and saw that Sam had purchased this gift over a year ago, rage coursed through her in hot, quick waves.

He'd wanted to end this *a year ago*. Yet he hadn't said a word until now. Humiliation made her want to sob. He'd wanted to move on and had delayed the breakup. Why?

A year ago, her beloved dog had died. Then her mom had broken her leg, and Bekah had had to help care for her that summer.

Rising from her chair, Bekah crumpled the receipt and tossed it in Sam's face. "You know, if you wanted to make this a clean breakup, you probably shouldn't have included a gift receipt dated from a year ago," she snapped.

Sam's face turned white. "Shit, Bekah—"

Bekah tossed back the rest of her wine, then did the same with Sam's glass. "You know what? Break up with me. That's fine. But don't feel sorry for me. I'm a big girl, Sam. I think I'll survive without you." Emboldened, she added, "God knows my vibrator has given me more orgasms than you ever did."

That remark earned her a sneer from him. "Don't act offended, Bekah. We both know you aren't marriage material, anyway."

She turned and left without another word. When she exited the restaurant, their waiter gave her a quick nod, as if he were telling her, *Good for you.*

It was a warm summer night on the island, the sun only starting to set. Hazel Island, population fewer than one thousand, was a small island in the Puget Sound that was as idyllic as it sounded. Bekah had grown up here for the most part, although she'd lived in Seattle to attend the University of Washington. She now lived here again, specifically to study the orca pods that lived in the surrounding waters. She was only a year away from earning her doctorate in marine biology.

Bekah considered going home, but she hadn't gotten another dog since Maybelle had died, so it was rather lonely. She was just glad she hadn't worn heels for tonight and had decided to walk to the restaurant. Sam didn't deserve her wearing heels and killing her feet. If anything, he deserved to be pushed off the nearest cliff into the freezing ocean.

The main street was bustling tonight, with both locals and tourists. Laughter and music floated around her, but she barely heard either. Mostly, she was telling herself she couldn't start crying right here in the street.

Three years down the drain. Three years playing second fiddle to Sam's career, hoping that once he passed the bar and began working as a lawyer, they could settle down together. Get married, start a family. But Sam had been reluctant to go to the next step in their relationship. *It's just not the right time*, he'd say. *I don't want to move too quickly.*

Well, the joke was on Bekah, because he'd had no intention of marrying her. He'd wanted to end things a year ago. A year ago! Bekah fumed. He'd thought she was too fragile to tell her the truth. She hated that. She hated pity. She preferred blunt honesty. It might hurt, but at least she knew where people stood.

Not marriage material. What the fuck did that even mean? Bekah rubbed her arms. She wasn't good enough to marry? She wasn't suited to being a wife and mother? She didn't understand. She'd thought she'd been a good, supportive girlfriend. She hadn't nagged, she hadn't pushed. She hadn't tried to make Sam change.

Maybe that had been the problem: she hadn't worked to make herself grow in the relationship, and she hadn't expected the same from Sam. They'd come to a place that was basically relationship stasis. Neither good, nor bad. It just...was. But as Bekah thought more about it, she realized that if she'd ever loved Sam, that love had dissipated like fog burned away by the sun.

When she felt sand beneath her feet, she realized she'd walked to the beach without thinking about her destination. She sighed, the sea air brisk, the setting sun's rays making the water sparkle.

Bekah had always loved the ocean. She loved how endless it seemed, how much of it remained unexplored. She marveled at all of the wildlife that lived within it. She'd known at an early age her fascination with marine life would be a defining factor in her life.

Her attention was pulled away from her musings when she heard a bird squawking in distress. Frowning, Bekah saw a large bird some yards away, and then she noticed that there was a person trying to do...something to it.

Bekah hurried toward the scene. As she got closer, she saw that the bird was a pelican, and that the person was attempting to extricate the poor thing from a net that had wrapped around its large beak.

"Come on, buddy, I'm just trying to help," said the man in low tones. He had a pocketknife in his hand, but the pelican kept thrashing, making it difficult for him to cut it loose.

"Give me the knife," she said to the man. When he looked at her in surprise, she added, "I'm a marine biologist. You can hold him while I free him. I've done this before."

The man's face had been shadowed by the bulk of the pelican's beak. But when he handed her the pocketknife, and she got a good look at his face, she nearly dropped the tool on the poor bird's head.

It was Elliot Parker. Her high school crush, the boy who'd stood up to her bullies for her and then had just as quickly ghosted her.

And to her immense annoyance, he was even more handsome than he'd been at eighteen. Now, he had the confidence—and muscles—of a man.

"Ma'am?" said Elliot. "What do you want me to do?"

Bekah had to stifle a hysterical laugh. He didn't recognize her.

Of course not. Why would he? It's been eight years since we've seen each other.

Shaking off the surprise, she directed Elliot to hold the pelican close, keeping its wings from flapping about. Kneeling in the sand, Bekah hardly noticed that her brand-new dress was getting soaked and dirty.

The net had somehow wrapped around the pelican's beak, making it nearly impossible for the creature to open its mouth. She began cutting at the net, making shushing noises when the bird tried to pull away.

"We'll get you free soon, promise," she kept saying. The net wasn't flimsy, and the knife wasn't all that sharp, so by the time Bekah had finished, sweat had begun to dot her forehead.

She looked at Elliot. "I'm about to get this off of him. You'll want to back away quickly so you don't get hit in the face when he flies off."

Elliot's lips quirked, which made her heart do a pitter-pat in her chest. "Noted."

Bekah forced her attention back to the task at hand. She cut one last bit of the lines, tugging the net off of it. Once she'd gotten out of the way, Elliot followed her.

The pelican opened its beak wide and then squawked loudly while flapping its wings. And then it was gone, flying into the horizon.

"Well," said Elliot a few moments later, "that was pretty cool."

Bekah still had his pocketknife in her hand. Handing it back, she looked around for a trash can to dispose of the net, but she didn't see any close by.

Looking down at herself, she realized that not only was she holding remnants of a net, but that she was covered in sand, water, and even some seaweed. She probably looked insane. Her cheeks were probably red; she was sweaty despite the ocean air, and she could feel her updo falling down.

She probably looked like a total crazy woman.

Of course, Elliot looked amazing: his dirty blond hair was perfectly windswept. If he was sweating, she couldn't tell. When he flashed her a charming smile, even his teeth seemed to gleam.

"Thanks for your help," said Elliot, making Bekah realize she hadn't said a word to him in minutes. "You've done that before?"

"A few times. It's not uncommon, unfortunately."

"You said you're a marine biologist?"

"Yes. Well, I'm finishing up my doctorate this year. I'm studying orca pods, especially their migration patterns and how they've shifted in the last decade." *Bekah, I doubt he cares about the mundane details about your research*, she told herself.

Elliot seemed like he was barely listening. "Cool. I'm Elliot Parker, by the way." He held out a hand for her to shake.

She didn't know if it was the remnants of her conversation with Sam, or her annoyance at not being recognized, or that this handsome, dreamy man seemed to look right through her, but Bekah didn't take his hand to shake it.

"I know who you are," she said simply.

Elliot blinked. "Do we know each other?"

"We did, a long time ago." She smiled, her expression sardonic. "Have a nice evening, Elliot."

CHAPTER TWO

Elliot wiped the sweat from his forehead and surveyed the wall he'd just finished painting. He only had one more room to go.

"You missed a spot," said his younger sister Gwen over his shoulder.

"Where?"

She pointed at a spot near the ceiling. "In the corner. See? I can still see some of the old peach paint."

Elliot squinted, not entirely certain his sister wasn't full of it, and decided that since she was the boss, he'd paint without protest. He made another pass with the roller.

"How about that?" he said.

Gwen frowned. "Let me get a brush."

Elliot rolled his eyes, but only because her back was turned. He took the brush from her and said, "I'll do it."

"Don't give me that tone. This is my bed and breakfast, and I want it to be perfect."

He patted her on the shoulder. "You've told me that at

least ten times now. But you're also not going to finish everything if you keep micromanaging me."

Gwen wrinkled her nose. "You're annoying when you're right."

"But I am right!"

Now it was Gwen's turn to roll her eyes. Elliot laughed, ignoring his sister muttering under her breath about how annoying brothers were.

Gwen was only a year younger than him. They'd grown up on Hazel Island. As children, they'd been close, but as they'd gotten older, they'd grown apart. It was only after Gwen had left her husband to move back to Hazel Island that they'd reconnected.

Elliot knew that his sister was still grieving her marriage, despite her assurances that she was doing fine. He'd heard her crying in her room more than once since he'd begun staying with her. He'd almost knocked on her door, but he'd changed his mind every time.

What did Elliot know about comforting someone with a broken heart? He was useless with challenging emotions. He preferred to keep those kinds of feelings at arm's length.

Gwen, in her return to Hazel Island, had impulsively bought a run-down house near Main Street and had decided to turn it into a bed and breakfast. She'd roped Elliot into helping her fix up the place. Considering that Elliot had wanted to take a long vacation from his demanding job as an architect in Seattle, he'd been happy to volunteer.

Elliot moved to the next room and began taping it off. He'd forgotten how much he enjoyed manual labor, although he'd never tell his dad that. He'd moved away from the island at age eighteen to escape his dad's attempts to get him to take the reins of the family tree removal service. His dad hadn't forgiven Elliot that slight, either.

Elliot began painting the south wall. The sea foam green color made him think of the green eyes of the woman he'd met on the beach two days ago. The woman who'd known his name but had declined to tell him who she was.

He'd racked his brain, wondering if he'd met her when he'd first returned to Hazel Island two weeks ago. It had been a flurry of people, many of whom were friends with his dad or had been close with his mom when she'd been alive. Most of them he'd recognized; when he'd forgotten a name, Gwen had helpfully supplied it.

But this woman—she hadn't been one of them. Had he known her in Seattle? He frowned. Then his stomach sank. Had he hooked up with her at some point? In his early twenties, he hadn't exactly been restrained in his pursuit of women and sex.

He was going through every hookup, every friend with benefits, that he'd slept with in the past five years, when Gwen returned. He was so engrossed in painting and in his thoughts that he didn't hear her approach.

"Earth to Elliot. You there?" she said, tapping his shoulder.

He jumped a little and flicked some paint on Gwen's shirt. "Fuck, sorry."

Gwen just laughed. "I'm already covered in paint and sawdust." She grabbed the roller from him and shook the roller near his chest. "There. Now we match."

"Was that really necessary?"

"No, but I enjoyed it anyway."

She cocked her head to the side. When she did that, Elliot couldn't help but see their mom in her expression. Gwen had Mom's curly, red hair and freckles, and she had the same smile. Sometimes it was hard for him to look at her when she smiled, a fact that he hated himself for.

"You've been out of it lately," said Gwen. "Is it Dad?"

"No. I haven't talked to Dad since I got here."

Elliot returned to painting, hoping his sister would get the hint. But his sister loved to pry. She claimed it was because she cared, but Elliot had a feeling she just liked keeping tabs on people.

"Then what is it? Is it a woman?"

Elliot shot her a dark look. "Stop meddling."

"That means it is a woman. This island is too small for you to keep any secrets, anyway." Gwen tapped her chin. "Who's single? Is it Jocelyn?"

Jocelyn Gray had recently returned from a year in Paris, attending one of the best culinary schools in the world. Elliot had only met her once. He could barely remember what she looked like, if he was being honest.

"Drop it, Gwen," he said.

"Felicity? No, she's too young. So is Alex. Unless you're a total creep. Is that why you look constipated?"

He glared at his sister. "I'm going to paint your entire face if you don't stop."

"Oh come on, tell me. I'm just going to pester you until you do."

He knew she would. Gwen could be as inexorable as death when she wanted to be. Sighing, he said, "I met a woman two days ago on the beach. She knew who I was, but I didn't."

"What did she look like?"

Elliot could see her in his mind's eye: dark hair tumbling from atop her head. Green eyes, skin a golden tan from being out in the sun. Based on the way her damp dress had clung to her, she had curves in all of the right places.

"She said she was a marine biologist. Dark hair, short." *Intelligent but as prickly as a cactus*, he thought wryly.

Gwen's eyes widened. "Oh my God. Are you serious?"

Now Elliot was confused. "Yes?"

"That was Bekah Matthews! You went to high school with her. Remember, Bekah? Glasses, black eyeliner, black boots Bekah?"

It took a moment for his brain to put the two people together into one. He remembered Rebekah Matthews. She'd been one of the weird kids, always drawing dolphins and whales in her notebooks. She'd dressed like the emo kids yet hadn't hung out with any of them.

Elliot had had a few classes with Bekah. He'd even sat next to her in World Studies sophomore year. He'd always asked to borrow a pen from her because he'd always lose his. One day, she'd gifted him a pack of pens and notebook paper, telling him she was tired of him taking hers.

That had been Bekah. Of course, he thought. Now it was obvious.

"I acted like we'd never met," he said with a grimace.

"Oh geez, how awkward. How did she react?" said Gwen.

"I don't think she's my biggest fan, let's just say that."

"You mean she cursed you and all of your descendants."

Elliot sighed. He'd majorly fucked this up. "To be fair to

me," he said grudgingly, "she looks *a lot* different than when we were in high school. And I haven't seen her in eight years. That's a long time."

Gwen laughed. "I wouldn't recommend telling her that. She'll probably take it the wrong way, and then I'll be searching for your body at the bottom of a cliff."

Elliot grumbled under his breath. She had looked different. In high school, she'd dyed her hair black and had worn black eyeliner that made her eyes look raccoonish.

Now, she'd given up the black hair dye, the intense eyeliner, and she'd shed the baby fat of adolescence. Her hair was a lovely chestnut brown, and without the eyeliner he'd seen how green her eyes were. Most of all, he'd realized how attractive Bekah Matthews was, even before he'd known who she was. He'd never seen what she'd looked like without all of the makeup and long, stringy hair in high school.

"She looks good," he said with a shrug. "That's what I'd tell her."

Now that caught Gwen's attention. "Are you interested? Because I hate to tell, but she has a boyfriend."

Elliot shot Gwen a dark look. "I'm not looking for a girlfriend, so don't try anything."

"I've always thought Bekah could do better, though. Her boyfriend is..." Gwen made a face. "Let's just say a cardboard box has more personality."

Elliot didn't need to hear about Bekah's relationship. No matter how attractive he might find her now, he wasn't going to be staying here on Hazel Island beyond the summer. And he knew from experience that few women wanted a quick fling. They wanted commitment. And Elliot was not a fan of the dreaded C word.

"Gwen? Are you in here?"

"Oh, Dad's here." Gwen hurried out, greeting their dad and quickly showing him the progress they'd made on the bed and breakfast.

Elliot continued painting. He and his old man weren't on great terms. The last time he'd visited, he and his dad had gotten into a fight that had nearly ended in a brawl.

"Elliot's painting the last room. Doesn't it look nice? I love this color." Gwen was talking quickly, and Elliot knew she did that when she was worried that he and their dad would get into it. Gwen hated conflict.

Walter Parker was in his late sixties now, a paunch overhanging his belt that had grown in the past decade. His hair had thinned to the point that his head shown in the sunshine. Gwen liked to tease him that the reflection of the sun against their dad's scalp blinded her. He was still as hardworking and dedicated to his family as he'd been thirty years ago—something that he'd found lacking in Elliot.

Walter grunted. "It's green," he said simply.

"It's sea foam green. I thought it was cheerful." Gwen shot Elliot a look. "Don't you agree? It's a fun color."

Elliot had zero opinions on what colors were fun. "I'm just following your lead, Sis. This is your project, after all."

"Still not sure what you'll get out of this. Lotta money you're putting into something that might not work out," said Walter.

Gwen's shoulders sagged. Elliot could've cheerfully punted their dad out the window. Even if their dad had a point, it wouldn't help to bring her down now.

"I think it's a smart idea." Elliot put down the paint roller, wiping his hands on a rag. "With the increase in tourism lately, there are people coming here who need a place to stay. With the motel closing, Gwen took an opportunity and seized it."

Gwen beamed at Elliot. "That's what I think, too. I'm not saying it won't be hard work, but I'm up for the challenge."

Walter's expression softened. He might not approve of his only son, but he was a softie toward his only daughter.

"I just don't want you to get in over your head. It's a difficult business to get into. It'll take years to be profitable, if at all."

"You don't know that." Elliot barely restrained a scowl. "Gwen has crunched the numbers, she's done her research, she has a small business loan from the bank. She's doing everything right. Why do you have to make her doubt herself?"

"Elliot—" said Gwen.

"I'm being practical. Something you both aren't good at." Walter crossed his arms. "Somebody needs to be a realist."

"There's being a realist, and there's being an asshole," Elliot shot back.

Walter's expression turned hard. Gwen's hands began fluttering.

"No, no, you both have good points," she interjected hurriedly.

"See, your sister understands me. She doesn't get defensive."

Elliot gritted his teeth. Their dad loved to twist his words to show that Elliot was always wrong.

"But Elliot is right, too." Gwen poked their dad in the upper arm. "I need encouragement right now. Not doubts. Believe me, I have enough of my own."

Gwen soon took Walter out to see the landscaping they'd been working on, leaving Elliot alone. Going to the window to watch the pair, Elliot forced his temper to go down.

When Elliot had refused to take on the family business at age eighteen and had left for Seattle, Walter Parker hadn't forgiven his son the slight. In his opinion, he'd built the business for the family and the family should be the ones to keep it going.

Elliot, though, had never wanted to become a tree surgeon. And he'd definitely not wanted to stay on the island, marry some sheltered island girl, and never see anything of the world. He'd packed his bags for Seattle and hadn't looked back. He'd gotten his degree in architecture and was now doing what he loved, designing buildings.

Elliot couldn't regret his decision to leave. But sometimes, doubt niggled at him, wondering if he'd made the wrong choice. He hadn't moved up the ladder at his firm as quickly as he'd thought. His boss had assigned him to another apartment complex design, something that Elliot found uninspiring. He worried that his career going into stasis meant that their dad was right about him.

Elliot watched as Gwen hugged their dad, waving goodbye as he walked to his standard lunch spot on Main Street. Gwen then caught Elliot's gaze through the window. She put up her hands and just shrugged.

233

CHAPTER THREE

Two weeks later, Bekah was sitting in the Gray family living room with her best friend, Jocelyn Gray.

"So that's the story of how Sam broke up with me, and then I ran into Elliot Parker," finished Bekah. "And I've yet to see Elliot since."

"Have you seen Sam?"

Bekah shook her head. "I'm pretty sure he'd already booked his ferry ticket before we'd gone to dinner."

"God, what an asshole. I never liked him. You were always way too good for him."

"You never said that you didn't like him."

Jocelyn shrugged. "I knew you wouldn't listen to me. You were infatuated, and I know when Bekah Matthews gets infatuated, there's nothing that'll stop you."

"Now you make me sound like I'm a crazy person."

"Crazy, no. Stubborn? Yes."

Bekah snorted. "Pot, meet kettle." Sighing, she admitted, "I think I gave Sam more credit than he actually deserved. I kept thinking he would change. He'd get more romantic, he'd care more about us having a life together. He just needed time."

"Can't make someone change if they don't want to. Especially men." Based on Jocelyn's expression, she'd experienced something similar.

Bekah felt like her insides were turning squishy, and she hated that feeling. She hated feeling vulnerable. Despite her tendency to become infatuated, she also wasn't great at taking risks with anything that could end in heartbreak. If she was being honest with herself, she'd admit that she'd stayed with Sam because he was safe. He was just fine—top grade mediocre boyfriend material.

"Speaking of men..." Jocelyn smiled devilishly. "I saw Elliot a few days ago at the market. I have to say, I wouldn't kick him out of bed."

Bekah scowled. "I'm not going after Elliot Parker. And did you miss the part where he didn't recognize me at all?"

Jocelyn shrugged. No-nonsense and frank, Jocelyn had always been the person to cut through Bekah's bullshit—or anyone else's. Bekah usually appreciated that personality trait.

"Elliot hasn't seen you in how long? Eight years? It took me a second to recognize him, and when I looked at his yearbook photo yesterday, he honestly doesn't look that much different." Jocelyn sipped her beer. "But you? You've changed a lot since high school."

Bekah didn't need logic right now. She wanted commiseration. "I don't look *that* different."

Rising from her chair, Jocelyn left and soon returned with the yearbook in question. Opening it, she found

Bekah's senior photo and held out the yearbook to her. "You aren't that goth girl anymore."

Bekah hadn't seen her senior photo since she'd graduated from high school. Seeing it now—her hair black, eyes lined with eyeliner, a fake nose piercing in her left nostril—she couldn't help but laugh.

"Oh God, why did I feel the need to wear four chokers?" Bekah moaned.

"It was definitely a look."

Gazing at that photo of her eighteen-year-old self, Bekah had to concede that she didn't look much like her anymore. She'd shed the black hair and clothes after her freshman year of college. Her mom had been so happy that Bekah had stopped dyeing her hair, she'd cried when she'd first seen Bekah with her natural color.

Bekah turned the pages to find Elliot's photo. He was tanned and golden, his hair long and shaggy. He looked like a surfer dude straight out of an early 00s romcom. He was even wearing a pooka necklace.

But he did still look like his high school self, more than Bekah did.

"Even if you're right," conceded Bekah, "I'm still pissed off at him. It's not like we never interacted, either. He *knew* me."

Jocelyn peered at Bekah closely. "Why are you so worked up about this? You don't usually care this much about other people."

Bekah felt a blush coming to her cheeks. "I'm not. It's not that big of a deal."

"Yet you not only called to tell me about it when it happened, but two weeks later, are still talking about it."

Bekah scowled. "You're annoying, you know that, right? Sometimes you just need to say, 'that sucks, I'm sorry.'"

"But you wouldn't love me if I was like that."

Bekah grumbled, which made Jocelyn laugh.

Jocelyn was staying on the island for the summer during her break from culinary school. She'd already regaled Bekah with all of her stories about living in Paris, learning French cuisine, and flirting with sexy Frenchmen. If Jocelyn seemed a little harder around the edges, Bekah hadn't had the courage to mention it.

Jocelyn was good at being frank with everyone but herself. And Bekah knew her friend hated admitting when she was struggling. Bekah had heard through the grapevine that her father, who'd been diagnosed with multiple sclerosis recently, wasn't handling the diagnosis well. When Bekah had tried to bring it up earlier, Jocelyn had immediately shut the subject down.

"You know what I think you need?" said Jocelyn, breaking Bekah's reverie. "I think you need to let your hair down. Have some fun. You've been in a rut for a while now."

"I've been working on my dissertation. How is that stuck in a rut?"

Jocelyn tossed a cashew in Bekah's direction. "I'm not talking about work or school. I'm talking about your love life. When's the last time you've just had some fun with a guy?"

Bekah was embarrassed to admit that she couldn't remember. The most fun she'd had with Sam was when he'd taken her to a dive bar on their first-year anniversary.

He'd forgotten to get her flowers, and had instead picked some roses that had been full of aphids.

"I really don't want to start dating again," said Bekah.

"I don't mean dating, trying to find another relationship. I mean, have some flings. Sleep around."

Bekah gaped at her friend. Jocelyn, queen of "I don't sleep around because I don't have time to waste" was suggesting *she* sleep around?

"How many beers did you drink tonight?" said Bekah.

"This is my first one." Jocelyn stuck out her tongue. "Jerk." The word held no rancor, though.

Bekah instantly recoiled at the idea of having sex with random guys. She wasn't that type of person: she was a planner. Planners didn't throw caution to the wind. Planners knew exactly where they'd be and when. You needed to be flexible to sleep around, and Bekah was about as flexible as a brick.

"Who would I proposition?" joked Bekah. "It's not like there are a ton of eligible bachelors on Hazel Island."

"There are some. And not only that, but there are plenty of tourists, too."

"Most of whom are over the age of sixty-five and collecting social security."

"Hey, don't count out the grandpas. They probably have money to make it worthwhile."

Bekah let out an incredulous laugh. "Jocelyn, this isn't like you."

Jocelyn wrinkled her nose, smiling. "I might've mentioned to Alex about you getting dumped. It was her suggestion."

Now it made sense. Five years younger than her sister,

Alexandra Gray was a firecracker who was the opposite of both Jocelyn and Bekah. She was the type of person who'd wake up and decide to go bungee jumping just because it sounded fun. Last Bekah had heard, Alex was on some Caribbean island, swimming with dolphins.

"Not sure I want to take advice from your sister. Didn't she set a toaster on fire in her dorm room her first week of college?" said Bekah.

"She's insane, but she has a point. Sometimes you have to get outside your comfort zone."

Although Bekah told herself she wasn't interested, she couldn't help but wonder if she *could* do something like this. Could she let her hair down and just have fun? Did she have it in her?

Maybe it was the beer, or maybe it was the fact that Bekah was tired of feeling like she was always in the shadows, but she found herself grabbing a nearby pad of paper and a pen.

"Okay, how about we make a list of eligible bachelors?"

Jocelyn clapped her hands. "Seriously? Are you going to do it?"

"I don't know. I'll have to think about it."

"That's the opposite of what you want to do. Just do something impulsive for once. You overthink everything."

"Once again: pot, meet kettle."

Jocelyn sniffed. "We're not talking about me, we're talking about you." She grabbed the pen from Bekah's hand. "Let's get started."

By the time they were finished, they had half a dozen men on the list. To Bekah's dismay, Jocelyn had written *Elliot Parker* at the top of it.

"Elliot? No way. I'm not going after him. It'd be too awkward after he didn't recognize me."

"He's eligible, and he's only here for the summer. Don't write him off."

Bekah ignored her friend. Second on the list was Jack Benson, who'd moved to Hazel Island a decade ago and who worked as a fisherman. Bekah had probably exchanged all of ten words with him. Jack wasn't known for his conversational skills, but he *was* attractive in a gruff kind of way.

"Has Jack ever had a girlfriend or anything?" said Bekah.

"Not that I know of. If he sleeps around, he's quiet about it. But as far as I know, he's always been single."

Bekah smiled. "Perfect. Jack goes to the top of the list." And before Jocelyn could protest, Bekah made a point to cross off Elliot's name.

CHAPTER FOUR

Bekah checked her makeup one last time before she entered Hazel Island's most famous—or infamous—dive bar. The Salty Shack was known for its cheap beer and perpetually sticky floors.

As Bekah stepped inside, she felt her shoe stick to one particularly sticky spot near the entrance. Had someone doused the floor with maple syrup? She didn't want to ponder the last time someone had used a mop in here.

Stop thinking about how dirty this place is. That's not why you're here, she reminded herself. Gathering her courage, she went to the bar, where a few men were gathered to watch some basketball game.

Jack Benson was furthest from the TV, nursing a beer, his expression blank. Tanned from working out in the sun, he was the essence of the word "rugged." Bekah had no idea how old the fisherman was. He could've been her age, or he could be a decade older.

Not only was Jack rugged, he had the cheekbones of a Greek god and the muscles of someone who knew the value of hard work. Bekah had often thought he was good-looking when she'd seen him in town, but he'd always been so reticent to talk that she'd never pursued him.

Until now.

Bekah slipped into a seat next to Jack. She waited for the lone bartender to ask for her order, but he was busy making a drink for someone else. Did they even make cocktails here? She thought The Salty Shack only served beer and maybe a cheap glass of wine if you wanted to be a little fancy.

Jack didn't even glance at her sitting next to him. He drank his beer, his expression distant, and Bekah struggled to think of something to say. When the bartender continued to ignore her, she tapped Jack on the forearm.

"Can you get his attention?" She pointed at the bartender and then batted her eyelashes for good measure. When Jack didn't speak, she added, "You're closer."

"Make more sense just to tell me what you want," replied Jack.

"Um." She smiled awkwardly. "Whatever you're drinking is fine."

Jack raised a dark eyebrow. "You like dark beers?"

"Sure. Of course. Who doesn't?"

Jack seemed skeptical, but he went to order her a drink. Returning to his seat, he proceeded to ignore her.

Bekah wondered if she'd been wrong to wear a pencil skirt and cardigan. Jocelyn had wanted her to wear something skimpier, but Bekah had balked. She'd be showing her legs, after all. She didn't need to show *everything*.

Now she realized that wearing what was basically a librarian's outfit didn't fit at all with the vibes of The Salty

Shack. The handful of other women in the bar were either wearing sundresses or crop tops with tiny shorts.

The bartender brought over her drink, Jack handing him a few bills.

"Oh, thank you." Bekah took a sip of the beer and couldn't hide her wince. A wince that Jack caught.

"I thought you liked dark beer?" he rumbled.

Bekah coughed. "I do. This one is just..." *Bitter? Thick? Hoppy?* "Potent," she said finally. She took another sip just to show she wasn't a total wimp.

Jack's lips quirked—just a brief quirk. Not a full smile, and certainly not a laugh. Bekah wasn't certain the man did laugh. Every time she'd seen him, he looked serious. Maybe he'd never learned how to smile—he was smile-deficient.

"You don't have to keep drinking it, you know." Jack looked her up and down. "You'd probably be better off with a cosmo or something."

"Excuse you, I do like beer. Just not this stuff."

Jack waved over the bartender. "Get the lady an IPA. Your palest one."

Fine, she did like IPAs, but she wasn't going to admit that out loud.

Jack drank the rest of her dark beer as she nursed her IPA. "You're the scientist, right?" he said out of nowhere.

"Marine biologist, yes. I'm Bekah Matthews."

"I know who you are. You're down at the docks a lot." He glanced at her. "Your boat looks like it tips a lot."

"What? No, it doesn't. My sail is only two years old."

Jack shrugged. "It's your boat."

Bekah wasn't sure if she wanted to throw her drink in his face or laugh. Maybe both. He didn't seem at all concerned that he'd gotten off on the wrong foot. If he knew she was trying to flirt with him, he was totally ignoring the attempt.

Bekah leaned toward him. "But as a fisherman, I'm sure you know even more than I do. How long have you been fishing?"

"Since I was a kid."

When no more information was forthcoming, Bekah asked, "Do you like it?"

"It's work. I'm good at it. I guess that means I like it."

Bekah had known Jack wasn't particularly chatty, but this was like pulling teeth. *Maybe if I tear off this cardigan and flash him my boobs, he'll get the hint.*

"I'm sure it takes a lot of strength to fish," she said, trying to sound breathy. "I couldn't haul in those nets."

Jack glanced at her arms. "Probably not."

This was clearly going nowhere. The man was totally obtuse. Sighing, Bekah drank the rest of her IPA and then placed a ten-dollar bill on the counter.

"To repay you for the drinks," she said.

Standing outside the entrance of The Salty Shack, Bekah sighed. That had been a bust, to say the least. Why had she thought this scheme was a good idea? *Let down your hair, have some fun. Except apparently I'm not even good at doing that.*

"That was a long sigh," said a man's voice.

Elliot Parker. Of course he'd be here. Then another thought occurred to Bekah: had he seen her pitiful attempt at flirting inside? Or worse, had he overheard their conversation?

A blush climbed up her cheeks. "It's nothing," she said quickly.

"Every time my sister sighs like that, I know she's basically asking anyone nearby to ask her what's wrong."

Bekah shot him an annoyed look. "If you're thinking I sighed to get some random person's attention, you're wrong. I sighed because I felt like sighing. There's no special meaning to the act of sighing."

Elliot looked like he was about to start laughing at her, which only made Bekah more irritated. Why him, of all people?

And why did he have to look so delicious, with his loose, cotton shirt unbuttoned, his hair perfectly wavy, strands falling across his forehead. He could be some model selling men's cologne. It was obnoxious.

"I disagree. Sighing always means something. No one sighs when they're happy," said Elliot.

"You seem very concerned about this subject. Weirdly concerned. Did sighing run over your dog?"

Now Elliot laughed. "Sorry. I might be projecting. My sister, Gwen, do you know her?"

"Yes, I know who she is." *Just like you still don't know who I am.*

If Elliot caught her jab, he ignored it. "Oh, well. She tends to sigh and sigh and then won't say what's wrong. It's annoying. Then she gets mad when I can't read her mind."

"Welcome to every interaction between men and women ever," said Bekah dryly.

Elliot eyed her. "You seem the type to speak her mind no matter what." His gaze trailed down her face to where her cardigan showed the little bit of skin she'd allowed for tonight. Based on the way he looked at her, she could've been wearing nothing at all.

"I do speak my mind. Most men don't like it. My boyfriend—my ex-boyfriend, that is. I'm pretty sure that's why he broke up with me."

Why are you telling him this? she thought. *He doesn't even remember who you are!*

Elliot raised an eyebrow. "Is that what he said?"

She shook her head. "No, but I could infer it. I've run into it before."

"Sounds like you dodged a bullet."

Jocelyn had essentially said the same thing. Had Bekah convinced herself that Sam was worth her time just because she was afraid to admit she might've been wrong about him?

"People keep saying that," she said, "but it doesn't make me feel better. We were together three years, that I wasted on him."

"It's funny, my sister said the same thing when she and her husband ended things. Have you ever heard of the sunk-cost fallacy?"

"No. Why?"

"It's when people think they have to stick out shitty situations—and relationships—because they've invested so much time already. That's the reason they stay."

"I can't fault anyone for wanting to work on things."

Elliot shrugged. "You can't fix something that's been crushed to bits." Standing straight up, he then said, "You never did tell me why you were sighing."

"You're like a dog with a bone." Suddenly exhausted and annoyed, all tact fled her mouth. "You don't even know my name."

At least Elliot had the good grace to wince. "I do know

your name. Rebekah Matthews. We went to high school at the same time, right?"

"Did you figure that out yourself, or did your sister tell you?"

"Would you believe me if I said it was a mixture of both?"

He had such a hangdog expression on his handsome, stupid face, that Bekah couldn't stay mad.

And when he added, "Sorry I didn't recognize you that night. You really don't look like you used to."

Now she cocked her head to the side, her eyes narrowed. "You're entering dangerous territory, Elliot Parker. Telling a woman you couldn't recognize her because she's *older*—"

"I never mention a lady's age."

"—is not a good look," Bekah finished.

Now he looked annoyed. "I meant that you look different because you aren't in all black, with black hair. You know, all that Evanescence, emo shit."

"I'm shocked you know who Evanescence is."

"I plead the fifth."

Bekah was mollified, although she wasn't going to mention to Jocelyn this little tidbit of their conversation. Jocelyn would lord it over Bekah for way too long.

She and Elliot watched the tourists wandering down Main Street for a few moments. One older couple stopped to pet a dog that had been tied to a lamppost, while another woman stumbled into the street, her partner catching her before she fell flat on her face.

Bekah rather felt like she'd fallen flat on her face

tonight. She'd failed miserably to catch Jack's interest, that was for sure.

Out of the corner of her eye, she could see Elliot assessing her. Was it because he found her confusing, or was he actually interested in her? It seemed too absurd to contemplate. She, the emo girl, with the beautiful football player? Those two things did not go together—even as adults.

"Since I do know your name," said Elliot, "then you can tell me what you were doing in there."

"I was having a beer."

"Your skirt is too short and tight." Elliot shot her a look. "You went in dressed to kill."

Bekah gaped at him. Her pencil skirt hit above the knee, so it was hardly *short*. Was he screwing with her? She waited for him to laugh at his joke, but the laugh never came.

"Why do you care?" said Bekah, genuinely confused.

"We're old high school friends. Can't friends just shoot the shit?"

"We barely spoke in high school. And I don't think this is 'shoot the shit' material."

"We spoke in high school. We did that project together, what was it about...?"

"It was a presentation on *1984*. Remember, you dressed up in a hat, trench coat, and dark glasses like Big Brother?"

Elliot smiled. "Oh yeah. I think that started that trend at school. I swear every guy was wearing a trench the week after."

Bekah rolled her eyes, then straightened up. "It's getting cold."

Elliot took off his jacket, handing it to her, but not

before saying, "Were you flirting with Jack Benson in there?"

Her blush gave her away.

"Thought so," added Elliot.

"Were you eavesdropping?"

"I might've overheard part of your conversation. Well, the part where you were talking." He grinned. "Jack didn't seem too interested."

"Keep the jacket," snapped Bekah. "I'm going home."

"Oh, come on. I'm teasing. Take my jacket and let's go to the beach. I can even give you tips for your next flirting attempt."

At that Bekah whirled on him. "Why are you acting like this? You don't even know me. Not really."

His expression turned serious as he replied, "Maybe I want to get to know you, Bekah Matthews."

CHAPTER FIVE

Elliot waited for Bekah to reply. Based on how red her cheeks were and how dilated her pupils were, she wasn't immune to him. But he had a feeling she was over-thinking things.

"I just broke up with my boyfriend," she stuttered.

"I'm not proposing marriage, Bekah."

She wrinkled her nose. "No, I mean, yes, I know." She slapped her forehead. "Oh my God, I'm making this so awkward."

"Yeah, you are."

At least that made her laugh.

"Let's walk. Maybe if we're lucky we'll find another pelican we can save," said Elliot.

Bekah didn't balk, at least. They went to the beach, near where they'd first run into each other. Under the setting sun, Elliot allowed himself to really look at Bekah Matthews.

She wasn't his type—not normally, at least. Elliot preferred tall, leggy blonds with names like Amanda. Stephanie, Madison. They carried Louis Vuitton bags and didn't like to get dirt under their acrylic nails. They tended to prefer casual relationships, and Elliot had never wanted anything more, either. Those women had had the same expectations as him.

Bekah, though, she probably didn't own any designer bags. Her fingernails were clipped short, a sign that she needed her hands to do her work. No stiletto nails for her. She wore little makeup, even now, and although Elliot found her librarian ensemble strangely alluring, even he knew that on any other woman, he would've found it decidedly dull. Frumpy, even.

"Did you mean it? What you said?" Bekah said quickly.

"That you're awkward? Definitely."

She rolled her eyes. "I can't tell if you're actually interested in me, or if you're just negging me. It's annoying."

"Negging you?" Elliot was offended. He never negged women. He didn't need to: a smile, a compliment, a drink bought and a hand on the knee, and he could usually take her home that evening. He was *good* with women. So why did he feel so tongue-tied around this one?

"Yeah, negging. You know, insulting me so I'll think badly of myself and feel like you're doing me a favor by being interested. I can't say any guy has ever tried it with me, though."

"I don't need to insult women to like me. I'm just likable on my own." Elliot held out his arms. "I mean, look at me. I'm a total catch."

Bekah looked him up and down, so slowly that he felt an electric current move through his body. When she looked away and shrugged, he had the feeling he'd just been *rejected*. Him, Elliot Parker.

"I guess you are. If you like guys like you," she said finally.

"Guys like me? You mean, handsome, confident, capable, intelligent—"

Bekah started laughing at him. "Don't get your feathers all ruffled. I really wasn't trying to neg you. I just meant we wouldn't go well together. We're too different."

"You don't even know me."

Why did he care? If she wasn't interested, well, it happened. Okay, it'd been a while since that had happened, but at the same time, Elliot had generally stuck with his type of lady companion these past few years. He didn't generally try to flirt with brainy scientists who knew how to free pelicans from nets.

"I know your type," she said.

"My type. What is that, exactly?"

"You want a woman who's sweet. Thoughtful. Soft. She's happy to stay home with your three kids. She loves to decorate and bake cupcakes. She's so cute it's nauseating. But she'll never outshine you, either. She's always in the supporting role."

Elliot stared at her, mostly because his brain couldn't come up with a response to what she'd said. Even worse, he couldn't deny the truth incapsulated in her statement. Bekah had described the exact type of woman he'd always dated. Hell, the last one, Courtney, had been an interior designer with her own line of accent pillows.

"So you're not sweet? Soft? You don't like to bake? What's wrong with those things?" Now he was just curious.

"Nothing. I just don't want them." Bekah shrugged.

"I'm just saying that you'd be the type of guy who'd get mad if his wife earned more than him, that's all."

Now Elliot was pissed off. She'd made a snap judgment about him from...what?

He moved so he stood in front of her, blocking her view of the sunset. "Like I said before," he said coolly, "you don't even know me."

"You aren't denying what I said, either."

He wanted to toss her into the ocean. He wanted to pull her hair like they were in elementary school. But he really, really, wanted to kiss her lush mouth to shut her the hell up.

"I'm not some dick who would hate seeing his wife being successful, or wants some cookie cutter partner who only gives, gives, gives." Suddenly, it dawned on him. "You're not talking about me. You're talking about your ex."

Bekah's expression hardened. "No, I'm not."

"Look, princess: I'm not your ex. I don't dump women because they're ambitious." Elliot took her hand, loving the way her eyes widened at the contact. "Women who go after what they want? That's sexy as hell. You're sexy as hell, Bekah Matthews."

He rubbed his thumb across her palm. She inhaled a breath when he massaged her hand and then entwined their fingers.

"Don't call me princess," was her only response.

He let out a laugh. "You're attracted to me. Admit it." He wrapped an arm around her waist, pulling her closer.

"I think you're arrogant and presumptuous—"

He silenced her with a kiss. She made a noise in her throat, but as he deepened the kiss, she melted in his arms.

In that moment, she was all softness and sweetness. Elliot licked inside her mouth, and she moaned, her fingers digging into his shoulder.

His cock came alive from that simple kiss. He cupped the back of her head and let himself indulge in this captivating, confusing woman.

When the kiss ended, it took Elliot a moment to return to the present. Bekah eventually broke their embrace. She was licking her lips, her gaze darting to the ground, and he had the sudden image of her darting off into the sunset without another word.

"Did that freak you out?" he asked.

"Um. No. I just—" She finally looked up at him. "I should tell you something."

Icicles dripped down his spine. *I'm married. I have a secret wife in the attic. I thought that kiss was terrible.* All kinds of thoughts flooded his brain.

"I'm not the type of person who kisses guys randomly," she explained. She tucked a stray tendril behind her ear.

"That's a shame. You're a hell of a kisser."

"Thanks. I think. What I mean, is that since Sam broke up with me, I've felt like I've been in a rut. I mean, my dissertation is going well. My research is progressing. But my personal life, it needs to be revived. It's nearly six-feet-under at this point. I think I kept dating Sam because it was convenient and I didn't want to be alone."

Elliot blinked. It felt like a river of words was pouring forth from Bekah, and he didn't know if he should stop the flood or just let himself get caught in the current.

"Anyway, I talked to my friend, it was her sister's idea, actually." Bekah blew out a breath. "I'm babbling, aren't I?"

"Somewhat, yeah."

"Okay, well, I decided to have some fun this summer. *Romantic* fun. That was what I was doing with Jack at The Salty Shack. I was trying to flirt with him." Her shoulders sank. "But he didn't even notice what I was doing."

At the thought of her sleeping with Jack Benson, Elliot saw red. That lumbering fisherman? She could do way better. She needed someone who could hold an actual conversation, not just respond with grunts.

Bekah was still talking. "So I think we should have fun. Together. We seem to have chemistry."

Elliot had to force his brain away from being jealous to being instantly aroused. Bekah Matthews had just propositioned him. Had the earth just been flipped upside down?

"Are you suggesting we have a fling?" he said, his voice raspy.

She nodded quickly. "I mean, if you want to. No strings attached. I'll be going back to Seattle by early September, anyway."

Elliot would be gone by then as well. It was perfect. They could fuck each other's brains out and go their separate ways. A thrill shot through him, and his still-hard cock somehow got harder at the mere thought of bending Bekah over the arm of his couch, or pushing her against the wall, or—

"You have a deal," he said, holding out his hand.

Bekah's smile made his heart flip. When she took his hand, he told himself that the electric current was just lust and nothing more.

CHAPTER SIX

B ekah only slept a few hours that night. She was woken up more than once feeling her body throbbing, her skin slick with sweat. Her dreams were all erotic encounters with Elliot, damn him.

She finally gave in and got up around five AM. Waiting for her coffee to brew, she wondered if she'd also dreamt last night. Had she really told Elliot Parker that she wanted a summer fling? And that he wanted one with *her?* It was unbelievable.

In high school, Elliot had been the golden boy: handsome, charming, and popular. He'd been the quintessential stereotype of the football player that would never notice someone like Bekah. What made him even worse was that he'd never been a bully. He was one of those teenagers who managed to make friends in almost every clique.

Bekah had been an emo kid, wearing black eyeliner and listening to My Chemical Romance, Evanescence, and Thirty Seconds to Mars. She'd mostly walked around school with her iPod and earbuds in her ears. More than once, teachers would scold her for listening to music during class, or sitting at her desk and doodling instead of listening to lectures.

Mrs. Wilson had even confiscated her beloved iPod one day and had only returned it at the end of the school day after Bekah had been made to promise she would keep it in her backpack during class.

Bekah and Elliot had both been in Mrs. Wilson's World Studies class. They'd ended up sitting next to each other, as Mrs. Wilson loved forcing students to sit next to other students they didn't know as well. When Elliot had first sat down next to Bekah, she'd turned her iPod volume up and made a point to ignore him.

Except Elliot couldn't be ignored. He started with asking to borrow a pen from her that day. He lost pens constantly, and Bekah found herself buying entire packs simply to share them with Elliot. Other days, he needed paper, or to borrow her book because he'd left it in his locker. He'd smile that charming smile and Bekah was too much of a human, teenage girl to say no.

"Hey, Matthews," said Elliot one day in World Studies, "did you do the reading?"

Bekah just rolled her eyes. "Duh."

"Can you tell me what happened? I had practice late and didn't have time to read." Elliot gave her his best puppy-dog eyes.

This wasn't the first time Elliot had asked her to show him her homework for him to copy it, or to tell him about the reading. Bekah refused to let him copy her, but she normally didn't mind talking about books.

Today, though, something devious inside her made her

say, "You know how Mr. Darcy proposed to Lizzy and she shot him down?"

Elliot nodded. "I read that far already."

Bekah leaned closer. "Darcy finds out that Lizzy is actually a vampire hunter. That's why she turned him down. If they married, he'd be in danger all the time."

"What? Are you serious?" Elliot at least was smart enough to look skeptical.

"Totally serious. I mean, *Dracula* was written around the same time." Untrue, but Elliot didn't know that. "People in the nineteenth century were obsessed with vampires, like *Twilight*-level obsessed. Jane Austen especially. I mean, her first book is basically about a haunted house."

Elliot had no reason to doubt her, so he took her at her word. Bekah had to restrain laughter throughout class, especially during the pop quiz about their reading.

A few days later, Elliot slapped his quiz down on Bekah's desk. It had a bright red F on it. "Mrs. Wilson wants to schedule a parent-teacher conference now. She thinks I don't take anything seriously."

Bekah's lip trembled, but when she read Elliot's answers, she started laughing. Elliot's expression was fearsome.

"Why would you screw me like that?" he demanded in a low voice.

"Because you always take and take. Pens, homework. I do all the work and you just mooch off of me." Bekah crossed her arms across her chest. "You should do the readings for once."

Elliot looked shocked. He hadn't said another word the rest of class to her.

Bekah had nearly apologized, feeling immensely guilty

for making him fail that quiz. Had she been too mean? Should she just have been honest with him?

A week later, they were paired together for a group project. Bekah wanted to melt into the floor.

Elliot, though, didn't seem fazed. When he told her calmly they should meet up in the library after school one day to talk about their project, she reluctantly agreed.

To Bekah's shock, Elliot had already divvied up what each of them was going to do. He'd already researched a few topics, and even provided a few books they could use for their paper.

"I know you think I'm just some dumb jock," he said as they got up to leave.

Bekah was looking at her shoes. "I don't think that," she whispered.

They'd finished the project and had gotten an A. Bekah had never gotten the courage to tell Elliot she was sorry. And when Mrs. Wilson had updated the seating chart, she never sat next to Elliot Parker again.

Had they been friends? Bekah mused as she sipped her coffee. She'd gotten along with him while they'd worked on their project. He'd proven to be a good partner and had carried his weight.

But after that, they'd barely spoken. So, not really friends. Just two students who'd had to work together but who hadn't had any friends in common.

Could we be friends now? As adults?

Bekah wasn't sure. Then again, friendship wasn't imperative to have sex with someone. You didn't even need to know their name.

Bekah finished her coffee and got dressed. Going down

to the docks, she readied her sailboat, needing to get some time out on the water. In all of this talk about flings, she'd neglected her research in the last few days. Normally, she'd go out in the morning to observe the orca pod that circled the island during the summer months.

Despite the bright morning sunshine, the wind off of the Pacific Ocean was cold. Bekah loved it: the blue sky reflected on the water, the smell of the salt air, the sound of the waves. She felt all of her worries melt away when she was out on the water.

She found the pod of orcas, making certain to stay far enough away so as not to get in their way. Despite the moniker "killer whale," the only known instances of orcas attacking humans were when in captivity.

Nearby, sea lions sunned on rocks. Their barks and calls filled the air. Although these orcas primarily ate salmon, they could easily kill a sea lion, too. Bekah watched as water sprayed from the orcas' blowholes.

A small orca, a baby, came above the surface. In recent years, the orca pod struggled to keep their young alive, what with the dwindling salmon population getting worse. This year, they'd successfully given birth to two babies that had survived so far.

Watching them, she felt like all of her worries about if she should go along with this plan for a fling melted away. Orcas didn't overthink things. They went with the moment. They hunted, they swam, they survived. They lived their lives without thinking about the "what-ifs."

Bekah wanted to be like that. She wanted to experience things she'd avoided in life because they could get messy. Maybe she needed to embrace messiness for once.

And maybe she needed to give Elliot Parker a little more credit. He wasn't that haphazard teenager who couldn't keep a pen in his backpack. He was a grown man, and he wanted her. Shouldn't she let herself indulge in that?

When she returned to the island, she didn't wait to get back home before she texted Elliot. Her heart racing, she sent a simple message: *I want to see you again.*

She had to wait five whole minutes for him to respond. But when he did, she smiled.

Me too. My place tomorrow, then.

CHAPTER SEVEN

"Elliot, the toilet isn't working!" Gwen called from the second floor. "I thought you fixed it?"

Elliot had to remind himself that he loved his sister, that she was stressed, and that throwing her out the nearest window wouldn't help anyway.

They'd been pushing themselves to hit their deadline to finish the renovations, but it seemed like when one thing was fixed, another five things broke. The latest was the toilet in the largest suite that had decided it was not going to flush.

Elliot found his sister standing over the toilet and fiddling around inside the tank. Gwen was many things, but a plumber she was not.

"Why isn't there water in here? There should be water, right? That's the whole point." Gwen grumbled, not even noticing Elliot's presence. Her red hair was sticking up every which way, and she had various stains on her pants and shirt. She looked tired and grubby. Elliot had a feeling she probably needed a snack and a bath, ASAP.

Elliot reached down and turned the water back on. Except, he didn't realize that Gwen had been messing with the hose, and a second later, Elliot got sprayed in the face with water. Sputtering, he turned the water back off and turned to see Gwen laughing.

"Did you do that on purpose?" He nearly growled.

She was still laughing. Wiping her eyes, she said, "I admit to absolutely nothing."

Little sisters were a menace. Grabbing a towel, Elliot wiped his face and attempted to dry his shirt, but it was soaked. At least the water was clean. The last thing he needed was to smell like sewer when Bekah came over tonight.

"You've been distracted all day," said Gwen when they went downstairs to drink beers together. "What's up with you?"

Did he tell her he was going to have a *fling* with Bekah Matthews? Elliot drank his beer slowly. *Telling my sister about my sexual exploits? No, thanks.*

"Working on this house has me distracted," he said finally. "And then you go and spray toilet water in my face."

"But now you're focused. So it worked." She smiled, not at all apologetic. "And I fixed that toilet earlier, by the way. Even though you said you'd do it this morning."

Elliot swore under his breath. Apparently, the thought of having sex with Bekah was enough to turn his brain to mush. It was like he was a teenage boy having sex for the first time. Even just the thought of having her underneath him, moaning and writhing, was enough to make his cock hard.

He tipped back his head for a long drink of beer. He

needed to cool his heels. He was getting way too excited about something that might not even happen. Bekah could back out. She was the type to overthink herself to death. She might show up and say she just wanted to eat ice cream and watch *Law and Order* reruns.

He felt a poke in his side. "Hello, earth to Elliot, are you there?" said Gwen.

"I'm fine," he said.

"You realize that you're just convincing me more that you aren't fine."

He looked his sister in the eye. "I'm *fine*," he emphasized. "I just have things on my mind. Just like you do."

"It helps if you talk about it."

"Like you talk about your impending divorce?" he snapped back.

Gwen's face whitened. Elliot immediately felt terrible. Gwen had been mostly mum about her splitting up with her husband of five years since she'd arrived on the island. At least with Elliot, she'd said very little about why their marriage was ending. Elliot hadn't pried because it was none of his business.

"Gwen..." He was about to reach out, touch her arm, hug her, something, but she got up instead.

She forced a smile on her face. "I'm hungry. I'm going to get a falafel from the food truck."

He noticed she didn't invite him to come along like she would normally. He had a feeling she'd probably avoid talking to him about much of anything for a while.

He glanced at his watch, realizing that he didn't have time to run after his sister if he was going to meet Gwen at his place. *Gwen probably won't even talk to me right now*, he said, guilt pricking him hard.

His sister might like to pry, but she could keep her mouth shut about her own problems as well as he could. It was a family trait, Elliot had discovered long ago.

Elliot returned to his one-room cottage that he was renting for the summer. After showering and shaving, he was in the middle of brushing his teeth when he heard a knock on the door. He nearly forgot to spit out his toothpaste in his haste to open the door.

"Calm down, man," he muttered to himself. "You're probably just having drinks with her anyway."

He opened the door to find Bekah standing there, wearing a simple summer dress, her hair braided. She was holding a bottle of wine and pointedly staring at her feet.

A memory came back to him, of when she'd told him that she didn't think he was just a stupid jock. She'd stared at her toes just like she was now.

He opened the door wide. "Come in," he said, his voice like gravel. He cleared his throat. "Do you want me to open that?"

Bekah looked at the wine bottle in her hand, like she'd forgotten she even had it. "Oh, sure. If you like white wine. Do you? I wasn't sure."

"I'm pretty much open to any alcohol," he said.

After he opened the bottle and poured them both glasses, he brought a cheese and fruit platter out that he'd bought last night. They sat down on his overstuffed couch, sipping wine and eating, neither of them speaking.

Why can I not think of anything to say? He was never tongue-tied. But he didn't know if he should simply have a regular conversation with her, or go about seducing her. The former would be less likely to scare her, but she might take it as him not being interested in her. The latter, well, that could send her running.

But Elliot didn't have to choose between the two, because suddenly, Bekah was scrambling into his lap and leaning down to kiss him.

Startled, Elliot nearly dropped his glass of wine on the floor. He then had to awkwardly reach around Bekah to set the glass down.

"What are you doing?" said Elliot, genuinely confused.

Well, his mind was confused. His body was not. Having her sitting on his lap, her heat so close to his cock, her breasts nearly spilling out of her dress...his body knew what to do.

"I'm seducing you," she said. Then she blushed bright red. "Wait, did I misunderstand? Do you not want to?" She tried to climb off of him, but Elliot wouldn't let her go.

"No, you didn't misunderstand anything." When she kept squirming, he said in a tight voice, "Keep doing that and I'll be pulling your panties to the side and be inside you in five seconds."

Bekah stilled. They were both breathing hard. Elliot was fascinated to see that Bekah's blush went all the way down to the tops of her breasts.

"So, what's the hold up?" Bekah was frowning at him.

He had to chew the inside of his lip to keep from laughing. She looked so adorably annoyed.

"I thought we could take things slowly. You know, build up to things. You might not even want to have sex tonight." *Please tell me I'm wrong. Please, please, please.*

"I want to have sex tonight."

He blinked, then laughed. "Well, I can't say any other woman I've known has been that straightforward."

"I wasn't planning to be, but you seemed confused."

"Have you ever heard of foreplay? Women tend to enjoy it."

Bekah stuck out her chin. "You mean a boob grab here and there? I'm okay without it. I just want to get this over with."

At that lovely remark, Elliot grimaced. Bekah quickly realized what she said and added hurriedly, "I mean, I want this, I do, but I'm trying to do it before my brain can tell me it's a terrible idea."

Elliot gently set her down next to him. "You need to relax."

"Wow, I've never heard that one before."

"Probably because it's true." He tipped her chin up, brushing his thumb against her lower lip. "I don't want to be something you just check off of your list. I want this to be fucking amazing for you."

"What about you?"

"Oh, I already know I'm going to have a hell of a good time."

Bekah smiled, clearly flattered. Elliot couldn't stop himself from kissing her. But when she tried to deepen the kiss, he ended it.

Elliot smiled devilishly at her flushed face, her wide pupils. He then said, "Have you ever played strip poker?"

CHAPTER EIGHT

Bekah might not be great at flirting or dating, but she was competitive. Although she'd nearly said no to Elliot's idea of strip poker, she realized soon after they'd begun playing it had been a great strategy for the evening.

Get out of her head. Stop overthinking. Just have fun, and let herself enjoy the company.

And Bekah really, really liked to win. Fortunately, so did Elliot.

"Goddamn," Elliot said, tossing his cards aside. He was about to take off his left sock when Bekah shook her head.

"The shirt," she said, surprising herself and Elliot. She licked her lips. "Especially for that hand I had."

Elliot cocked an eyebrow. He didn't protest, though, and he made a point to very slowly take off his shirt. Bekah took in his rippling muscles, the sprinkling of blond hair across his chest and down his abdomen. She had the intense urge to trace her tongue all along the ridges and valleys.

Elliot shot her a heated smile. "Enjoying the view?" He made a point to flex his biceps.

Bekah had already had to strip off her shoes and her earrings. She was glad that she'd worn jewelry for once. She would've been taking off her top within the first half hour otherwise.

And she didn't know if she was ready to do that in front of Elliot yet.

"You know you're hot as hell," said Bekah. She wrinkled her nose. "I'm not sure if it's sexy or annoying."

"Oh, it's definitely sexy. I ooze sex appeal."

"I'm not sure 'ooze' is the sexiest term."

"Saturate. Drip." Elliot's eyes darkened. "Soak."

Bekah cleared her throat. She was turned on, dammit, and he'd barely touched her.

When he hadn't immediately kissed her back after she'd climbed onto his lip, she'd wanted to die right then and there. She'd gotten enough courage to throw caution to the wind for once. And he'd rejected her.

It had taken all of her pride not to run all the way home. But now, with the way Elliot was looking at her— especially when she bent over and flashed him her cleavage —she knew he wanted her. He was just enough of a good guy to go slowly for her.

Her heart flipped in her chest. *This is just a fling,* she reminded herself. *By the end of the summer, we probably won't see each other again.*

"Are my rippling pectorals that hypnotizing?" said Elliot. "You're nearly drooling."

"I am not drooling." Bekah finished the last of her wine. "Let's get your pants off, Parker. I'm getting impatient."

Near the end, they were both only wearing their underwear: Elliot in his boxers, Bekah in her bra and panties. She said a silent prayer of thanks that she'd made a point to wear her sexiest thong. Normally, she'd wear some beige, cotton panties that were hardly seductive.

Bekah uncrossed her legs, which Elliot watched with avid interest. She hadn't intended to flash him, but she shivered a little at his reaction. If she touched herself, she knew she'd be wet.

"How about we up the stakes?" said Elliot.

"Oh?"

"Last game. Loser has to strip completely naked and stay that way the rest of the night."

Bekah flushed, mostly because she wasn't sure if she was more turned on by Elliot getting naked or being naked in front of him. Trying to hide her trembling, she said, "You're on."

They were silent as they played, stealing glances at each other.

"Cards down," said Elliot. He fanned out his cards with a flourish.

Bekah's heart sank. She'd been sure her hand would be the winner, but somehow, Elliot had managed to get a full house. She set her own cards down and lifted her chin up.

Elliot's smile was wide, his eyes glittering. "You need help taking the rest off?"

"No." Bekah reached around to unsnap her bra, but before she could, Elliot stopped her.

"Stand up." His voice was a growl. "Do it slowly. I want to enjoy the show."

They'd been sitting on the carpet while playing. Bekah rose, Elliot kneeling in front of her. Despite the fact that she was the one standing, she felt like the one prostrate before him. She found herself suddenly frozen.

When she'd slept with Sam, they'd always had sex with the lights off. Bekah wasn't ashamed of her body, but she'd never been comfortable having anyone look at it so openly. Brazenly. What if Elliot didn't like what he saw?

"Do you want me to do it?" he said quietly.

Bekah nodded, words having fled her.

The top of Elliot's head reached to her shoulders. She felt his hand go around her back, his fingers unsnapping her bra with deft skill. As the band loosened, she let her arms hang loose so the bra began to fall away.

Elliot tossed the bra away. With him only a breath away from her bare breasts, she had to clench her fists to keep from covering herself up.

But then he leaned forward, kissing her sternum, before his tongue laved a path across her breasts. He circled her nipple until she was close to begging him to take it into his mouth.

"You're gorgeous," he breathed. He looked up at her. "Now the panties. But first, turn around."

Bekah inhaled sharply. But she obeyed. Turning around, she slowly bent over and slipped her thong down. When she heard Elliot suck in a breath, she widened her legs to give him a quick peek.

"Temptress," he growled. Then he was standing and wrapping an arm around her waist. "Your body is stunning." He took her hand and pressed it against his hard cock. "See what you do to me?"

She cupped him and then rubbed him through his boxers. He kissed her as she felt him lengthen further. Then, she delved below the elastic of his boxers to feel his bare flesh. His fingers dug into her waist when she squeezed his cock.

She'd never realized how powerful it was to have a man like him want her like this. Sex had always been nice, but it had never felt like this. And they'd barely even started.

"I wanted to take this slowly," said Elliot. His eyes were glazed over. "I don't want to rush you."

Bekah squeezed him again, and he groaned. "Does this seem like you're rushing me?"

"Bedroom. Now."

Bekah was apparently too slow to comprehend his command, because a moment later she was being thrown over his shoulder and carried. She laughed breathlessly, which earned her a hearty smack to the ass. That just made her squeal.

Bekah Matthews, squealing, laughing, and making out with Elliot Parker? Elliot Parker, feeling up her breasts and rubbing his cock against her mound? It was surely a dream. She couldn't believe it.

But then Elliot was sucking on her nipple as his fingers delved between her legs. Bekah moaned, arching against him. Her body was already on fire, and as he stroked her, she had to bite her lip to keep from crying out.

"I want to taste you." He said the words against her mouth.

"Aren't you already doing that?"

He let out a laugh. "You're adorable."

Bekah wanted to protest that remark, but before she could, he was moving down her body and lifting her legs onto his shoulders. Then his mouth was on her core, and the entire English language fled her mind completely.

Elliot knew what he was doing with a woman's body. Bekah writhed and moaned as he licked and sucked. When he began to flick her clit while pushing one, then two, fingers inside her, it didn't take long for her to reach her peak.

She started shaking before she even climaxed. It hit her, hard and fast, seeming to go on forever. Elliot kept laving her clit, drawing out the pleasure until she nearly begged him to stop.

They were both panting now. Bekah kissed him, feeling so many things that she couldn't even name, and reached down to stroke his cock.

"Do you want to have sex?" she said, her voice hoarse.

"I wanted to eat you out. I got my wish."

She kissed him again, stroking him at the same time. She'd never been a fan of giving handjobs, but this somehow was one of the most erotic things she'd ever done. Maybe it was the way Elliot was whispering her name, or the way he licked at her mouth and sucked her tongue as she quickened her movements.

When he came, he swore, his body convulsing. Bekah felt wetness against her palm. Triumph filled her. She felt like she could rule the world.

Elliot eventually rolled over onto his back, Bekah's head lying on his arm. As she cuddled next to him, his fingers stroking her hair, she wondered, *what the hell have I gotten myself into?*

CHAPTER NINE

Elliot didn't see Bekah again for a week, although not for lack of trying. He was busy helping Gwen, to the point that he found himself having to cancel his plans with Bekah. Bekah had seemed to understand, but he worried she would think he was going to ghost her. She'd assured him that she had her own work to do and they'd see each other that Saturday.

It's not like you're dating, he reminded himself. *You just fooled around* once.

"Fooled around" didn't really describe what had happened that night. Elliot still didn't know how he felt about it, except that it had exceeded all expectations. And they hadn't even had sex yet. Would he just explode into a millions pieces once they did?

Early in the morning on Saturday, he met up with Bekah at the docks. She wanted to take him sailing. Seeing her in a bikini top and shorts, her hair in a messy braid, he wanted to tear off their clothes and have her right on the beach.

"Hi." Bekah smiled at him, almost shyly. "Are you ready to go?"

"As long as you know what you're doing. I'm not exactly an expert sailor."

"You've never been?" Bekah looked surprised.

"I have, but maybe three times. I prefer swimming. Or surfing. Sailing takes too much work."

She snorted. "Well, then, Mr. Lazy Bones, I guess I'll be the one working hard this morning."

"I promise not to fall asleep." He winked.

As they sailed through the crisp, blue waters, Elliot wasn't at all close to falling asleep. He was entranced, watching Bekah tend to the sails and navigating the boat. She was in her element. The woman who'd thrown herself into his lap had disappeared.

This Bekah was self-assured, confident, and sexy as hell.

"I've never gone whale watching," Elliot admitted.

"Never? Weren't you born here?"

"Born and raised. Just never got around to it."

"Well, then today's your lucky day." Bekah pointed. "There's the orca pod."

Elliot forced himself to turn his attention to the whales. When they began jumping above the surface, though, he was captivated. Bekah began explaining orca behavior in detail. Her cheeks were pink, and he could tell by her voice how excited she was just talking about the subject.

Then, one of the orcas began swimming toward their boat.

"They don't actually kill humans, right?" said Elliot, only half joking.

"No, but better keep all of your limbs inside the boat just in case." She shot him a smile.

The orca was a juvenile based on its size. It began swimming circles around their boat. When it came to the surface and sprayed them, they both laughed.

The orca even got close enough to touch. Elliot had to resist the urge. He knew that the juvenile's mother was probably watching it like a hawk. He didn't want to get in between a calf and its mother.

Eventually, the juvenile swam back to its pod, and he and Bekah watched the orcas swim away.

"That's never happened before," said Bekah. Her tone was awed.

"They must know you're just here to watch them, not bother them."

"They definitely know who I am at this point, but they've never approached me like that." Bekah wiped her eyes. "Sorry, I'm kind of emotional. I'm a weirdo."

Elliot couldn't help but take her hand. "You're passionate about something. That's nothing to be embarrassed about." He almost added that he wished he was that passionate about his career.

He liked his job, but it hadn't felt fulfilling in a while. He'd never admitted that out loud, though, because that would mean his dad had been at least partially right.

"Did you always want to study marine biology?" said Elliot.

"Since I went whale watching in second grade. I fell in love. I became obsessed with reading every book I could find about whales and dolphins. It got to the point that the librarians would let me know if a new book came in that week."

"So instead of being a horse girl, you were an orca girl."

"Too bad I can't ride an orca." She glanced at him out of the corner of her eye. "Did you always want to study architecture?"

Elliot rubbed the back of his neck. "I didn't get interested in it until high school. My dad hated the idea, though. He wanted me to take over the family business. When I refused, he pretty much disowned me."

"I'm sorry. That doesn't seem fair."

"The ironic thing is that my job isn't everything I'd dreamed of. It's a job. I make good money. I like creating building designs, but..."

"But what?"

He shrugged. "I'll never talk about architecture like you talk about whales."

Bekah was silent a long moment. Elliot wondered if he'd stepped in it, but then she just said, "Maybe you just need to pivot. Or maybe there's some other hobby you could pursue, if your job isn't making you happy."

"It isn't making me *unhappy*."

"Still. I think of that kid you were, playing football. You clearly loved it."

Surprised, he said, "You attended football games in high school?"

"I went to every single home game." At his look, she laughed. "I was in marching band, remember?"

Had he thought she'd attended because of him? *Don't be stupid, Elliot.*

"I'd forgotten. What did you play?"

"Clarinet. I was terrible, but my friends were in band, so I stuck around." She nudged his shoulder. "Why did you stop playing football?"

"Oh, I wasn't good enough to get a scholarship somewhere."

"I find that hard to believe. You were the star player."

"In a tiny high school. Compared to the rest of the players across the state, I was a small fry. When I didn't get any offers, I gave up football."

Elliot hadn't thought about playing football in a long time. When that dream had ended, he'd decided to go with Plan B and getting a degree in architecture. In his mind, unless he was moving up the ladder, continuing to play was a waste of time.

"You could play again, or maybe coach. Have you ever thought about that?"

He had to admit he hadn't. "It's been too long since I've played."

"It's never too late to pick it up again." She shot him a smile. "How about if I start playing my clarinet again, you'll play football again."

"Only if you'll become a one-woman marching band to cheer me on."

She just laughed and began to steer them back to the docks. Since it was a beautiful morning on a Saturday, the beach nearby was packed.

"I know a spot," said Elliot.

Bekah had packed a cooler with drinks and food that she retrieved from her car before getting into Elliot's. He drove them to a spot he'd found as a teenager that usually secluded.

From the road, it seemed like there was no beach at all, but only tall rock formations. It was only when you got closer that you'd see that there was a small patch of beach situated between formations.

"I had no idea this existed," said Bekah as they settled on a blanket in the sand. "It's like some secret hideaway."

"It's popular at night with high school students. We smoked a lot of weed down here."

She snorted. "Of course you did. Smoked weed, drank, had sex. You were a bad, bad boy then."

Grinning, he replied, "Guilty as charged."

Bekah had stripped off her shorts. She wore a high-waisted bikini, modest yet alluring at the same time. Her braid had come undone, and her hair fell softly down her back.

Reaching over, he twined his fingers in her hair and kissed her shoulder.

"I haven't stopped thinking about that night," he admitted. He trailed a finger down her spine. "Have you ever had sex on the beach?"

Bekah shook her head. "Too much sand. I've never understood the appeal."

That made him laugh. "You're missing out. Besides—" He turned her face so he could kiss her. "I bet I can get you so desperate for me that you won't even notice the sand."

"Oh, is that a challenge?" Her eyes sparkled. "Go for it."

Elliot wasn't about to turn her down. Kissing her, he untied her bikini top, massaging her breasts. They were so soft, the perfect handful. Her nipples were already hard and swollen like berries.

"You smell so good," he said, inhaling against her skin. "Like vanilla."

"And probably ocean water."

He sucked a nipple into his mouth, which made her gasp. "Definitely sweet."

It didn't take long for him to strip her of her bikini bottoms. She was soft all over, from her calves, to her ass, to her breasts. He found out that she had a mole on the back of her knee, and a mole on her pelvis. He kissed both.

"Do you have a condom?" she said breathlessly. "I didn't think to bring one."

He pulled one from his wallet. "I'm going to let you think that I always have one in my wallet," he said lightly, "and not that I put one there last night in anticipation of having sex with you."

"You're ridiculous." Despite her words, she wrapped her arms around him and kissed him.

It took all of Elliot's self-control to break their embrace to slip the condom on. But when he was finally pressing inside her tight sheath, all thoughts fled. He was only pure sensation.

"Elliot." Bekah's eyes were wide.

"Okay?" He gritted his teeth, forcing himself to still.

"What? Yeah. Don't stop." She bucked her hips. "It feels so good."

Elliot slammed into her. She moaned, and it only made him quicken his pace. They kissed hungrily, their bodies moving in tandem, the sounds of the ocean and the sounds of their movements creating a seductive soundtrack.

Sitting up, Elliot sat up. He couldn't help but enjoy the view, with Bekah's breasts bouncing as he thrust inside her.

He reached down and rubbed her clit, and he felt her tighten around him. She came hard, her body shuddering, and then Elliot's release hit him, too.

Sparks exploded behind his eyelids. Pleasure ricocheted through his body. It was too much and not enough.

It took a while for his brain to come back online. Both of them were slicked with sweat, and when he found Bekah's back and legs covered in sand, he started laughing.

"What?" She looked over her shoulder. "Why are you laughing?"

He wiped sand from her shoulder. "Good sex makes you forget all about the sand," he said with a grin.

CHAPTER TEN

The weeks passed in a blur of sex, laughter, and more sex. Bekah couldn't remember ever having a summer more exciting. It was like something out of a movie. Sometimes when she woke up in the morning to see Elliot asleep next to her, she'd have to pinch herself to make sure she wasn't dreaming.

In mid-August, Bekah had drinks with Jocelyn one warm Sunday evening. It was rare for the temperature to get above eighty degrees in the summer, but today it'd been close to ninety. Bekah fanned herself with a random brochure she'd snagged from Jocelyn's coffee table. Jocelyn, for her part, preferred to keep drinking very cold beers to cool down.

"You're practically glowing," said Jocelyn, a wide smile on her face.

"That's just the sweat."

Jocelyn snorted. "I've never seen you this happy. Ever. Sam definitely never made you look like this."

Bekah had to concede that her friend was right: her ex

282

had never made her feel like this. It was like comparing a stale Twinkie with a pastry straight from Paris. Elliot was her dream macaron.

"Sam never gave me these kinds of orgasms." Bekah then clapped a hand over her mouth. "Sorry. TMI."

Jocelyn just laughed. "I like this side of you. You've loosened up. That was the whole point of this idea, right? Bekah with her hair down and just having fun. And based on that dumb grin on your face, it's been *a lot* of fun."

Maybe it was the margarita, or maybe it was just butterflies, but Bekah couldn't help but gush. "I didn't think sex could be like that, you know? I always assumed amazing sex was for romance novels. You could have good sex, maybe really good every once in a while. But amazing? No way. That was just a fantasy."

"Now you're making me jealous. I haven't had even mediocre sex in..." Jocelyn thought. "Way too long."

"And not only is he great in bed, he's smart. He's funny. He doesn't think I'm intimidating." Bekah shook her head. "It's almost too good to be true."

Jocelyn propped her chin on her fist. "Sounds like you're falling for him, my friend."

Bekah felt her heart pinch. She'd had the same thought more than once. But it was too soon: this was just infatuation. Soon enough, the sex would get stale. Elliot's jokes would rankle. She'd find out that he only changed his boxers once a month or that he never washed his dishes and just bought new ones.

That was what had happened with all of her previous boyfriends. It was great in the beginning, until the rose-colored glasses came off and you saw who the other person really was.

"It's just sex," said Bekah, almost like she was trying to convince herself. "Good sex. I'm not going to make any decisions when my hormones are the driving force here."

"Sounds like a cop-out. If you're feeling this, why not tell him? He might want something more, too. You never know."

"He already told me he's leaving the island by the end of the month. He'll go back to his job in Seattle."

Jocelyn frowned. "You're going back to Seattle, too. I mean, that isn't a sign?"

"It's a big city."

"Sure. Way too big to coordinate a relationship." Jocelyn got up. "Want another margarita? I'm getting one for myself."

"I'm good. I'm seeing Elliot tonight so I don't want to get there tipsy."

"Oh, no, you might make very bad decisions otherwise." Jocelyn winked.

Bekah wondered if Jocelyn had a point. What if they could turn this into...something? Bekah immediately dismissed the idea. They'd already agreed that this was for the summer. She wasn't going to change the rules now.

Besides, what if Elliot didn't want a relationship? Then he'd probably break things off now and they'd lose these last two weeks.

Bekah wasn't willing to give him up yet. Even if it meant keeping her mouth shut about her true feelings.

"What if you asked him if he'd be interested in continuing your arrangement in Seattle?" said Jocelyn when she returned to the patio.

"You're like a dog with a bone."

"I know. It's why you like me. I mean, you could see how he reacts. Do it all casual like. If he shuts it down, then there's your answer."

Bekah considered. It didn't seem that crazy of an idea. "I guess I could make it seem like he'd just be one of my friends with benefits," she mused.

"Oh, now you're going to have an entire harem? God, I need to get off this island. My vagina is probably going to shrivel up and die at this rate."

"Don't worry. I'll share."

An hour later, Bekah was putting on lip gloss, fluffing her hair in the mirror. Her makeup—and lingerie—collections had expanded since she'd begun sleeping with Elliot. Not because he wanted her to wear makeup or skimpy underwear, but because Bekah enjoyed how he looked at her when she did. Besides, she realized that she had fun primping for him.

I should ask him if we can keep this going in Seattle, she told herself. Her heartbeat sped up at the thought.

She had to say it casually, like she didn't mind if he said no. Just a random comment. She thought she could do that. If he said no, well, no harm, no foul. They'd remain as they were. She could even tell him that she probably wouldn't have time, anyway, what with her dissertation and her teaching commitments.

When Elliot arrived, Bekah opened the door to see him holding a bouquet of flowers. "I saw these and thought you'd like them," he said.

This was the first time he'd gotten her flowers. Something inside her twisted. The feeling was simultaneously painful and exhilarating. Every time she saw Elliot, it was like a rollercoaster of emotions.

At dinner at a famous seafood place, Bekah struggled to gather the courage to ask Elliot her proposition. More than once, she opened her mouth to ask, when Elliot interjected with some hilarious story, or the waiter arrived to serve them.

Elliot had just paid the bill when Bekah said, "Where do you live? In Seattle?"

"I just moved from West Seattle to Ballard, actually. Why?"

Ballard would be even closer to the university. A thrill went through her. "Um, just curious. I'm in Ravenna. Just north of the university."

Elliot nodded, but he didn't comment further. He didn't mention that they wouldn't be that far from each other. Was that on purpose? Or was he just not paying attention?

Don't overthink this. You'll tie yourself up in knots.

"We should get together, in the city. If you have time." At his silence, she let out an awkward laugh. "It's hard enough finding friends in Seattle to begin with."

The waiter returned with Elliot's card, stalling his answer. It seemed like an eternity for him to sign the receipt. Bekah felt sweat break out on her forehead, even though the night was already cooler than it had been just a few hours prior.

"I'd be down to get drinks sometime. I tend to get really involved in my work, though. I'm not great with socializing." Elliot shrugged.

Was that a no? A reluctant yes? Bekah suddenly wanted to grill him, to ask him what he meant.

But she didn't have the courage to ask him. Instead, she just smiled, forcing herself to seem calm.

"Well, relying on me to socialize is probably not a great idea," she said, "but I'd like to try."

CHAPTER ELEVEN

I t was another unusually hot day, and Elliot was already sweating buckets before noon. It didn't help that he and Gwen were having to move furniture upstairs today. They'd already taken up three beds, three nightstands, countless tables and chairs, rugs, curtains—anything you could possibly need and then some.

Elliot wiped his forehead with the bottom of his shirt. He normally didn't mind manual labor. In fact, he usually enjoyed it. But he hadn't slept well last night, and he'd woken up in a bad mood. And now, Gwen wanted him to start *assembling* the furniture.

Apparently, his little sister wanted to make him suffer today.

As Elliot began to work on the first bed, he couldn't help but think of Bekah and what she'd said last night. When she'd asked if they should continue their fling in Seattle, he hadn't exactly answered smoothly.

I was caught off guard. We'd made a deal that this would end when I left.

Had Bekah caught feelings for him? Although normally that thought alone would send him packing, this time, it didn't. It made him wonder: what if there was potential here? The sex was amazing. He enjoyed her company. She was smart, beautiful, funny.

So why was he hesitating?

Elliot started using a drill head, mostly hoping that the noise would drown out the noise in his head.

He didn't want to think about his feelings. He didn't want to untangle the reasons why he felt like saying yes to Bekah's question would end in disaster, and why that thought scared the shit out of him.

When someone tapped his shoulder, Elliot nearly drilled a hole straight through the bedframe. "What the hell—?

His dad stood behind him, arms crossed, eyebrow cocked. "I said your name."

Elliot scowled. "Did you not hear the drill?"

"You should always be aware of your surroundings."

Of course his dad would criticize him for something so small. Shaking his head, Elliot grabbed his bottle of water, taking a long drink, before asking, "What do you want?"

Walter was the one scowling now. "Don't speak to your father like that. Can't I come down to see my kids without the attitude?"

Elliot now felt all of ten years old. Gritting his teeth, he forced himself not to take his dad's bait. Anytime Elliot was defensive, his dad used it against him.

Why are you so sensitive? Calm down. I'm just telling you my opinion.

"Fine. Can I help you with something?" Elliot's tone was sickly sweet now.

Walter began moving around the room, mostly empty now except for the boxes of furniture that were going to be assembled. "I wanted to see how you two were progressing." Walter ran a finger down the side of the window, as if searching for dust.

"And?"

"It's probably going to be a bad investment," said Walter, "but Gwen's put in the work. I wasn't sure she would. She didn't with her husband." He shook his head. "Too bad about that. Not sure why she didn't work it out with him."

Elliot crumpled the plastic water bottle in his fist. "As far as I can tell, her husband isn't worth the effort."

"That's what's wrong with kids these days. You hit a speed bump, and you give up. And then you get a trophy just for trying. Whatever happened to grit? Gumption? Getting your hands dirty and working hard?"

Elliot splayed his hands out. "Isn't that what we're doing? Working hard?"

"And when it starts bleeding cash, she'll let it go." Walter turned back to face his son. "It's what both of my children seem to do."

Elliot hadn't always understood the phrase "seeing red," but in this moment, he did. His temper was already on a short leash. Apparently, his dad seemed determined to let it mangle him.

"I'm not having this conversation," Elliot gritted out. He picked up the drill. "I have work to do."

"Always running away. I didn't teach you that. Fine, turn your back on your dad. You've done it once already."

"That's where you're wrong. I made a choice that you didn't like. That doesn't mean I ran away."

Walter shook his head. "I created my business for you to inherit. But you left your family behind. For what? I gave you everything, and you repay me by slapping me in the face."

They'd had this argument so many times that Elliot had already lost count. Normally, he'd ignore his dad's complaints.

Today, though, his temper was riding high. "I'm not going to let you make me feel guilty because I didn't want to take over the business."

"Who doesn't want to help provide for their family?" Walter sounded genuinely incredulous.

"Do you think that's why I left?" Elliot's temper finally snapped free. "I left because I'd rather live on the street than have you control me for the rest of my life."

Silence descended. Elliot knew he'd gone too far, but he didn't care. He wasn't going to apologize.

His dad opened his mouth, then apparently decided against his response. Then, muttering under his breath, he left without saying goodbye.

Gwen found Elliot sitting on the floor, staring at nothing. She sat down next to him. She didn't need to ask what had happened.

"He's never going to understand me," said Elliot quietly.

Gwen just laid her head on his shoulder and sighed.

WHEN THERE WAS a knock on his door that evening, Elliot was surprised to see Bekah there.

"Is something the matter?" was his first thought. She never showed up out of the blue.

"Oh, no. I just wanted to see you." She suddenly looked hesitant. "Is this okay? I can go home if you're busy."

Elliot had been busy: drinking, and having a pity party. He hadn't responded to Bekah's texts because he'd been in such a foul mood.

Seeing her, though, he didn't have the strength to send her away. He wanted to wrap his arms around her and hold on.

Somehow, in such a small time, she'd become an anchor. He already knew intuitively that she'd understand why he was so angry.

And that realization scared the piss out of him.

Elliot turned off the show he'd been barely paying attention to, glad that he'd put the bottles of beer in the recycling before Bekah had shown up.

But Bekah, being way too observant, said, "Are you drunk?"

Elliot considered the question. "Not as much as I'd like to be," he said finally.

"What happened?" She eyed him up and down. "You look terrible."

He laughed, a little harshly. "Thank you. But it's not worth getting into. Just family drama."

"It must've been more than a little drama to get you looking like this."

At that comment, Elliot needed another beer. He got

one out of the fridge and brought one for Bekah, which she declined. Fine, more for him.

Despite his intense desire not to talk about the subject, Elliot found himself telling Bekah the whole sordid tale. She listened intently, her focus solely on him. When he finished, she squeezed his hand.

"So, I'm in a shit mood right now. You might want to go back home," he said.

"I have a feeling you don't actually want to be alone right now."

Elliot almost hated how understanding she was. Those beautiful green eyes of hers were filled with empathy. It made him feel like he could drown in them.

She's not for you. You knew that from the beginning.

"Maybe you're the one who doesn't want to be alone." He gave her a heated look. "Pretty sure this could be considered a booty call, showing up unannounced at a guy's door."

"I don't think that's what that term means. Besides..." She sat forward. "I'm not going to have sex with you when you're like this."

"Then why are you here?" His tone was sharp, sharp enough that she flinched a little.

"Can't I just want to see you? Is that so bad?"

He swigged his beer. "Maybe it is."

She looked at him like she didn't know who he was. And that was the crux of the matter: she didn't know him. Not really.

No matter what, he'd always been a failure. In his father's eyes, and maybe, in his own, too. Bekah wasn't going to put up with that. She deserved better.

"Why are you pushing me away?" Her voice was soft.

"I never asked you to come over. You're the one who showed up."

She was shaking her head, and Elliot was dismayed to see tears in her eyes. "You're pushing me away. It was me asking about Seattle, isn't it? I wanted this to keep going, but you obviously don't want it to."

"I don't know what the fuck I want." His voice was a growl.

"I think you do. And I'm an idiot for thinking this fling could be something more." She rose, wiping her eyes. "Well, that was my mistake. I overstepped. I shouldn't have assumed you'd want more than this."

"No, you shouldn't have."

Bekah, despite her tears, looked regal and proud as she got her things. She didn't beg or scream. She didn't tell him to go to hell, which he knew he'd deserve. Even in his drunken haze, he thought she was a queen.

"Goodbye, Elliot," she said. "I won't bother you again. I promise."

Elliot stood paralyzed as he watched her leave. He wanted to chase after her, yet it was like his body was frozen.

And then, in a fit of rage—mostly directed at himself—he threw his empty bottle of beer at the door, shattering it.

CHAPTER TWELVE

B ekah stared at her laptop screen and realized she'd typed the same line from her notes three times in a row. Sighing, she closed her laptop. She wasn't going to get any of her work done at this rate.

Since her fight with Elliot, they hadn't spoken. Bekah had been wallowing, trying to tell herself she'd dodged a bullet. It hadn't helped assuage the heartbreak.

Yes, heartbreak. I'm an idiot for falling in love with him.

"Bekah! There you are!"

Bekah, sitting on her deck, looked down to see Jocelyn waving at her. She waved back, albeit with little enthusiasm.

"I brought ice cream. A lot of ice cream. So you should let me in so we can watch movies and talk!" said Jocelyn.

Bekah wasn't going to say no to that offer. When Jocelyn burst into Bekah's apartment and handed her a pint of her favorite ice cream flavor—butter pecan—she started crying.

"Oh dear. Is it that bad? Come and tell Jocelyn all about it," said Jocelyn, patting the couch cushion next to her.

Bekah spilled her guts. Jocelyn made the appropriate

remarks, mostly about Elliot being a bastard who needed to have someone bash in his kneecaps.

Bekah wiped her eyes. "So, I shouldn't have said anything, because I ruined everything."

"That's what you got out of that?" Jocelyn snorted. "What I got was that you were dealing with some man-child who needs to get his head out of his ass."

"I pushed him too hard. I know I did."

"Hun, you didn't ask to get married tomorrow. You asked to continue being friends with benefits. That's hardly a deep commitment." Jocelyn licked her spoon of ice cream. "Sounds like he's got his own commitment issues."

"And yet, I still want to see him. I miss him. We haven't talked in a week. We'd text all day when we weren't together."

"That's adorable. And nauseating." Jocelyn set her ice cream down. "Are you in love with him?"

Bekah felt her heart crack further. She hung her head and whispered, "Yes."

"Shit, I was afraid of that." Jocelyn sighed. "Now I feel bad. I shouldn't have persuaded you to start this thing. I should've known you'd fall in love with the guy."

"That's not fair. I made the decision myself. I don't regret it, either."

"Maybe, but I doubt you wanted to get your heart broken."

"It doesn't matter, though, does it? Elliot doesn't love me. That's obvious. He doesn't even want to keep sleeping with me. It's clear that he's done, and when I pushed, he freaked out."

Bekah's lip started trembling again. "I'm too much,

aren't I? I'm too pushy with guys. They get intimidated and run in the other direction." In a murmur, she added, "I don't think I'll find any guy who'll love me for those things."

"Bckah Matthews, that's the stupidest thing I've ever heard you say."

Bekah looked up to see her dearest friend red-faced and her eyes glittering. Jocelyn didn't get angry very often; her younger sister Alex was the one with a quick temper. But when Jocelyn did get angry, Bekah knew to get out of her way.

"Do not change who you are for any guy," continued Jocelyn, her finger wagging. "You're amazing, smart, successful, gorgeous. You're the dream package. If I were gay, I'd date the hell out of you. And if an idiot like Elliot Parker can't see that, he can choke. That's *his* problem, not yours."

Bekah marveled. "I can't remember the last time you got so worked up."

"Yeah, well, you're making me cranky. Cry about Elliot if you want, but he's clearly not worthy of you."

Bekah pondered Jocelyn's words throughout the evening and into the night. Although one part of her agreed with her friend, the other part—the insecure part—wasn't so sure. Maybe there was something inherently wrong with her that made her unlovable.

Maybe she was too blind to see what she needed to change. Did she really want to be alone because she had blinders on?

Her alarm woke her up right after sunrise. She'd forgotten that she'd planned to go sailing. She hadn't gone to see the orca pod since her fight with Elliot. Glancing out the window, she saw gray clouds, but shrugged them off. Even if it did rain, it would be brief. Summertime was wildfire season for a reason around here: it was dry as a bone until the rains began again in the fall.

Bekah was too wrapped up in her own thoughts to notice that the docks were essentially deserted. It was early, earlier than she usually went out. Most people would be arriving later in the morning.

Bekah readied her boat and started sailing. She couldn't help but think of Elliot the last time she'd seen him. He'd looked so distraught when talking about his fight with his dad.

Had he lashed out at her solely for that reason? That his anger had nothing to do with her, but with his dad?

Hope, that dangerous thing, bubbled inside her. She had the sudden urge to turn around and find him. She'd been so afraid of rejection that she'd assumed that he'd rejected her because of something she'd done. But what if that wasn't true? What if he was just as scared as she was?

Don't get your hopes up, she told herself sternly. *You're just going to get your heart broken a second time.*

The winds picked up as Bekah traveled further, forcing her to concentrate on sailing and not on Elliot.

When the rain began, she pulled up her hood and kept going. She had the brief thought that she should turn around, but she was already behind on her research. The pod wouldn't be here for that much longer. Besides, she'd sailed in the rain before. She was hardly a novice: she knew what she was doing.

It was only when she realized that she didn't know where she was that she began to feel afraid. The rain was falling harder and harder, the winds increasing. The sound of their howling made the hairs on the back of her neck stand up.

She carried a compass with her, but the rain was falling so hard and the waves were so choppy that she struggled to get an accurate reading. And with the thick cloud cover, she had no way of knowing where the sun was in the sky.

I'm going to die out here, she thought. *I'm going to die out here, alone, without telling Elliot that I love him.*

Bekah felt like laughing, except the laugh came out as a sob. When a crack of thunder made her jump, she lost her grip on the tiller.

And then she was spinning, like she was caught in an endless whirlwind, and then everything went dark.

CHAPTER THIRTEEN

After Elliot had managed to mess up the caulking of one of the bathtubs and window, Gwen banished him to work on cleaning the finished rooms.

Elliot didn't protest. He didn't much care what he did lately. He'd never been this despondent. A week without Bekah in his life, and he was a mess. He didn't know what the hell was wrong with him.

"You've already dusted that corner," said Gwen behind him. "I think this is the third time, actually."

"Sorry. My head is just not on straight lately."

Gwen came around him, mostly to peer into his face, like she could extract the truth of things from his expression alone.

"Is this about your fight with Dad? Or did something else happen?" Gwen cocked her head to the side. "Because I've never seen you like this. It's kind of freaking me out."

"It's nothing. And it's not Dad. I haven't spoken to him since the last time."

"You're distracted, moody, and sad. You look like a

zombie. It's unsettling. Are you going to be okay?"

Elliot pondered the question. Would he be okay? Probably, in the long run. But strangely, he didn't want to feel okay. That would mean he'd moved on from Bekah. It would mean they were officially over.

Then why did you treat her like shit? his mind whispered.

Shame made his gut twist. Considering Bekah hadn't texted him since their fight, he knew she didn't want to see him. He figured he'd respect that she needed space.

"This is about Bekah, isn't it?" said Gwen.

Elliot blinked. "How did you—?"

"Oh, come on. There are no secrets in this place. You two weren't exactly discreet."

Elliot felt himself reddening, wondering if someone had seen them fooling around on the beach. But, based on his sister's expression, she was referring to something more mundane. At least, he hoped that was the case.

"I told you not to mess around with her," said Gwen with a sigh.

Elliot's fists clenched. "Why? Because I'm not good enough for her?"

"What? No. Of course not. But she's not the type who wants a brief affair. I know you don't like commitment. It just didn't make sense."

His shoulders slumping, Elliot leaned against the wall, his head making a thumping noise as it made contact. "We broke up," he admitted. "If you could call what we were doing dating. But we ended things a week ago."

"And, you're not okay with that?"

"No. I'm not." He hated saying the words, yet at the same time, it was freeing. "I fucked up. I pushed her away. I got drunk, and she came over out of the blue, and then I said some stupid shit. I can't even remember now. But she left crying and I haven't heard from her since."

"I've never seen you this upset over a woman."

"When is the last time we've spent this much time together? Maybe I get this bent out of shape all the time," he said, trying to joke.

"My brother? Who hops from one bed to another?"

Elliot grimaced. "God, please don't say those words ever again."

"I'm aware of your reputation. Believe me, any female friend who's straight and single has asked me if you were single and ready to mingle. The thirst is real, apparently. I don't get the appeal, but——"

"What's your point, exactly?"

Gwen wrinkled her nose. "My *point*, is that you must have feelings for Bekah if losing her friendship is this devastating to you."

Elliot felt his mouth go dry. He didn't want to feel devastated, but it'd been like he'd been walking through a thick, endless fog for the past week. When he woke up, he reached for Bekah, only to find his bed empty. He thought of her all day long, wondering what she was doing or thinking in that moment.

When he'd see something she'd probably like—a large hydrangea bush, a brightly colored bird—he wished she was there to see it. He missed the way she got excited talking about orcas, or how deft she was when sailing.

He just missed her, period.

"Is this what love feels like?" Elliot rubbed his chest. "Because it kind of sucks."

"Love doesn't suck. It only sucks when it ends, or it isn't reciprocated." Gwen's expression turned sad. "Or when it disappears. But unless you go to Bekah, grovel like hell, and tell her how you feel, you'll never know if she loves you, too."

"She hates me. I saw her face."

"She might be angry with you. But love isn't about being perfect: it's about apologizing and then working to do better. Show her that you have a good heart. Because I know that you do."

Elliot knew his sister was right. He couldn't keep wallowing: he needed to fight for Bekah. For the woman who'd captured his heart. He couldn't just let her go without trying.

Before he could tell Gwen that he needed to go find Bekah, the front door of the bed and breakfast burst open. Jocelyn came in, soaked to the skin, her eyes wild.

"Have you seen Bekah?" she said.

Elliot was instantly on alert. Gwen replied, "No, we haven't. What's wrong?"

"We were supposed to meet for brunch this morning, but she isn't answering my texts or calls. She never does that. I went to her place, but there's no answer." Jocelyn's chin wobbled. "I'm really worried something happened."

Elliot didn't hesitate: grabbing his parka, he quickly put on his rain boots as he tried calling Bekah. No answer.

"Maybe her phone died," suggested Gwen. "And with this storm, cell towers could be messed up."

Elliot said to Jocelyn, "Did you go inside her place?"

Jocelyn shook her head. "I don't have a key."

"Then maybe her phone died and she was just sleeping." Gwen bustled to a nearby closet and grabbed a towel, which she wrapped around Jocelyn's shoulders. "Have you called the police?"

"Not yet." Then, Jocelyn's eyes widened. "You don't think—?"

Elliot did think. Bekah must've gone sailing this morning despite the storm warnings. Why, he didn't know. The thought alone made his stomach clench with terror.

Bekah was an experienced sailor. She knew better. But if she'd been distracted... Elliot could barely think about it without feeling paralyzed.

"Do either of you have Jack's number? Because we're going to need a boat," said Elliot.

JACK DIDN'T NEED MUCH convincing. Both he and Elliot knew that time was of the essence, and Jack was even more experienced on these waters than Bekah.

And Elliot was the only person who knew where to take Jack.

Jack's boat, the *Perseverance*, was worn but clearly well-loved. Standing on board in the pouring rain, Elliot watched as the rugged fisherman untied the anchor.

Jack normally would've been the last man Elliot would've asked for help, considering that Bekah had wanted to sleep with him at one point. Elliot wasn't above petty jealousy when it came to Bekah Matthews.

"This is going to be a bumpy ride," grumbled Jack as he began to steer the boat. "Maybe say a prayer we don't capsize."

"I don't pray," said Elliot.

Jack grunted. "Maybe you should start."

Jack wasn't kidding about it being bumpy. The waves rolled and bounced the boat, and Elliot was eternally grateful that he didn't get seasick. But with the undulations under his feet, Elliot wasn't so sure his stomach would manage to keep its contents inside it.

"You sure this is the right way?" yelled Jack. Thunder boomed around them.

Elliot squinted. Through the wind and rain, it was difficult to see, but he could just make out the large rock formation where those sea lions had rested.

Elliot pointed. "Keep going. If we don't see anything, we can turn around."

When the boat nearly tipped over from one huge wave, both Elliot and Jack tumbled to the floor of the boat. It was only Elliot's quick action, grabbing the tiller, that kept the boat from spinning like a top in a bathtub.

That was when he saw a shape in the water. A shape that looked like a sailboat.

Jack grabbed the tiller as Elliot yelled, "There! She's out there!"

Jack turned the boat, the waves doing their best to pull them in the opposite direction. Elliot went outside of the galley, his heart in his throat. He couldn't tell if there was anyone on board.

"Bekah!" he cried, all the while knowing she couldn't hear him. "Bekah, are you out there!"

And then, he saw it: something red waving in the wind, and a small, white hand was holding it.

CHAPTER FOURTEEN

Bekah awoke to the sound of beeps. Trying to roll over, she realized there was something stuck to her arm. It took her another moment to figure out that the something was an IV, and that the beeps were from a nearby monitor.

She was in the hospital. Why was she in the hospital? Then everything came back, in one intense wave of memories. She felt the chill of the water, the fear that had gripped her, the feeling of a hand on her arm—

How had she gotten here? She couldn't remember. The last thing she remembered was seeing a boat on the horizon and frantically waving at it. She remembered tearing a piece off of her red shirt, then a hand on her arm. That was all.

She must've fallen asleep again, because when she woke up, Elliot was sitting next to her bed.

Why was Elliot in her hospital room?

He'd nodded off, his chin on his chest, but his eyes flew open when he sensed she was awake. They stared at each other. Bekah couldn't figure out what to say. It was like all words inside of her had fled.

Elliot leaned over and took her hand, squeezing it. "Thank God," he said, "thank God."

"Why are you here?" Bekah's voice was a croak.

"You almost drowned out there. If Jocelyn hadn't realized you were missing, you could've died." Elliot sounded...angry. His eyes were wild now, red splotching his cheeks.

Bekah licked her lips. "Can I have some water?"

Elliot went and fetched her a cup of ice, handing it to her with that angry expression on his face. Shouldn't she be the one who was angry? He'd been the one to say those cruel words to her.

"I can't remember," said Bekah, gesturing vaguely. "Tell me?"

Elliot's expression cleared somewhat. He began to recite what had happened: Jocelyn, going out with Jack, finding Bekah. When he got to the part when he'd pulled her into Jack's boat, he stopped talking.

"I've never been that scared in my entire life. I thought you were dead." Elliot swallowed hard. "You weren't moving. Jack was the one who took you inside the boat to see if you were still breathing."

"Did I drown?"

"We're not sure. You must've fainted. You were still in the boat when we arrived. I don't know how you stayed inside it."

Bekah closed her eyes. She could feel the rocking of the boat, the rain hitting her face so hard it felt like needles. She could hear the wind howling. Shivering, she forced herself to open her eyes.

"You saved me," she said simply. She took his hand.

"You could've died out there, too."

"When I realized that I might never get a chance to tell you how I felt..." He shook his head and looked down.

Bekah's heart flip-flopped in her chest. She waited for Elliot to finish, the anticipation nearly painful.

Elliot was tracing invisible drawings on her palm. "I was an idiot. No, I am an idiot. What I said to you last week—I was an ass. I'm sorry, Bekah. I don't know if you can forgive me, but I want to try to show you how sorry I am."

"I don't care about last week." The words burst forth from her unexpectedly. Elliot looked up in surprise. "How do you feel about me? Because I love you."

The smile that Elliot gave her right then was like looking into the sun. He kissed her, the kiss long and sweet. Bekah knew in that moment what he was going to say next.

"I love you, Bekah Matthews," he said against her lips. "I want more than just a summer fling with you. I want a fling in every season. Flings galore. I want to be the only man you have flings with—"

"Now you're just talking nonsense." Even as she said the words, she didn't mean them. "Does this mean you want to keep seeing each other in Seattle?"

"If by 'seeing each other,' you mean 'date,' then yes."

"I do mean date. A boring, monogamous, committed relationship." She cocked an eyebrow. "Are you up for the challenge?"

Elliot kissed her forehead. "More than up. I can't wait."

EPILOGUE

The summer eventually came to a close. Bekah was released from the hospital after two nights of observation. She had somehow managed to escape relatively unscathed, with only bumps and bruises from her adventure.

Unfortunately, her boat wasn't so lucky. It had sunk to the bottom of the ocean. Bekah had found herself mourning its loss, mostly because she couldn't afford a new one any time soon.

Even without her boat, Bekah couldn't remain unhappy for long. She and Elliot saw each other every day—and almost every night—until Elliot had to return to Seattle for work.

The night before his return, Gwen hosted the unofficial opening of her new bed and breakfast. Jocelyn had offered to cater, and nearly the entire island—along with the tourists—came out to see the finished hotel.

"You guys did an amazing job," said Bekah after Elliot

had given her a tour. "I can't believe you still finished it on time."

"It took some extra help. I was a little distracted these past two weeks," he said.

Bekah put her arms around him, hugging him. "Are you ever going to forgive me for that?"

"Probably not. You'll just have to get used to me grumbling about it."

The sun had already set, and the island sky was streaked with the colors of twilight. Laughter and conversation flowed around them.

"Do you really have to go back to Seattle?" said Bekah with a pout.

"Do I have to go back to work? Yes. But you'll be there in a month." He looked a little hesitant now. "I've realized that I want to have what you have. Passion for your job. So I've started looking for another position."

Bekah smiled. "I'm sure you'll get tons of offers. You're amazing."

"I'll be thinking about you during every interview before you get to town."

A month apart felt like a lifetime, but Bekah knew they'd survive it. And when she returned to the city, she and Elliot could really start this relationship they'd begun.

Bekah couldn't wait.

"I just hope I can find a rental boat," said Bekah.

"No luck yet?"

She shook her head. "They don't have any to spare. I'm not surprised, given it's the summer. But I don't know how I'll go to see the pod without a boat."

"Jack said he'd take you." Even as Elliot said the words, he made a face.

Bekah laughed. "Are you still jealous? You really don't need to be."

"I'm not jealous." He squeezed her ass. "But do I want you spending one-on-one time with him? Hell no."

Later in the evening, Gwen came up to her brother and whispered something in his ear. Before Bekah could ask him about it, he took her hand and guided her away from the party.

They went toward the parking lot, Bekah asking questions the entire way. Elliot stayed mum, however.

"Okay, close your eyes. I want this to be a surprise," said Elliot.

Bekah shot him a look. "What are you up to?"

"Nothing. Now, close your eyes."

Bekah finally complied, letting Elliot lead her forward. When he told her to open her eyes finally, she let out a gasp.

It was a brand-new sailboat. And inside the tractor-trailer was Jack.

"Sorry I was late," he said to Elliot. "The ferry was late."

"Is this for me?" Bekah whirled on Elliot. "Seriously?"

"Of course it's for you." He gestured at the boat. "You needed a boat, so I got you a boat."

That was when Bekah saw the name inscribed on the side: *The Stuck Pelican.*

Laughing, she threw her arms around Elliot and kissed him.

Best summer ever.

Gwen Parker didn't consider herself to be a daring person. Buying and renovating an old, dilapidated house and turning it into a bed and breakfast was about as daring as it got for her.

So the morning she watched a man swimming nude, she found herself staring, instead of immediately turning around and giving him privacy.

It was early in the morning, and although it was summertime, the water had to be freezing. What person in their right mind would go swimming *naked* in the Pacific Ocean? Gwen shivered just thinking about it.

There was no one else about. Gwen had been going for a walk, unable to sleep, the opening of her new business weighing on her mind.

Now, she was arrested by the sight of this naked man diving beneath the waves and then surfacing moments later.

She was at least twenty yards away and standing on a rockface above the beach where the man was swimming. She couldn't tell who it was, especially with the sun reflecting brightly off the water, obscuring her vision.

Fortunately for her, there were plenty of rocks to hide behind, in case he looked back and saw her gawking. She just hoped he wouldn't recognize her if he did look over his shoulder.

Gwen giggled. She was acting like some horny teenager. But as the man slicked his dark hair away from his face, his back muscles rippling deliciously, she felt her heart speed up.

As if he'd heard her giggle, the man turned.

Gwen ducked down. Had he seen her? She waited for a while, listening, not sure how much time had passed.

When she stood up, the man was gone.

LATER THAT MORNING, Gwen was pouring herself a cup of coffee in the kitchen of the bed and breakfast when someone knocked on the back door.

It was Jack Benson. His hair was wet, she noticed.

"I thought you might like these." He handed her a pair of old binoculars. His bland expression never wavered.

"Um, what?" She blushed as realization crept upon her. "I'm not much for bird-watching," she stuttered.

"Never said anything about watching birds."

She stared. Then she started laughing, because what else could she do? This made Jack smile—just a little, wry smile, but a smile nonetheless.

And thus an unexpected friendship began.

ABOUT THE AUTHOR

A coffee addict and cat lover, USA Today bestselling author Iris Morland writes sparkling, swoon-worthy romances, including the Flower Shop Sisters and the Love Everlasting series.

If she's not reading or writing, she enjoys binging on Netflix shows and cooking something delicious.

She currently lives in Seattle with her boyfriend, two cats, and an excessive number of houseplants.

Made in the USA
Monee, IL
05 March 2022

92318798R00189